DUTY BOUND

AGENTS OF THE CROWN BOOK III

LINDSAY BUROKER

Duty Bound
Agents of the Crown, Book 3

by Lindsay Buroker

CHAPTER 1

S OMEWHERE OUTSIDE THE DARK CAVE, *pots clanked and the wind moaned. Harsh, guttural voices spoke, rising and falling in a discussion. Zenia couldn't understand them. Were they even human?*

Fear flowed through her veins. Where was she?

She lifted her head, and chains rattled. For some reason, she lay on her belly, looking toward the misty gray sky outside the mouth of the cave. She tried to rise, but the chains held her down. The shackles bound her limbs and ran across her back, pinning her to the rough earthen floor. Her fear grew stronger as she realized how little she could move. Again, she tried to rise, muscles bunching and flexing in her haunches.

Haunches? Strange. Her body did not seem to be her own.

A grunt came from the cave entrance, and a large, muscled figure stepped into view, straight white hair hanging to its inhuman shoulders. She couldn't see the face, but the hint of a tusk protruded from its silhouette. An orc?

Zenia had heard stories of orcs, trolls, ogres, and how they hated humans, elves, and dwarves, and had once battled great wars with them, but those races never came to the capital anymore. They had not been welcome for many generations, with people hunting them until they fled the continents that men claimed, and sightings were rare throughout the kingdom.

Wherever Zenia was, she doubted she was in the kingdom anymore.

The orc lifted a sword and pointed the sharp tip at her. It spoke in the guttural language. She heard herself growl, the deep growl of a dangerous predator, but the orc wasn't afraid of her. It strode in, lifting the sword as it—

A knock sounded at the door. Zenia bolted upright in bed, her fingers clenched in a blanket that fell to her waist. She peered around the dim room, struggling to get her bearings. The shadowy figure of the orc remained all too prominent in her mind, and she expected to see it crouching behind the armoire, poised to drive that sword through her heart.

The knock came again, and she managed to push the memory—the *dream*—away, rational thought overriding the fear that lingered. She was in her room at Alderoth Castle where she worked as captain of His Majesty's Crown Agents. There weren't any orcs within hundreds of miles.

Dim light filtered through the window and signaled dawn's approach. Who was knocking on her door so early?

Jev?

Excitement stirred in her breast at the possibility, and she hurried to grab her robe and don it.

She hadn't spoken to Jev in two days, not since she'd pulled away from his kiss and told him they couldn't date, not when there was no possibility of marriage between her—a common woman—and him— zyndar and heir to his family's estate. She hadn't been deliberately avoiding him, even though part of her was tempted since she didn't know what to say to him now, but he hadn't been around the castle much. She'd had to hear from Zyndar Garlok in the office that Jev's friend Cutter and the dwarven gem cutter Master Arkura Grindmor were missing. First, her magical diamond-encrusted carving tools had disappeared and now the dwarf herself.

As Zenia opened the door, she wondered what she would say if it was Jev. What if he wanted to convince her that she'd been wrong, that they should date and enjoy each other's company even if marriage wasn't a possibility?

But it wasn't Jev.

"Oh," Zenia said.

Rhi Lin, former monk of the Water Order and current rookie Crown Agent, stood in the hallway. She gripped her six-foot-long bo staff in one hand and held a pack over her shoulder with the other.

"*Oh?*" Rhi asked. "I realize it's early, but you needn't sound disappointed to see me. Unless I'm interrupting something?" Rhi cocked an eyebrow and peered around Zenia and toward the bed. "Your sheets are certainly rumpled enough to suggest vigorous lovemaking was going on last night, but I don't see a naked zyndar. Unfortunately."

"No. I had a dream."

"A dream or a nightmare?"

The sheets *were* a tangled mess, and her blanket had fallen to the sheepskin rug beside the bed.

"I'm not sure." Zenia rubbed her face, memories of being chained and of the hulking, sword-wielding orc returning to her mind. "It doesn't matter. Your arrival here must mean it's time to get up." Thank the founders. She didn't want to go back to sleep and risk the dream returning. Wherever it had been heading, she knew she wouldn't have liked it. "Though you're earlier than necessary, Rhi. Are you trying to earn the approval of the king and your fellow agents by being extremely punctual?"

"Actually, I'm looking for someplace to throw my stuff until I can find a room to let. Archmage Sazshen kicked me out of the temple almost as quickly as she kicked you out. I told her I'd gotten a job up here and tried to give her a week's notice, and she fired me on the spot."

"I'm sorry," Zenia said, guilt welling in her chest. "That's because of me. I'm..."

"A delightful person who's going to let me stash my belongings here for the day. And perhaps recommend to the king that his newest and sexiest agent would love a room down the hall from yours here at the castle."

"Sexiest?"

Rhi no longer wore her monk's gi from the Water Order Temple, but she had chosen a crisp, long-sleeved shirt and trousers that snapped in a similar manner when she punched and kicked people. The new outfit didn't show off any more skin than the gi had.

"Sexiest," Rhi said firmly. "I've seen the bulbous blowhards that work in your office. The competition is scant."

"*I* work there."

"Yes, and you're quite pretty and you have those perky bosoms, but the more rugged sex finds you distant and unapproachable. Also, you walk like a man. To be sexy, you need to sway your hips in a way that rivets men's eyes to your backside as you walk away."

"Hm."

Zenia didn't think she was as unapproachable as she had been when she'd worked as an inquisitor for the Water Order but admitted she wasn't the best judge. Had she ever truly been distant? She was inclined to deny that but then thought of the way she'd pushed Jev away, not willing to let him get close out of the fear that their kisses might turn into something she'd long ago vowed to avoid as long as she was an unmarried woman.

"Go ahead and put your stuff down," Zenia said, having the urge to change the subject. She waved for Rhi to set her pack inside the door. "As for the rest, I don't think it's within my power to get you a room here. None of the other agents stay in the castle, and I barely know King Targyon, so I would feel awkward asking him for a favor."

"Zyndar Dharrow stays here."

"Yes, but Jev is the king's army buddy. The rest of the agents stay in town with their wives or girlfriends."

"Alas, I don't have one of those to impose upon."

Zenia smiled faintly. She was glad Rhi was coming to work in the office, especially since the only other female agent had turned out to be instrumental in the deaths of King Abdor's sons. The day before, Lunis Drem had sailed away from the harbor on a ship bound for another kingdom. Though horrified at what the former agent had done, Zenia was glad she had been exiled instead of executed.

"Did you know your chest is glowing?" Rhi asked.

"Uh." Zenia looked down.

The dragon tear that King Targyon had given her to use while in his employ lay under both her nightshirt and robe, but a faint blue glow was indeed seeping out. She glanced at the bed again, wondering if the dream could have anything to do with the gem. Her *old* dragon tear had never prompted odd dreams, but in the few days she'd had this one, she'd quickly come to realize it was different from the norm. More powerful and… she wasn't sure exactly. The dragon tear almost came across as sentient.

A faint vibration emanated from the gem.

"Yes," Zenia said, "it does that sometimes."

"Do people find it alarming?" Rhi spoke in her usual joking tone, but her brown eyes held a hint of concern.

Had Cutter told Rhi what he'd told Zenia and Jev? That the gem, its oval surface intricately carved with the likeness of a dragon instead of a typical dagger or quill, might take on some aspects of the creature?

"Only if they're looking at my chest," Zenia said, hoping if she kept her own tone light Rhi wouldn't worry.

"But doesn't that happen a lot? Due to the previously mentioned perkiness?"

"I don't encourage it. If you're not sure where to stay," Zenia said to change subjects again, "my old room may be available. It's only been a few days since I moved my things up to the castle."

"The room that's actually the hayloft of a stable?"

"Yes."

"Behind a farmhouse that burned down?"

"The stable didn't catch fire."

"Comforting. Any chance to get a discount on that room? Due to the view of a charred and smoldering house?"

"I'm sure it's stopped smoldering by now." Zenia stepped back into her room, waving for Rhi to come in and close the door. She might as well get dressed for the day and start work. The king hadn't yet assigned her to look for the missing dwarf master, but she expected he would soon, so she had better get a start on gathering information. One of the few dwarves living in the city, Master Grindmor was the most skilled carver of dragon tears—for those able to afford the gems and the carvings that added specificity and potency to their innate magical powers.

A soft knock came at the door.

"My room is popular this morning." Zenia stepped around Rhi to open it, once again thinking it might be Jev.

A female page of thirteen or fourteen stood in the hallway holding a silver tray with an envelope on it. The edges were curled up as if it had been rolled like a scroll at some point.

One of the castle's ubiquitous guards stood next to the page, frowning deeply as he looked at Zenia.

"Is there a problem?" She lifted her chin, prepared to defend herself if need be. Only a second later did Rhi's words come to mind, making her realize the expression might be construed as *unapproachable*.

"Inappropriate delivery of mail," the guard said. "Messages are to be delivered to the post room for inspection, not shot over the castle wall tied around an arrow."

Zenia stared at the envelope, understanding the curl to the paper now, if not why it had been sent that way.

"Are you going to punish her?" Rhi asked dryly from behind Zenia. "Because I'm not sure she appreciates spanking as much as I do."

The guard's mouth dropped open, his sternness shifting to surprise, then contemplation as he met Rhi's eyes, her smirk slightly inviting.

"It's addressed to me?" Zenia asked.

"Yes, ma'am." The page lifted the tray.

"Did you see the person who, uhm, shot the arrow?" Zenia asked the guard.

"I wasn't walking the parapet when it happened, but Sergeant Dakru was and said he didn't see who did it. The person must have worn dark clothing and shot the bow when it was still full night. He found the arrow sticking out of a crack in the mortar in one of the crenellations. He didn't think it had been there for long but couldn't be positive."

"I see. And it's been inspected?"

"No, ma'am," the guard said. "Seeing as how you're captain of the Crown Agents now..." His lips twisted. Did he not approve?

Her chin twitched upward again before she could stop it.

"It's usually someone from your office that gets all the suspicious mail anyway," the guard said. "And *this* is suspicious." He turned his disapproving frown toward the tray.

"I agree." Zenia used the tips of her thumb and forefinger to lift the envelope. She had read two-thirds of the thick Crown Agents' handbook and remembered seeing a section on the appropriate protocol for handling and searching suspicious mail, but she hadn't yet read the section.

"Afraid it's poisoned?" Rhi asked. "I don't think you've worked here long enough to irk people into wanting to poison you and get you out of the way. Unless the elven ambassador counts. I bet he wants you dead. I rode past the embassy the other day. Almost all of the courtyard garden burned down."

"Yes, thank you, Rhi." Zenia gave her friend a quelling look, then nodded to the page and the guard. "And thank you. I'll handle it from here."

The page recognized a dismissal and scurried away without hesitation. The guard was another matter. He frowned at the envelope dangling from her fingers and looked like he wanted to follow it into her room.

Zenia stepped back and closed the door firmly. He didn't stop her.

She turned and took the envelope to the dresser where her wash basin, brush, and a small folded piece of paper rested. The *last* mysterious message she had received.

"Think it's from the same person?" Rhi trailed her over and nodded to the old message, the one that had warned Zenia to keep an eye on Lunis Drem.

Zenia had received it too late for it to be useful, but she'd kept it, wondering who had sent it. Rhi had picked it up at the temple and brought it to Zenia in the castle, so she knew all about it.

"The writing looks similar, doesn't it?" Rhi waved at the name on the front of the envelope, *Captain Zenia Cham.*

"We'll find out."

Zenia gingerly opened the envelope. If it had come from the same person, she didn't suspect poison, but being careful couldn't hurt.

The message inside contained only three words: *'Ware the wealthy.*

Rhi, reading over her shoulder, grunted. "File that under *obvious.*"

Zenia gazed down at the words, not finding anything obvious in the message at all. She was positive it wasn't some vague fortune teller's warning but a hint about a crime. Something to do with Master Grindmor's disappearance? Or something related to a crime she hadn't yet heard about?

"The writing is definitely the same." Rhi pointed at the new message and then the old.

Not only was the elegant writing the same, but both messages had been penned in blue ink on the same unadorned beige stationery. Unfortunately, the stationery was unremarkable, and she doubted going hunting for the store that had sold it would be easy.

"Yes," Zenia said.

"Any idea who would want to send you clues?"

"No."

CHAPTER 2

J EV SET THE AXE ASIDE and helped his father lift the freshly
hewn rail into the top position on the fence they were repairing.
The sun had been up for less than an hour, but the day promised
to be hot. He and the old man were shirtless, sweat dripping down their
chests, and Jev already longed to run up to the pond beside the castle and
fling himself into it. If he gave in to the urge, he had no doubt his father
would sneer and imply it was a sign of weakness to want to cool off. Jev
was in good shape, but he admitted he hadn't fully reacclimatized to Kor
after his years at war in the chillier northern forests of Taziira.

"How long you staying?" Father asked as they picked up another
long rail.

"I can't stay long. It's a work day, so I have to head to the office after
I meet with the comrades I invited out." Men Jev had worked with in the
army—and that Cutter had also known. He hoped one of them had seen
Cutter more recently than he had and had an idea where he'd gone. Or
had been taken.

"Office," Father grunted. "Sitting at a desk. There was a time when
zyndar spent their days out on the battlefields, practicing at arms. That
and keeping up the estate were their only duties. Now, they sit at desks
and shuffle papers around."

"Sometimes, I sit on the papers and shuffle the desks. To keep it
interesting."

His father skewered him with a hard look. Someday, Jev would learn
to rein in his wit around the old man. Heber Dharrow, zyndar prime and
overseer of the family and all their land, always seemed like he'd come

from the previous century rather than the previous generation. Maybe it was because he had married late and more than forty years in age separated them.

Jev had never learned the art of conversing with his father without feeling awkward and uncomfortable. And they were picking up right where they'd left off when Jev had sailed away from home ten years earlier. He wouldn't be out here at all if not for something he desperately needed to discuss with the old man.

"I'm surprised you came home last night when you've got to go back to the castle this morning." Father eyed him shrewdly.

"I wanted to talk to you about something," Jev admitted as they picked up their axes to hew more rails.

"I figured. Got something to tell you too."

"Oh?"

A faint giggle drifted up from a copse of trees beside the road a quarter of a mile away. A gaggle of teenage girls was down there, languidly filling their arms with firewood, though they hadn't seemed to accumulate any more branches than they had ten minutes ago when they first showed up.

Father looked at them, and Jev half expected him to yell for them to return to their chores. Jev didn't know who they were but assumed they came from one of the villages on this side of the property. Everyone who worked on Dharrow land was a tenant and paid taxes for zyndar protection and a stable place to stay, so Father technically had the right to tell people what to do. Jev had a feeling he would holler at kids to get back to their chores whether he had any right to or not.

"Zyndari Nhole came by yesterday," Father said.

Jev dropped his axe.

"What? Why?" His voice came out squeaky with alarm, and he rushed to clear his throat and pick up the axe as Father frowned at him.

"Made a marriage offer for you and her daughter, Ghara. She said you'd met and got along well."

"Got along— Uh, no. She's a strange research doctor who keeps cadavers in her laboratory basement." Jev hadn't *fought* with her, but he certainly hadn't found the woman charming or appealing. It was *Zenia* he'd kissed the night they had visited the Nhole estate to do research for their case.

Zenia, who had decided they shouldn't date or kiss ever again. He stared bleakly down at the stack of split wood.

"The Nholes aren't a prominent or powerful family, and they have little sway in government," Father said, as if he hadn't heard Jev mention the cadavers. To Jev, that was far more important than familial prominence. "We can do better. You're still young enough and appealing to the women, I gather."

More giggles drifted up from the copse. Father grunted and nodded as if they reaffirmed his reasoning.

Jev had his mouth open to protest the marriage topic, but he paused and glanced down the slope. The girls all looked away and pretended to hunt for wood. Dear founders, was his father insinuating those girls were there because of *him*?

Jev had the sudden urge to find his shirt and yank it back over his head. He didn't think they were more than fourteen or fifteen. In the old days, that had been considered a marriageable age, but he rarely heard of anyone under twenty marrying anymore, and he'd always thought it repulsive to see a lecherous old zyndar strolling around the city with a teenage girl on his arm. Maybe because he knew the young woman was only there because of the man's status and money. Jev wanted someone attracted to him, not to his status. Or even—he thought of Zenia again and how she loathed zyndar—*despite* his status.

"I'm glad you rejected the offer," Jev said, eyeing his father. "Marriage is what I wanted to talk to you about today."

"You've got someone else in mind?" His father eyed him right back. Warily. "Someone from an appropriate family? Someone from a long line of noble warriors? Not from one of these zyndar families full of town flops. I want my grandchildren to have superior blood. Like ours."

Jev held up a hand. "I don't want to marry at all. Not now," he rushed to add when his father's eyebrows flew up. "I just got back, and I've got a new job, new duties to the king. I want to relax and not worry about weddings and children, at least not this year."

Father frowned and grabbed a rail by himself and hefted it into place, his muscles still wiry and strong at seventy-five. "Having a woman in your bed ought to be relaxing, not stressful, or you aren't doing it right."

Jev grimaced. "I'm not ready to marry the very month I returned from ten years at war. Give me some time, Father. There's no rush, right?"

There hadn't been when he'd been twenty-three instead of thirty-three, but back then, he'd been madly in love with Naysha and she with him. Or at least he'd believed that. They had been engaged, due to marry in scant months, when King Abdor had declared war on the Taziir and ordered every zyndar family to raise a company from their lands and bring the men to fight in the army. Naysha, Jev had learned not from her but from his cousin Wyleria's letter, hadn't even waited a year before taking another lover and eventually marrying the man.

"I'm not getting any younger, boy," Father said. "I'd like to see grandchildren before I pass, to know our estate and the Dharrow family legacy are secured for generations to come."

"I know, Father. And I understand that. I'm only asking for a year." Jev hated to lock himself into even that, as he didn't want to feel rushed. He wanted to marry a woman he loved, not someone his father or relatives picked out for him. "And I'd like to choose someone, not have it be arranged."

Father made an exasperated noise. "Nothing wrong with having it arranged. This isn't about love or any other storybook nonsense. It's about producing superior heirs."

"And you're convinced a zyndari woman from a less prestigious family, or even a woman of common birth, couldn't bear good children?"

"*Common* birth?" Father blurted, almost knocking off the rail he'd placed.

Damn, Jev shouldn't have said that. He hadn't meant to suggest it, not yet. Maybe not ever since Zenia didn't want to date him. But her reasoning had been that he could never propose to her, not that he was odious. If that changed, perhaps she would reconsider—

"Did you get hit in the head when you were overseas, boy? Dharrows do *not* marry common women."

"I was hit numerous times," Jev said. "Stabbed and shot too."

"Save your lip for someone who appreciates it, Jevlain. You'll marry an appropriate zyndari woman, and that's that. You want to take some common mistress, fine. I'm no prude, and I won't object to that. Just be discreet. But first, you marry a zyndari woman and plant your seed in her womb. You want a firstborn legitimate heir before you get a child on some mistress and she starts begging you to legitimize him. Or her." Father frowned in the direction of the girls, though they had drifted farther down their slope now, their arms full of wood.

With an alarmed start, Jev realized one or more of those girls could be half-sisters to him. He knew of three his father had sired before the war, but Jev wouldn't recognize any of them after ten years. And there could be more by now. It had been a long time since his mother had left—since she'd been *killed*—and he knew his father hadn't been chaste that whole time.

"You hearing me, boy?" Father asked. "No common women. We are Dharrows, not some lesser zyndar family, the likes of which let themselves get written up in gossip publications. If you don't find someone appropriate this summer, I'll set your aunts to finding someone for you."

"This *summer*?" What had happened to his year?

"You heard me. It's your duty to produce grandchildren, Jevlain. You gave up ten years to the king and his war, and that was an honorable act and not a duty to be shirked, but now it's time to do your duty to the family." Father swung his axe, lodging it in the top of one of the fence posts, and stalked off.

Jev rubbed the side of his head. When did he get to do a duty to himself? Never?

He wished his brother were still alive. The castle didn't feel like home without Vastiun and his sarcastic mouth commenting on everything, and it wasn't fair that his life had been cut so short. Further, if Vastiun were still alive—and Jev admitted this was an entirely selfish thought—he wouldn't be his father's only son. Maybe it wouldn't have made a difference, since Vastiun had been younger and not the natural choice to become zyndar prime after Father, but it would have made Jev feel better, knowing Father had another potential heir, in case he did something… crazy. Like forgoing his inheritance and responsibilities and running off to marry a common woman.

Jev sighed. He couldn't truly consider that. Even if he wanted to. Even if he loathed his *duty* sometimes, he couldn't shrink from it. He'd always known he would take his father's place as zyndar prime one day. He'd just hoped that, somehow, he could marry and have children with someone he loved.

Hoofbeats on the road pulled his focus away from the subject. Thankfully.

Recognizing three of the four riders as his expected guests, Jev lifted a hand. Zyndar Krox, still serving as Captain Krox in charge of the vaunted fighters of Wyvern Company, led the way, riding a stout black stallion almost as muscular as he was. Zyndar Hydal, formerly Lieutenant Hydal of Gryphon Company came next. He had served as Jev's slight, spectacles-wearing second-in-command. Zyndar Captain Tuoark, former leader of Tuoark Company, followed him, the burly man an artisan metalworker who'd turned into an armor- and weapons-smith during the war. He reputedly had dwarves in his ancestry, and he'd gotten along well with Cutter.

The fourth rider was a woman Jev didn't know. She rode sidesaddle, a yellow dress flapping in the breeze as the group trotted up the road.

Jev grabbed his shirt and headed across the field to meet them. His father had disappeared from sight, but the thwack of a distant axe suggested he'd found tools and work elsewhere. No doubt someplace where he wouldn't have to listen to his son's crazy desires.

Jev had to force an affable smile onto his face for the approaching riders.

"Nice of you to put a shirt on for us, Dharrow," Krox growled in his typical baritone. "I didn't come up here to see sweaty men. Had enough of that in the army."

Jev would have been shocked if Krox wasn't still throwing sandbags around and dragging people off to wrestle with him.

"I did it for the lady." Jev extended a hand, assuming she was related to one of them. He thought she might be Tuoark's little sister, but she had only been ten the last time Jev had seen her. She wore a lot more makeup now, and he wasn't sure it was the same person.

"My sister," Tuoark said. "Zyndari Elle. She wanted to come along to visit with your cousins."

The twenty-year-old woman smiled shyly at Jev.

"She's welcome, of course." Jev nodded at her but focused on the others. "I've breakfast if you want it and coffee at the castle. I invited you up here to see if you've had any news about Cutter. He's been missing for three days. Master Arkura Grindmor, the city's prominent gem cutter, is also missing."

"You sure they didn't intentionally go missing together?" Krox asked. "Romantically?"

"I don't think so," Jev said. "My understanding is that Master Grindmor found Cutter's beard lacking, and he was trying earnestly to prove himself to her but hadn't yet."

"His beard?" Krox asked.

"As you may know," Hydal said, "a dwarf male grows out his beard with great care in order to help attract a mate. It's akin to the male peacock spreading his tail and displaying his plumage to draw the females."

"I hope Cutter wasn't spreading anything," Krox said. "Nobody wants to see that."

Jev didn't smile. He didn't have a lot of love for Krox and had only invited him up because Cutter had occasionally joined in with his company's dice and chips games. Even though Cutter was missing a hand, he was a solid fighter, and he'd liked wrestling and boxing with the highly trained men of Wyvern Company. Jev thought it possible Cutter would have sought some of them out to help with his quest to find and retrieve Grindmor's valuable magical tools.

"Have you seen him?" Jev asked. "Have any of you?"

"Not since we sailed into port," Krox said.

"Same here," Tuoark said.

"I saw him, oh, it was about four days ago," Hydal said. "You know that old quarry in town that was abandoned last century and turned into shops about twenty years ago?"

"Yes." Jev leaned forward. It had been three days since Lornysh reported that Cutter was missing. Hydal might have been one of the last people to see him.

"I waved when we chanced across each other, but we didn't speak. He was heading into the clockmaker's shop in there. I had business with my tailor across the way and didn't see him again when I came out."

"Thank you, Hydal." Jev had hoped for more, but he could visit that clockmaker easily enough and see if anything suspicious had happened while Cutter had been there. For that matter, maybe he could find out *why* Cutter had been there. He was staying in a fully furnished room in Dharrow Castle. Cutter shouldn't need a clock.

"You going to feed us now that you've interrogated us?" Krox asked.

"That was a modest interrogation," Jev said, "as any inquisitor would tell you, but yes. Head on up. I'll meet you there."

As Krox and Tuoark nudged their horses into motion again, Hydal swung down from his mount.

"May I have a word with you in private, Captain?"

"Of course, and it's Jev, eh? We're back in the realm of civilians now."

"Certainly, sir."

Jev snorted. *Sir* wasn't any better than captain. But he knew what a stickler for social rank Hydal was, and that since he came from a smaller and less established zyndar family, he might have sirred Jev even if they had never served together.

Hydal, the breeze riffling through his short brown hair, moved his horse to the side of the road and gazed pointedly at Zyndari Elle, who hadn't yet followed the others.

She smiled shyly again, glanced at Hydal, grasped her thick braid of brown hair, then spoke to Jev. "Zyndar Dharrow, am I invited to your breakfast? I... didn't think to eat this morning before heading out, and I'm famished."

"Of course," Jev said. "Wyleria and the others may have eaten already, but you're welcome to have your fill before finding them."

"Thank you." She smiled at him again—she certainly liked to smile a lot—then guided her horse up the road. She glanced back a couple of times before disappearing around a bend.

Jev looked at Hydal, expecting him to speak immediately, and was surprised to find a dyspeptic expression on his fine-featured face as he looked off toward that bend.

"You all right?" Jev asked.

"Yes." Hydal smoothed his face, though his lips remained wryly canted. "I've decided I'm too mature to lament that the younger sisters of my fellow zyndar don't flirt with *me*."

"Oh." Jev was either obtuse or had been away from female company for too long because he hadn't realized flirting was what she'd been doing.

"I know I'm not the typical warrior zyndar." Hydal waved at his slender form. "But with there being so many men who didn't return from the war, the unmarried women to unmarried men ratio skews heavily to one side right now. You wouldn't think the ladies could afford to be so picky."

"Ah." Jev hadn't thought about the topic, but he realized right away it was likely true, that there was a shortage of available men right now. That might explain why he'd received a marriage offer so soon. The last ten years had to have been something of a drought for women seeking marriage prospects, not only for the zyndar class but for the commoners as well. A lot of men from all social ranks had gone off to fight and die.

"That's not what I wanted to speak with you about, I confess," Hydal said.

Jev nodded, hoping he had suggestions about how to find Cutter. Hydal might not be an unparalleled warrior, but he was intelligent and clever. There was a reason he'd been moved into Gryphon Company. Jev was a little surprised he hadn't been made captain of the unit over him, though he was a couple of years older and related more easily with the men, so he did understand the king's choice. Still, he had deferred to Hydal often over the years.

"You may already be aware of this, since you're captaining the Crown Agents now," Hydal said, not surprising Jev with his knowledge of the organization or its new leaders, "but there are rumors circulating about you. It's likely nobody will act on them—who would dare pick a fight with a Dharrow?—but I don't want you to be blindsided."

"Go on." Jev's first thought was that someone had found out he'd taken Zenia on a date and might think to share the news with his father, but he found it hard to believe that was gossip Hydal would worry about. Besides, nobody knew they'd spoken of marriage; anyone watching them from the outside would likely assume he wanted a temporary physical relationship with her.

"A few people, Krox included, are pointing out that it was rather brilliant of you to befriend Targyon."

"They all had their opportunities, as I recall," Jev said.

Targyon, more scholar than warrior, had a lot in common with Hydal. Targyon had been sent out for a couple of years of *hardening*, at his uncle King Abdor's suggestion, but Targyon had never turned into a natural soldier. He'd been relieved when Jev, at Hydal's suggestion, had offered him a spot in Gryphon Company, and he'd been able to escape from under Abdor's overbearing leadership. Targyon had tried to get himself transferred into other companies first, but nobody had wanted to babysit the king's nephew.

"Yes, but *they* don't recall that. What they remember is that you had your arm around Targyon's shoulder for two years, mentoring him. And they—a couple of Targyon's brothers' wives reputedly started this rumor—find it suspicious that Targyon has been made king and that you're now working for him in the castle with daily access to him."

Jev frowned, getting the gist. "It's not like I could have known he would end up on the throne. Nobody could have. He has five older brothers."

"Who were oddly passed over in favor of him."

"By the hands of the Orders. I've found it odd, too, as has Targyon himself."

"Some are suggesting that you may have been the mastermind behind him being chosen."

"How would I have managed that when I was out there in the field with him? You were on the ship with us. We all found out together about the deaths of Abdor's sons and about the Orders' choice of Targyon."

"I know." Hydal lifted his hands defensively.

Jev realized his voice had grown loud and agitated. He forced himself to take a slow breath and relax his shoulders.

"You know as well as I do that people see what they want to see," Hydal continued, "what agrees with their views of the world."

"And people want to see me somehow manipulating the succession and Targyon on top of that?" Jev asked.

Hydal spread his hands. "You've been away a long time. People don't know you anymore."

"People, as in zyndar people, I presume. Where did you hear the gossip?" He hadn't been invited to any zyndar social gatherings lately, but he had been too busy to notice. Was he being ostracized because of his association with Targyon? Or was it that he simply hadn't sought out any events? He had been at the coronation, but he'd been thinking more about Zenia and his new job than about socializing with old acquaintants.

"Zyndar Gorgin Alderoth held a gathering at his townhouse the night before last."

"I see. Targyon's oldest brother. The one who doubtless thinks he should have been chosen."

"Correct. Most of Targyon's brothers are less vocal in their displeasure, if they're displeased at all. I got the feeling Tibbs and Trevon are more puzzled than upset, but they've both followed in their parents' footsteps and have academic careers in different cities. They reputedly have little interest in politics."

Jev wished he could have no interest in them, but zyndar second sons and beyond were the only ones who could get away with ignoring them. The heir to the prime? No. He'd take his father's place one day with a seat in the king's court, and he'd have to attend the quarterly meetings, vote on laws, and share his thoughts on domestic and foreign affairs.

"As far as I heard," Hydal said, "nobody's thinking of acting against you or accusing you of anything at this time, but you may want to set an agent to watching the zyndar social scene."

"Zyndar Garlok is the only one who could." Jev grimaced, imagining asking the crusty former captain of the agents to head to nightly parties and listen to the vapid conversations of those who chose not to work and had no reason to rise before noon.

"Or yourself."

"Yes, I'll start attending to listen in on the latest gossip about me."

Hydal smiled faintly. "Are you at liberty to hire more agents? Perhaps you could find a diligent zyndar you could trust."

"Are you lobbying for a job, Hydal?"

Hydal blinked. "Me? Not at all. I wasn't in Taziira quite as long as you, but eight years was plenty. I intend to spend the next year contemplating my navel while drinking copious amounts of brandy and port. Perhaps after that, I'll return to handling my father's books."

"Is that what you were doing at Gorgin's house? Drinking port and navel gazing?"

"It was sherry, and it was wretched. I'd rather lick the bottom of that still Targyon made in the field. What was he fermenting? Some kind of elven berry?"

"I don't remember, but it was potent."

"And dreadful. I'd rather consume that. Gorgin has the taste of a commoner."

"Such an insult." Jev eyed his old second-in-command thoughtfully. He hadn't truly meant to go on a hiring spree, not until he and Zenia had fully assessed the agents currently working for them, but he could likely talk Hydal into taking the same salary as he did: none. So, it wasn't as if adding him to the staff would tax the office's coffers. "Can I talk you into spending the summer working part-time with us? For the sake of Targyon and the kingdom?" Surely, that was a plea no zyndar following the Code of Honor could reject.

Hydal's lips twisted again.

"I'll have Lornysh select a port for you. You know he has a good palate."

"He does," Hydal admitted, not sounding sold yet.

"And I'll introduce you to the new female agent in the office." Jev couldn't imagine the muscular and athletic Rhi Lin falling for the bespectacled Hydal, but maybe he could convince her that one date wouldn't be so bad.

Hydal's eyes sharpened with speculation. "I've seen her. She is a beauty, and nicely athletic. But common-born, right?"

Jev was surprised Hydal already knew about Rhi and wondered how many rumors about the castle—and its Crown Agents—were circulating at these social gatherings this month. "Yes, but I wasn't suggesting marriage. Just that you might enjoy asking her to dinner."

Jev kept himself from mentioning that, given how sketchy Rhi's celibacy oath had been as a monk, a man's odds might be good for more than dinner. It wasn't his place to imply Rhi might sleep with Hydal. He already felt like a procurer for trying to arrange a date for her without her permission.

Hydal patted him on the arm. "If you need my assistance, sir, all you have to do is ask. I owe you my life. Twice."

"See you at the office soon then?" Jev asked. "I'll make sure the guards know you're on the roster."

"Very well." Hydal mounted his horse and turned it toward Dharrow Castle where breakfast was likely growing cold. "She'll be there?"

Jev smirked. "I'll introduce you."

CHAPTER 3

R HI YAWNED.

Zenia hoped that wasn't a sign that she was already bored with her new job. They were walking through the city, visiting the informants on the Crown Agents' payroll. In the future, Zenia would send junior agents to collect whatever news and gossip the informants gathered from week to week, but she first wanted to acquaint herself with them, to make sure they were trustworthy and that they were *worth* paying.

"Do we need to pick a fight with some thug to keep your interest?" Zenia asked when Rhi yawned again.

"I'd welcome a fight, but I'm only tired because I was up early getting kicked out of my room. I don't think Archmage Sazshen ever sleeps."

"Ah."

They walked through a busy intersection, passed a steam carriage wafting black smoke into the air, and headed toward the clanks and whistles of Anvil Row.

"Is one of your quirky informants a smith?" Rhi waved toward the columns marking the entrance of a street lined with the workshops of carpenters, smiths, and furniture makers.

"No. We're taking a break to visit Master Grindmor's shop. And they're your quirky informants now too."

"Lucky me." Rhi glanced back toward a tenement building, the home of the informant they had just visited. "They're not at all what I imagined assistant spies would be."

"They're normal people who happen to work in jobs where they see and hear a lot. That last fellow collects the fees at the docks."

"Normal? Did you see all the *collections* he had? That's not normal."

"Not everybody follows the Codices of the Monk and has been instructed to live a simple life with few material belongings."

"I don't have to follow those anymore, but I'm still not going to start collecting dead butterflies to frame and hang on the walls. Or ancient ogre jewelry pieces. Or pressed autumn leaves to turn into a book. By the founders, you shouldn't have asked him about that book. I didn't know there were that many species of trees in the world, and I didn't want to know."

"He's very observant. I put a checkmark next to his name." Zenia waved the notepad she carried. "We'll definitely want to keep him on the payroll."

"I'm sure he'll be pleased," Rhi said. It grew harder to hear her as they passed smithies with open rollup doors, the bangs of tools echoing out into the streets. "I think he liked you. I got the impression few girls ask him about his collections."

"You'll have to learn to ask questions and speak to people, you know. As an agent, you'll be expected to gather information, not simply thump on people with your bo."

"I can gather all kinds of information by thumping on people."

"There's Master Grindmor's shop." Zenia spotted a brown-haired dwarf with a knapsack and toolbox standing outside the shop and peering through a narrow window beside the closed rollup door. At first, she thought it was Jev's friend, but Cutter had more red in his hair and beard, and he also had a hook in place of his right hand.

But this dwarf might know something. Zenia quickened her pace.

"Hello," she called to him. "Is the master in?"

The dwarf jumped and spun toward her, his gray eyes widening. He glanced over his shoulder, as if he had been caught doing something wrong and might race off down the street, but he settled down and met Zenia's gaze.

"I was looking for her," he said. "Shop hours say she ought to be in."

"What do you want to see her for?" Zenia kept her tone casual, not wanting to sound like an inquisitor, but he seemed suspicious. Should she draw upon her dragon tear to test whether he was lying or telling the truth?

His bushy brows drew together. "What do *you* want to see her for, human? Your dragon tear is already carved."

Something he couldn't know without drawing upon some magic of his own—she wore her gem under her blouse.

"I'm here on the king's business. And you?" She offered her friendliest smile, but she also silently willed the dragon tear to aid her in pulling the truth from him.

"Just want to talk to the master." He backed away. Could he sense her prying? "But if she's not here, I'll come back later."

As he spun and strode away, Zenia got a strong feeling of embarrassment from him. He didn't want to admit... Oh. He was a young dwarf who'd seen her work back in his home city and had grown smitten with the master carver from a distance. He'd arrived early, ahead of a shipload of dwarves coming to Korvann for work, and he'd hoped to make her acquaintance before other male dwarves came and swarmed her.

"You want me to catch up and thump him?" Rhi fingered her bo as she watched the dwarf's hasty retreat.

"No."

"No? He's oozing suspiciousness like a slug oozes slime."

"He doesn't have anything to do with her disappearance," Zenia assured her.

Rhi frowned over, glancing down at the faint bump under her blouse where the dragon tear lay. "The rock tell you that?"

"It did indeed. Apparently, he has a romantic interest in the master carver and wished to make himself known to her before the competition showed up." Zenia stepped into the spot the dwarf had vacated so she could peer through the narrow window.

"A what?"

"A romantic interest."

"Has he *seen* Master Grindmor? She has a beard you could strangle a horse with."

"I don't know much about dwarves. Perhaps that's an appealing trait."

"Not if you're a horse with your throat being threatened." Rhi stepped up to the window on the other side of the rollup door.

Zenia couldn't see much in the shop's shadowy interior. A few large tools and a counter in the back. Was that the entrance to another room behind the counter?

She bent and tried to tug up the door, but a padlock looped through the handle kept it from opening. "I guess this means she wasn't likely kidnapped at her workplace."

"You don't think kidnappers lock doors on their way out?"

"I suspect Master Grindmor was trouble enough that they would have their hands full subduing her. She has magic in addition to being rather sturdily built." Zenia did not know the extent of the dwarf's powers, but she had caused a tunnel-boring drill to operate on its own in Iridium's underground lair while she also brought a ceiling down on Jev's guards.

"I could bust that lock with my bo."

Zenia eyed the metal clasp of the padlock and willed her dragon tear to unlock it. She didn't know if it could, as she'd yet to discover its full abilities, but she had learned that it was capable of far more than detecting truths. The week before, it had sucked the water out of a well to put out a farmhouse on fire.

A soft *snap* sounded, and the padlock opened. Before Zenia could reach for it, a similar *snap* rang in her head, a crack of power accompanying it, like something using a bullwhip on her brain. Pain stabbed between her eyes, and she tipped over, landing on her back on the sidewalk before she could catch herself.

"Zenia!" Rhi blurted, kneeling and gripping her shoulder.

The sharp pain disappeared, but a harsh throbbing remained. A voice rang out in her head.

Trespassers and thieves will know the wrath of Master Arkura Grindmor!

"Zenia?" Rhi squeezed her shoulder. "Your eyes are open. I know you're in there. You *are* in there, aren't you?"

"I—yes." Zenia swallowed and let Rhi help her into a sitting position.

Several passersby looked curiously in their direction, but only one spoke. "You don't fiddle with a dwarf's shop when she isn't there."

"Thanks for the sage wisdom." Rhi made a shooing motion at him. "Move along and mind your own business."

The man gave her a rude gesture.

"I hate people," Rhi grumbled.

"And yet you want to heroically save lives and be immortalized in song?" Most of the pain, along with the dwarf's voice, had faded from her mind, and Zenia found she could talk again. She wiped a few tears from her cheeks. That had been as abrupt and painful as a fist to the nose.

"Songs aren't required. I'd settle for being immortalized in print. Can you get up?"

"I think so."

Zenia shifted toward her hip so she could push herself to her feet, but Rhi hoisted her up as if she weighed no more than a child.

"I forget your strength sometimes." Zenia straightened her clothes and turned her back toward the street and the passersby.

"Scrawny heroes don't get immortalized."

Zenia scratched her cheek thoughtfully as she eyed the broken lock. She had hoped the dragon tear could open it without destroying it. Maybe she should have been more specific with her thoughts.

"Since we tripped the booby trap," Zenia said, "it seems unlikely that anyone has been in the shop since the last time the master locked it up."

"Probably not. Should we barge right in? What if there are more booby traps? We could bring down one of your junior agents to go in first. Got anyone who is expendable?"

"You know you're the most junior agent in the office, right?"

"That can't be true," Rhi said. "I'm almost twenty-eight."

"It goes by how long you've been working there, not age."

"Oh, damn." Rhi shrugged and bent to unhook the padlock.

"Wait," Zenia said before her friend could pull the door up.

She drew out the dragon tear on the leather thong she'd found in the castle—one day, she would buy a silver chain worthy of the fine gem—and clasped her fingers around it. It warmed her palm and vibrated faintly. Almost... hopefully?

It still disturbed her that the dragon tear had a personality, but at least it always seemed eager to work. She wasn't sure how to request that it spring other magical attacks before she stumbled into them, but she pictured the inside of the shop in her mind, then envisioned padlocks popping open. Maybe that would convey the idea.

Soft creaks, snaps, and groans sounded. The rollup door fell off its frame and almost crumpled to the sidewalk on top of them. Rhi grabbed Zenia, yanking her to the side to keep her from being battered.

"Thanks," Zenia muttered, staring from the collapsed door on the walkway into the shadowy interior of the shop.

"If you were going to rip the door off the hinges, what was the point in breaking the lock?"

Zenia sighed. "Nothing. That was unintentional."

A breeze came from inside the shop, tugging at her braid, and white flashed a step inside the doorway. Another flash brightened the back door behind the counter. The hair rose along Zenia's arms. She wasn't positive magical traps had been triggered, but she'd definitely felt surges of power along with those flashes.

"Is it safe to go in?" Rhi scowled at more passersby who had stopped to gawk into the shop and at them.

"Maybe?"

"That's the confidence that inspires junior agents."

Zenia would have walked in first, but Rhi strode inside, her bo extended like a blind man's cane. Maybe she hoped it would trigger any remaining traps.

A feeling of indignation came from Zenia's dragon tear. Because she still worried there might be traps?

Shaking her head, Zenia followed Rhi inside. She wished she could reaffix the door since she had inadvertently made it much, much easier for looters to take advantage of the master carver's absence. She would have to find someone to repair it, at her own expense if necessary.

The shop abruptly grew darker, and a clang sounded behind Zenia. She jumped and spun toward the entrance. The door was attached again, attached and somehow repaired.

Smugness emanated from her dragon tear.

Rhi looked at Zenia, her face highlighted by a sunbeam slanting through one of the narrow windows. "Going places with you didn't used to be this eerie."

"It's not eerie." Zenia tapped the dragon tear before lowering her hand. "It's useful."

"Uh huh."

"You did request this job."

"Don't remind me. What are we looking for?" Rhi walked to the glass counter in the back of the shop and peered inside. "Not that we can see anything in the dark."

The dragon tear glowed blue, creating enough light to illuminate the area several feet around Zenia. She joined Rhi at the counter, earning another dubious look.

"Eerie," Rhi muttered.

The combination counter and display case held watch bands, jewelry chains, and clasps, and Zenia looked wistfully at one that would go nicely with the predominantly blue-green coloring of her dragon tear. Once they found the master carver, she would reward herself by purchasing it.

"Boring," Rhi announced and walked around the counter toward the door.

Zenia took a longer look at the outer shop, at the shelves and bins full of tools, books, and raw materials. Nothing appeared amiss. Given the value of those materials, it was interesting that the shop hadn't been ransacked after Grindmor had disappeared. If she had been kidnapped, the kidnapper did not care about wealth.

"Hells, this is alarming," Rhi said from the back room.

Zenia hurried through after her and almost bumped into her back. A high window on the alley-side wall let in light, and it was brighter than the front room. She could easily see a desk, chair, shelves, and bulletin boards on one side and a small forge taking up most of the rest of the space. It was the bulletin boards that Rhi stared at.

"What did you find?" As far as Zenia could tell, the inner room was as undisturbed as the outer, with no signs of a skirmish or a hasty departure.

Rhi leaned forward, pulled a tack out of a piece of paper, and handed it to Zenia. "*That.*"

"A picture of a dwarf?"

Someone had sketched a bearded dwarf on the paper. It might have been Master Grindmor, though the artist hadn't been overly blessed with ability, so it was hard to tell.

"That's Grindmor, I think, and there's a *heart* around the picture."

"So?"

Zenia checked the back and found a poem. A love poem from what she could decipher. It had been written using a combination of dwarven and Korvish, switching mid-line depending on the demands of rhyme and meter. Since dwarven words tended to be a couple of feet long, she imagined finding good rhymes in that language was difficult.

"It looks like she has an admirer," Zenia said. It was signed Dorbok Minehafter. Was that the dwarf they'd bumped into outside? Or another admirer? "You find something suspicious about it?"

Zenia had seen jilted lovers involved in revenge crimes, but it was early to assume this Minehafter was involved. Unless he was someone who had seen Cutter getting close to Grindmor and had acted out of jealousy.

"I didn't say it was suspicious. I said it was *alarming*. Who falls in love with a bearded woman?"

"Bearded men, I suppose." Zenia drew out her notebook and wrote Minehafter's name down. It wouldn't hurt to look him up and see if he lived in the city. If nothing else, he might know Grindmor's usual haunts around the capital, places they could check for information.

"Are these love letters?" Rhi pulled a box full of letters and envelopes, some opened and some not, from a shelf.

"Probably receipts or copies of invoices. She does run a business."

Rhi lifted a page. "This one is in Korvish. Mostly. An Ode to an Artist of Unparalleled Renown. Doesn't sound like an invoice."

"The work of Minehafter?"

"No, this is signed by someone else. Rockcrusher. Another dwarf, presumably." Rhi flipped through the letters. "He's written several times. So have others. By the founders, Zenia. There must be twenty different dwarves that have sent her love letters or poems. This one sent a schematic of a... mandoline?"

"A vegetable slicer?"

"Yes, with a giant flyer and all manner of gears. According to the notes, it slices, dices, and juliennes. I guess nothing says love like kitchen tools."

Zenia left Rhi to root through the love letters and poked into the desk drawers, looking for more concrete clues. She found the invoices and receipts she'd expected, along with an accounting book with tidy rows of columns. It didn't take her long to deduce that the business was profitable, and Grindmor didn't seem to owe anyone any money. They didn't find any blackmail threats among the letters or any crossly written messages by spurned lovers. They also didn't find any clues to suggest that Grindmor had returned the affections of any of the admirers, unless it was significant that the drawing had been pinned up instead of in the box with the letters and poems.

"I don't think there's anything here that's going to help us." Reluctantly, Zenia stepped away from the desk.

Rhi returned the love letters to the shelf. "Just proof that Master Grindmor has far more allure to dwarves than she does to humans."

"How can you be positive human men don't find her alluring?"

"I know what men like." Rhi patted her backside.

"A woman with a big bo?"

"Exactly."

Zenia formed thoughts in her mind and tried to ask the dragon tear if there was any magic in the office beyond the booby traps it had disarmed. Powerful artifacts one might kidnap a person for? Hidden cubbies that held arcane secrets? Magical maps leading to distant treasures?

The dragon tear pulsed once against her skin, conveying a negative. Too bad.

Zenia headed for the exit. "Let's finish visiting people on our list of informants before going back to the castle."

She'd hoped she would be able to take clues about Grindmor's disappearance back with her. She hadn't yet been given the assignment to search for the master carver, but she believed it would land on her desk soon, if it hadn't already. Master Grindmor was an important person that many people in the city relied upon. Nobody else could carve dragon tears the way she could.

Zenia wished she could have solved the mystery of her disappearance preemptively since she still felt she had to prove herself to their new king. Rhi might be the junior agent, but Zenia had only been on the job a week longer and felt she'd bumbled the way to solving her first case. She dearly wanted to once again have an employer consider her invaluable.

CHAPTER 4

A S SOON AS JEV REACHED the castle that afternoon, a
page accosted him and escorted him to Targyon's office, saying
only that the king had been looking for him that morning and
wanted to see him as soon as he arrived. That made Jev feel delinquent
in his duties for coming in late.

He thought Targyon would understand that he'd needed to talk to anyone
who might have information about Cutter, but he could have invited Hydal
and the others to see him in Alderoth Castle rather than Dharrow Castle.
He also could have come in sooner instead of staying after the meeting to
play horses and knights with his cousin's children, Drayon and Teeks. But
Teeks, in particular, had taken to Jev and constantly asked for stories about
the "noble battles" he'd engaged in during the war. Even if they weren't
his children, Jev would have felt bad not making time for them, the way
his father had so rarely made time for him when he'd been a boy. One day,
Drayon and Teeks would likely work for the estate—and for him after his
father passed—in some capacity or another, and he wanted to have a good
relationship with them. With *all* the people he would one day be responsible
for. He didn't want to be some distant hard-to-approach liege lord.

Jev hoped Targyon wouldn't think him derelict in his duties here. A
part of him wondered if he'd made a mistake by accepting this job, but
he had obligations to his king and the kingdom too. That was an oath
he'd sworn at fifteen, during his Ceremony of Manhood, and he'd sworn
it again when Targyon took the throne.

He wondered what it would be like not to have any obligations to
anyone. As he passed into Targyon's outer office, he wiped the wistful

expression off his face and reminded himself that he had been awarded a very good life because of the position he'd been born into. It wasn't seemly to complain, even to oneself. The Code of Honor spoke of selfless sacrifice as the noblest of all qualities a zyndar should strive for, and strive for it, he would.

As soon as the secretary knocked on the inner door, two men who had been exchanging parting words with Targyon walked out. They were both zyndar primes and nodded polite greetings at Jev, but after speaking to Hydal, Jev couldn't help but wonder if every zyndar he passed now believed him a schemer with his hooks in Targyon.

"Come in, Jev." Targyon paced in front of his desk instead of sitting behind it.

Seeing him agitated made Jev feel guilty all over again for coming in late.

"Sorry, I wasn't here earlier, Sire. I was at Dharrow Castle. I didn't realize you needed to see me today."

"Family business?" Targyon stopped and pushed his fingers through his hair. Judging by its disarray, he'd been doing that often today. At least he had mostly recovered from the flu that had laid him low earlier in the week. The one hint that he might still be tired and napping often were the slippers he wore instead of his usual boots.

"In a manner of speaking. My father has threatened to arrange a marriage for me if I don't find myself a suitable zyndari lady by the end of summer."

"Ah. My condolences. Though maybe that's easier than propositioning women and being rejected." A fleeting grimace crossed Targyon's face.

Jev assumed any propositioning he'd done had been before the coronation and likely before he'd joined the war effort.

"It's worth risking rejection to find someone you love. Uhm, Sire. Did you know that Cutter is missing?"

"Cutter? I know Master Grindmor is missing. That's what I called you here about."

"You want the agents to look for her?" Jev guessed.

"I want the agents to *find* her. *Soon*."

"You think she's in danger?"

"I don't know, but having her missing could start… an incident."

"With whom? The dwarven embassy?" Jev didn't know where in the city the dwarven embassy was, but since the elves had one, he assumed the dwarves did too.

"Them, too, I suppose, but I was thinking of Preskabroto, the most predominant and most powerful dwarven nation. In the hope of fostering goodwill between our nations, I sectioned off some royal land in the city and offered it to any industrious dwarves that were willing to relocate here. Free land essentially, with the only stipulation being that they would set up shop and sell to the people of Korvann. Kor's subjects would have access to superior dwarven workmanship, the crown would have more businesses to collect taxes from, and it would foster racial diversity, something that the capital and kingdom as a whole have been sorely lacking in the last generation or so."

Jev nodded. "It sounds like a good idea."

"I thought so. Good for the economy, good for foreign relations. That was before a prominent dwarf—not just prominent here but prominent among her own people too—went missing. I fear the dwarves who have accepted my offer will not be pleased to hear this when they arrive."

"How many are coming?" Jev was surprised Targyon had managed to set this in motion so quickly. He must have sent off the offer before he'd officially been crowned. Though surprised, Jev was pleased that Targyon was already working toward the good of the city and the kingdom.

"Five hundred."

Jev stared. "Five *hundred*?"

"On a big dwarven steamship that's due to dock in a few days." Targyon pushed his hand through his hair again. "When I made the offer to King Bladrocknor, I thought he'd put up a poster in his city and that maybe a handful of dwarves would trickle in each year for the next few years…"

"Do you have enough royal land to accommodate that many?"

"Oh, yes. The Alderoths own a large portion of the city. There should be plenty, and I offered them a couple of old mines in the royal mountain forests too. I didn't realize it would be such an enticing offer to so many."

"Hm, a new opportunity for them, perhaps? Cutter has mentioned that his home city is heavily populated and full of master craftsmen and women, so it can be difficult for dwarves to get work. Especially if they have any kind of impairment. That's why he left."

"I didn't know that."

Jev well remembered when Cutter had first ambled into Gryphon Company's camp, offering to carve for the soldiers or repair watches and the like for a small fee. He'd been traveling solo across the war-torn continent and barely making a living. A zyndar officer had needed a rifle repaired, and Jev had been so impressed with the quality of the work and the speed in which Cutter had done it that he'd offered him a job on the spot. Cutter had accepted and often said he appreciated that the soldiers didn't assume he wouldn't be good at his work because he lacked one hand. Jev hadn't expected Cutter to go into battle alongside his people, but he'd taken his job—and the new friendships he quickly made—seriously. Jev owed him for his loyalty and the way he'd often risked his life for the company.

"Yes," Jev said. "I imagine others of his kind have felt the same way."

"Five hundred others, apparently. Jev, I need you and Zenia to find Master Grindmor before the dwarven ship arrives."

"Yes, Sire. We'll find her. I'm sure Cutter knows where she is."

"That would be reassuring if you hadn't opened by saying he's missing too."

"I know, Sire, but at least if they're missing together, we won't have to divert our resources to search for them separately." Jev decided not to ask Targyon if he would have minded Jev using his resources to search for a simple visitor to the city. He didn't think Targyon would object since he'd known Cutter for two years. "Did you already tell Zenia?"

"No, Zyndar Garlok reported that she and Rhi Lin had gone out for cocktails and to play chips early this morning." Targyon's lips twisted. "Which I assumed to mean they were doing work in the city."

"Ah, that's likely. I've yet to see Zenia consume more than a sip of anything alcoholic. She seemed unimpressed by the fine elven wine I offered her."

Targyon arched his eyebrows. "After hours, I assume."

"Yes, Sire. I don't ply women with wine when we're both supposed to be working."

Targyon's expression grew difficult to read. Jev hoped he wouldn't object to his two Crown Agent captains dating each other. Not that they were now. Jev regretted bringing it up. Or alluding to it. Whatever he had done.

"Glad to hear it," Targyon said.

"I'll find her and let her know we're officially on assignment. Oh, do you have any objection to me hiring Hydal from the company?"

"Not at all. Is he willing? I wonder if he'd come up and play a game of Castles and Knights with me."

Jev remembered the two playing out in the Taziira forests on a makeshift board using rocks instead of sculpted figurines. "After he's done snooping on our fellow zyndar, I imagine so. Apparently, I need an agent attending social gatherings and collecting the latest gossip from zyndar and zyndari lips."

"Yes, that would be a good idea. If you want him to be useful, he should be a secret agent, not someone with a desk at the castle."

Jev nodded, realizing he should have thought of that. If people knew Hydal worked for him, they wouldn't gossip about him around the man.

"Good point, Sire. I did promise to introduce him to Rhi, but then I'll shimmy him out of the castle."

"Rhi? The monk?"

"The monk who is even now fantasizing about you in your silk pajamas."

"I hardly think that's true." Targyon scoffed, but his cheeks turned slightly pink. That would teach him to avoid mention of the odd feel of his lush new royal wardrobe in front of ladies. "You're dismissed, Jev."

Jev bowed politely and strode out, wondering if it was early enough in the day to visit the clockmaker's shop Hydal had mentioned. He also wondered where Zenia and Rhi were now. He wanted to let Zenia know about their new assignment.

Deciding to check the agents' office in the basement first, he headed in that direction. He was at the intersection of one of the broad hallways on the main floor when the call of a woman made him pause.

"Jev?" the familiar voice asked, sounding surprised.

He was surprised too. By the founders, he hadn't heard that voice in ten years.

Jev swallowed and turned to face Naysha, his former fiancée and presently another man's wife. She was walking down the hallway, escorted by a guard. Judging by the way the guard pointed at Jev, they had been looking for him.

For some silly reason, his heart started hammering against his rib cage. His armpits pricked, breaking out in a sweat. He felt like the teenage boy he'd been when he first fell in love with her, years before he'd managed to convince her that she, two years his senior, found his attention flattering and loved him back.

"Hello, Naysha." Jev hoped his voice sounded casual.

Did he still have feelings for her? He didn't know. He'd spied on her a few days earlier—her and her three children—but only so he would know she was doing all right. He hadn't knocked on her door, hadn't wanted to interfere in her life.

Logically, he shouldn't want anything to do with her ever again. Even if he could understand her not waiting for him, it still rankled that it had taken less than a year before she'd married someone else. Presumably far less than that before she'd started seeing that Grift Myloron and finding comfort in his arms. How true could her love have been if she'd gotten over Jev and forgotten the promise they made to each other so quickly?

Logic didn't keep sweat from slithering down his spine as she approached, smiling the smile that had made his heart flutter long ago. It didn't have quite the same effect now, but she hadn't lost any of her beauty. She was a little plumper and more motherly, but she'd been but a wisp when they had been together. The padded hips and bosom looked good on her.

"Hello, Jev," she said quietly, drawing close. She stopped at arm's length and slanted her escort a pointed look.

"Zyndari," the guard rumbled politely and retreated back down the hallway.

Jev didn't think the man would normally have let a random woman, even a zyndari woman, roam the castle hallways unattended, but Naysha had a regal I-belong-here bearing. It was also possible the guard assumed that if she was in a Crown Agent's company, she was being watched.

"It's good to see you," Jev offered inanely. He had no idea what to say, nor any idea what she wanted.

Likely not to tell him that her husband was odious and she was leaving him.

She lifted a hand, as if to take his, but ended up threading her fingers together in front of her instead. "I'd heard most of the men who went off to war returned this month. I wasn't sure if you were among them until Grift mentioned reading in the paper that you'd been appointed to an office by the new king."

"That is true."

"I was glad to hear that you're alive and well. I wish... I guess I can't be surprised that you didn't come to see me." She looked down at her clasped hands.

A faint clink came from down the hall as a maid carried dishes toward the kitchens. Jev thought about drawing Naysha aside for a more private discussion, but since she was a married woman, he feared that might give the appearance of impropriety.

He clasped his hands behind his back. "I did think about it, but I didn't know if you would appreciate it if I showed up on your doorstep." He especially hadn't known if her *husband* of nine years would appreciate it.

"I understand."

She was still studying her hands, or perhaps the two gold rings on her fingers. They hadn't been there long ago. Casual jewelry or gifts from her doting husband?

"Jev? I've wanted to tell you for a long time... I'm sorry." Naysha lifted her gaze, meeting his eyes. Hers were wary. Did she expect him to lash out? To turn his back on her?

He might have once, early on, but too many years had passed. The pain was mostly a dull ache now, a wistful wondering of what might have been. His father, he recalled, had approved of Naysha. An appropriate zyndari woman from a bloodline full of great warrior heroes of the past.

"I'm sorry for not writing and telling you myself," she continued. "It was cowardly of me not to. I was so nervous about it, I was making myself sick, and when your cousin mentioned that she had written you... I don't know. I was horrified that you would hear first from her, then relieved that she'd broken the news so I didn't have to. I still planned to write, but somehow the months passed, and I didn't, and then it seemed like it had been too long and that it would be strange to write then. That you wouldn't want to hear from me."

"It's all right, Naysha." Jev made his voice as gentle as he could, though a petty part of him didn't want to let her off the hook so easily.

But no, it was enough that she was distressed over this ten years later. She must have thought of it at least a few times while he'd been gone. "We were young. It was a long time ago. I hope you're happy with Grift?" Jev was proud of himself for using his name rather than calling him by some dismissive derogatory term.

She hesitated but only for a second before nodding. "We're doing well. We have three children, and they're wonderful. Trying at times, but you know how it is."

No, he did not, alas. But he nodded and smiled. "Of course. I'm glad you're well."

"Thank you. That's all I have to say. I just wanted to apologize for being so immature back then."

Not for leaving him, he noted, but he carefully kept his smile fixed in place. He'd been gone. Things would have been different, he was certain, if he hadn't been sent away. But the past couldn't be changed now.

"I admitted to my mother a few years ago that I never told you, and she lectured me terribly about how shameful that was. She'd assumed I'd written and gone to tell your father in person. She said your family would likely never talk to ours again."

"Well, my family isn't that scintillating, so that couldn't have been much of a loss."

She snorted softly, appearing more relaxed now that she'd offered her apology. A part of him almost regretted that she'd felt bad all these years, but it wasn't as if he could have done anything. He could have written her, he supposed, but anything he might have penned back then would have been full of feelings of hurt and betrayal. Better simply to let her go, he'd always thought.

"I hope you'll come by sometime," she said, unlacing her fingers and offering her hands. "Meet the children."

Meeting the children she'd had with another man sounded like one of the more horrifying experiences he could conjure up, but he made himself clasp her hands and nod. "If you need anything, let me know."

He was aware of a side door opening and two people walking into the hallway, but he didn't think much of it, assuming more castle staff were passing through, until he heard a soft gasp. He released Naysha's hands and was surprised to see Rhi and Zenia standing a short distance away.

A guilty lurch assaulted his gut, though he didn't know why. He and Zenia weren't dating, and even if they had been, Jev hadn't been doing anything romantic with Naysha. Even someone walking in on them should have recognized it as a platonic hand clasp. Right?

Zenia, he was certain, had been the one to let out the little gasp, but she recovered quickly and continued forward, her chin tilted upward. Rhi strode along beside her, a frown on her face mingling with a confused wrinkle to her brow as she looked at Jev, then Naysha, then back to Jev.

"Captain Dharrow," Zenia said formally as she and Rhi entered the intersection. They looked to be heading through it toward the stairs on the far side that led down to their office. Her gaze shifted to Naysha, but she paused, probably not certain how to address her.

Jev had the urge to hasten Naysha down the hall and not have the two women meet, but it was too late for that.

"This is Zyndari Naysha Elan," he said. "Naysha, Captain Zenia Cham and Agent Rhi Lin."

"Ah, colleagues?"

Jev hesitated. Zenia was more to him than that, even if she didn't want to be, but he couldn't have explained things to his best friend much less an ex-fiancée from the distant past.

"Yes," he said.

"Nice to meet you, Zyndari." Zenia curtsied, then started past them.

Rhi grunted what might have been a greeting or indigestion. Naysha frowned, and Jev lifted a hand, hoping to forestall some zyndarish correction of etiquette.

"Zenia," Jev said—she'd already hustled past, as if eager to give him and Naysha their privacy. "Are you heading to the office? The king just gave us a new assignment. I need to share the details."

She gave him a look back over her shoulder that was hard to read. "I'll be there."

Jev watched as she and Rhi turned the corner toward the stairs, tempted to run after them and explain that nothing had been going on. Again, he reminded himself that he and Zenia were not seeing each other, that he owed her no explanations regarding Naysha.

"Will you see me out, Jev?" Naysha asked.

"Of course."

She offered her arm, and after hesitating, he linked it into his. They walked out side by side, their talk conversational and meaningless, which was good because Jev didn't have to focus to follow it. He found himself trying to think of what he would say to Zenia.

Nothing, he decided. He would tell her the assignment, and they would discuss work matters, as was appropriate for co-workers to do with each other. That was what they were. Nothing more.

"I feel like I should have punched that woman in the nose on your behalf," Rhi announced as they stopped in front of the door to their office.

"I'm glad you didn't." Zenia didn't reach for the knob, not yet. Other agents would be at their desks inside, and she needed a moment to compose herself. She didn't know why, but seeing Jev clasping hands with that woman had rattled her. They hadn't been kissing or doing anything romantic, but they'd seemed to have a connection, and for some reason, she had no trouble imagining them doing those things. And that disturbed her.

She fully acknowledged that she'd rejected Jev's offer to date, so she had no right to feel disgruntled if he had a relationship with someone else, but she couldn't dismiss the wild I've-made-a-horrible-mistake-in-telling-him-no thoughts that flooded through her mind.

"Are you sure?" Rhi asked. "I thought you two were—"

"We're not."

"Oh? Why not?"

"I'd rather not talk about it here." Or at all, Zenia silently amended. Even though Rhi had always spoken openly about her interests in men, her monkly vows of chastity aside, Zenia had rarely spoken of such things with her. In part because she'd been Rhi's superior in the Water Order organization and in part because there had been so little interest from men. Her inquisitor's robe and reputation had acted as a shield to keep men and women alike from approaching her, and she'd never known how to lower that shield and approach *them*. Zenia always found herself hesitant to admit to Rhi that she'd never had sex, because she didn't know if Rhi would understand her reasons or the vow she'd made, not when Rhi's own vow to the Water Order regarding celibacy had meant so little to her.

"Even if we were seeing each other," Zenia added, mostly because Rhi was staring at her as if she'd grown a third nostril, "there wouldn't be anything wrong with him platonically touching some other woman."

"Even if she's a beautiful woman?"

"Even if." Zenia reached for the knob to end the conversation.

The door opened before her fingers wrapped around it. The stocky, glowering Zyndar Garlok stood there.

His scowl deepened when he saw them.

"Where have you been all day?" he demanded of Zenia.

She bristled at the lack of respect in his tone.

"Zyndar Garlok," she said as calmly as she could, hating that she had to zyndar him when she was his superior, at least in this office. "As I clearly told you this morning, we went into the city to check in with the office's civilian informants. I understand that our chat was six hours ago, but if you forgot about it in that time, you may want to see one of the castle's doctors. Perhaps they can prescribe a potion to enhance your memory."

Garlok's nostrils flared. He looked like a horse after a hard run.

"For all I know, you were off lollygagging all day," Garlok growled.

"I fail to see how it would be your concern even if we were, though I assure you that I don't lollygag. Ever."

"It's true," Rhi said. "She works even on holidays. It's a little sad, really."

"Thank you for the support," Zenia murmured to her.

Rhi slapped her on the back. "No problem."

Garlok grumbled something under his breath, then strode forward, clearly intending to mow them over if they didn't move. Zenia thought about calling upon her dragon tear to form a barrier around her so she could hold her ground and he would bounce off, but that would be immature. Besides, the dragon tear didn't always do things exactly how she wished. She gritted her teeth and stepped aside.

As Garlok passed, still managing to bump her shoulder with his, he startled her by slipping on something. Before he could catch himself, his feet flew up, and he fell onto his back. Zenia and Rhi barely managed to jump out of the way.

Belatedly, Zenia thought she might have caught him and kept him from falling, but she'd been more worried the huge man would hit her.

Garlok cursed and pushed himself to his feet immediately, pausing to turn his glower onto the stone floor. From the way he'd pitched backward, Zenia wouldn't have been surprised to spot a moldering banana peel down there, but she didn't see anything.

A smug feeling of contentment emanated from her dragon tear.

She stared down at it. *Did* you *do that?* she asked silently.

The gem had never spoken to her—that would have alarmed the founders' gifts out of her—so she didn't expect an answer. But the smug feeling shifted to a faint sense of innocence. One she didn't quite believe.

"Having trouble walking today, Garlok?" came Jev's voice from down the hallway. "Maybe you shouldn't stay out so late drinking."

Garlok turned his glower on Jev. The fall hadn't done anything to improve his mood.

"I'd accuse you of greasing the floor, but a zyndar wouldn't stoop so low," Garlok said, then squinted suspiciously at Zenia.

She did her best to mentally convey to the dragon tear that she didn't want anything else to happen to the man.

"I would," Rhi said cheerfully. "I'll have to start carrying cans of the stuff around to rub all over the boots of annoying zyndar."

Jev snorted. Garlok's eyes narrowed further—it was amazing he could still see out of them. Finally, he stomped past them. It was careful stomping with much surveying of the floor as he jammed each foot down.

Zenia didn't relax until he disappeared up the stairs. Though she didn't relax entirely then, either, for Jev remained, as did her thoughts of that woman. Naysha. Why was that name familiar? He'd mentioned her once before, Zenia thought. Oh founders, wasn't that the name of the woman he'd intended to marry but who had married someone else when he'd gone off to the war? What would *she* be doing at the castle?

Jev smiled tentatively at her. Zenia nodded professionally at him. Rhi looked back and forth between them, as if she wanted to say something, but she didn't.

"I met with the king a little while ago." Jev pointed toward the ceiling and the floors above them. "We're to prioritize finding Master Grindmor.

There are hundreds of dwarves on their way—Targyon invited them to open up shops in Korvann—and it would be politically inconvenient if our most prominent dwarf in the city was missing when they arrived."

Zenia nodded again. "We went to Master Grindmor's shop today, hoping to find clues about where she's gone—or who might have taken her."

"Already? Did you know we'd get this assignment?"

"I guessed, and I knew your friend Cutter was missing."

Jev frowned. "Yes. I'm hoping we'll find him when we find her."

"The shop hadn't been disturbed at all. At least until we disturbed it." Zenia held back a grimace. She didn't want to admit that she and her dragon tear had broken the lock—and the magical alarms. Even though they had searched the premises in order to find clues to *help* Grindmor, she felt like a burglar who'd gone thieving in the night.

"I don't know about that," Rhi said. "I found the love poems disturbing."

"Disturbing isn't the same thing as disturbed." Zenia waved at her, hoping she wouldn't go into details. Again.

"No? Are you sure?"

"Yes."

"Rhi," Jev said, "would you mind giving us a couple of private minutes?"

"In the hall?"

"Well, we don't have a private office of our own." Jev's expression grew wistful, and Zenia wondered what he was imagining. Maybe just being able to shut a door to keep out Garlok.

Rhi reached for the knob. "Want me to scowl ferociously at anyone who tries to leave while you're getting private out there?"

"That's not necessary," Jev said. "This won't take long."

Rhi shrugged and stepped inside, her bo clunking on the door frame. A few agents in the office had been talking, but their voices stopped. Zenia imagined them peppering her for gossip.

The door closed, leaving her standing in front of Jev and wondering what to do with her hands. Clasp them behind her back? Stuff them in the pockets of her dress? Why was she even worrying about it?

"I'm surprised there weren't any clues at her shop," Jev said, "but I trust you would have found them if they had been there."

"Yes," Zenia said before realizing that sounded arrogant. "I mean, Rhi and I poked through everything thoroughly, and my dragon tear didn't sense any magic outside of the traps Grindmor likely set herself."

"I've got another lead. I met with some of the officers I worked with—and that Cutter also knew—in the army. One saw him going into a clockmaker's shop four days ago. I don't know what Cutter would want with a timepiece, so I'm guessing he was following a lead of his own in his quest to find Grindmor's special tools."

"You want to go check the shop?"

"Before it closes today, yes. Do you want to come with me?"

"Yes," Zenia said, before she could question if he truly wanted her to come or was simply being polite in asking. She wouldn't want to miss a chance to investigate a lead.

"Good. Are you ready to go out again now?"

"Yes."

He continued to stand facing her instead of heading toward the exit. She'd suspected the clockmaker lead wasn't the reason he'd asked Rhi to leave, so she patiently waited for him to say more.

"Are we all right?" Jev asked quietly, pointing to her chest, then his. "Or do we need to, uhm, talk about things?"

"I don't need to talk."

"No?"

"You're the one who's been avoiding the office." Zenia didn't add *and me*, not out loud. She didn't want to accuse him of anything, and she truly hoped her decision wouldn't make their relationship awkward going forward.

"I have not." His spine straightened, a touch of that zyndar arrogance bleeding into his stance. Usually, he only got that when someone accused him of not intending to keep his word.

"There's dust on your chair."

"I have a dusty butt."

Zenia arched her eyebrows.

He turned his hand palm up. "I went out to Dharrow Castle yesterday and spent the night. I needed to talk to my father about a few things."

Zenia almost asked him if the possibility of an arranged marriage was one of those things, but that was none of her business. Even so, she caught herself asking, "Is it settled?"

Jev sighed. "Not in the long term, but for the moment, I hope."

That sounded ominous.

"Shall we go look for red beard hairs in the clockmaker's shop?" Jev smiled and extended his hand toward the stairs.

"Such long, coarse things might muck up the inner workings of a clock."

"Of that I have no doubt."

CHAPTER 5

N O SIGN OF BEARD HAIR yet," Jev announced.
Zenia cocked an eyebrow at him. They were walking through the Earth Dragon quarter, following the wide cobblestone street leading to a series of shops carved into an old quarry that had once been outside the boundaries of the city.

"You think you'd notice it amid the dirt and cobblestones?" Zenia asked, willing to go along with his humor.

"Oh, absolutely. You'd trip over it."

"What are we going to do when the king's five hundred dwarves—and their beards—arrive?" she asked.

Jev had filled her in on more of the details of his meeting with Targyon on the way over.

"Spend our days getting tangled up and tripping. It's the price we have to pay so the world learns to once again see Korvann as welcoming and friendly rather than xenophobic and belligerent."

"Do you think that's truly how the other races see us?"

Zenia had rarely traveled outside of the city and had never been outside the kingdom. According to the newspapers, Kor's relationships with neighboring kingdoms along the coast and the desert tribes over the mountains to the south weren't exactly cozy and comfortable, but there had been peace among the human nations since before she'd been born. But Jev, far more traveled than she, might have a different perspective.

"The elves and dwarves certainly do right now." He raised his voice to be heard over a steam wagon clattering across the nearby cobblestones. "We started the war with the Taziir, and dwarves have long been allies to the elves. I doubt my invasion of the elven embassy in town helped anything." Jev spread his hand in a helpless gesture, then turned it into a point. "There's the clock shop."

They had reached the mouth of the quarry. The street descended into what had been turned into a brick square full of tables, potted trees, and a hulking bronze fountain of the Earth Dragon, its curving tail poised in the air behind it like a whip about to crack. Shoppers strolled around and occupied most of the tables while the scents of spiced lamb and fish drifted from a vendor's tent.

The clockmaker's shop was easy to spot, thanks to a wood and copper tower clock built into the wall beside its front door.

"It looks like it's open." Zenia waved to someone walking out. This was already more promising than Grindmor's locked and abandoned shop.

They walked around the fountain and through the front door. Ticks, tocks, and the bings of bells echoed from dozens of clocks in all manner of sizes.

Jev led the way to a counter along one side where a boy of fifteen or sixteen used tiny tools to repair a pocket watch.

The owner's apprentice, Zenia assumed.

"I'll talk," Jev murmured to her before stepping up to the counter and giving the spot where her dragon tear lay a significant look.

Zenia nodded and stopped behind his shoulder. She didn't like appearing like anyone's assistant but reminded herself that this was about Cutter, Jev's friend. Besides, she believed she could suss out truths easily enough even if she wasn't the one doing the questioning.

"Hello, friend. I'm Zyndar Jevlain Dharrow, here on the king's business."

The boy, engrossed in his work, hadn't noticed them approach, and he dropped his tools with a clatter.

"Zyndar, sir," he blurted. "The king?" He bowed clumsily, almost clunking his forehead on the counter.

"Yes. Is your master or employer around?"

"Mr. Horinth should be back in an hour, Zyndar." The boy looked at Zenia. "And, er, Missus Zyndar? Zyndari."

"Captain Cham." Zenia decided to be pleased the kid acknowledged her presence, rather than only talking to Jev, however fumbling his address was.

"Captain?" The boy's eyebrows disappeared under his scraggy bangs. "Are you with the watch? I didn't—I mean, it's been three years since I took that food. I work for Mr. Horinth now. I don't thieve. Ever. I swear!"

"Relax, boy," Jev said. "What's your name?"

"Uhm." The kid eyed Zenia warily. Thinking she would arrest him for the heinous crimes he'd committed as a twelve-year-old? "Sashan."

"We just want to ask a couple of questions, Sashan." Jev made his tone soothing.

Zenia wondered what it said about her that she was less good at soothing tones than he.

"Were you working here four days ago?" Jev added.

"All week. I'm learning how to repair watches and clocks. And I interact with customers when Mr. Horinth is doing deliveries. Oh! Do you want to hear about our specials? Those clocks near the window are ten percent discounted, and—"

"No." Jev lifted a hand. "Thank you. Four days ago, did you have a dwarf customer come in? He would have had a hook instead of a right hand."

The boy paused and glanced over his shoulder at what appeared to be a solid stone wall. Zenia didn't see a door anywhere along it that would have suggested a back room.

"I think so," the boy told Jev, "but he didn't talk to me. He met with another customer over there for a few minutes, and then they left."

Sashan had been nervous since they'd introduced themselves, but now, his anxiety grew more noticeable, both visibly, as he repeatedly wiped his hands on his trousers, and through the dragon tear. Zenia sensed his distress and that he was... if not lying, then not telling the whole truth. He was afraid to, she realized.

"Neither of them purchased anything or spoke to you?" Jev asked.

"No, they went outside. Left the shop. I wouldn't have even remembered them, but dwarves don't come into the shop often. They both left," the boy repeated.

Jev looked at Zenia. Even though she hadn't alerted him of what she sensed, he must have also felt the boy wasn't telling the whole truth.

Zenia stepped closer to the counter. A feeling of eagerness emanated from her dragon tear, and it warmed against her skin.

"Had you seen the person the dwarf met before?" she asked.

"No," Sashan blurted. A lie.

"Was it a man or a woman?"

"A man." True.

"And how often does he come in the shop?"

"He doesn't." The boy shook his head vigorously. "I told you, ma'am—uhm, Captain. He was never here before."

Zenia knew the dragon tear wanted to sift through his mind—she felt like a handler with a dog on a leash, fighting to restrain it—but she didn't want to use so much force on someone so young. She let a bare trickle of its mind-manipulation energy out. Enough, she hoped, to entice the boy to tell the truth.

"What's his name?" she asked firmly. "And how often does he come in the shop?"

"Morash," Sashan whispered, his eyes growing glazed as they locked onto hers.

Zenia recognized the name—or nickname. It belonged to a higher-up in one of the city's criminal guilds. Night Travelers, that was it. She hadn't dealt with him in her previous investigations for the Water Order, but she knew most of the names of the top troublemakers. She was fairly certain he was second or third in charge after Digger.

"He pays Mr. Horinth not to say anything," Sashan said, "and I'm not supposed to say anything either. I'll get in trouble." An anguished expression leaked through the glazed look.

"We won't tell anyone you told us," Jev said gently. "But we need to know the truth, especially if my friend Cutter was involved. We're on a mission for the king."

The boy's expression only grew more anguished.

"What does Morash pay your master for?" Zenia asked, trying to make her tone as gentle as Jev's. She had questioned children on occasion but felt more comfortable using her firm tone on adults.

"Not to see him."

"See him doing what?"

"Passing through. And I think he promised Mr. Horinth protection if he ever needs it."

"Passing through?" Jev looked pointedly around the shop carved into a cliff. The front wall, made from wood, was the only one with windows and a door. A *visible* door.

Zenia looked at the stone wall behind Sashan, at the spot he'd glanced toward earlier.

"On his way to and from." The boy shrugged. "I don't know where he goes. I was told not to ask."

Jev's brow furrowed.

Zenia directed her dragon tear to focus on the wall, silently willing it to explore, to let her know if it sensed anything back there.

Right away, the image of a dark tunnel carved into the cliff came to mind. She envisioned the secret door hiding it opening, and the dragon tear hummed against her skin, a faint blue glow escaping through the front of her dress.

The boy noticed, and his eyes bugged out.

A rumble came from the wall, and a door carved from the stone ground open. The boy yelped and ducked behind the counter.

A dark tunnel exactly as the gem had shown Zenia stretched into the cliff.

"Passing through," Jev said. "Now I see. Where does it go?"

Sashan shook his head, only his eyes above the counter. Genuine fear seeped into his voice as he whispered, "I don't know. You can't open it from this side. I never tried, but that's what the man said."

Another image sprang into Zenia's mind, this time of a scar-faced man gripping the boy by the collar and nearly yanking him from his feet as he growled a warning. If the boy ever went into the tunnel or told anyone about it, the man would skin him alive, then kill his sister and mother too.

Indignation flared in Zenia's chest, and she vowed to arrest Morash if they encountered him. After punching him repeatedly.

"Did Cutter—the dwarf—go down the tunnel with this Morash?" Jev asked.

"I don't know," Sashan said, but a memory rose to the surface along with the words, of Cutter following the scarred man into the tunnel and the door shutting behind them.

Zenia nodded once at Jev.

His jaw firmed in determination, and he moved around the counter and toward the tunnel.

"I'll get in trouble if he finds out I told," the boy whispered.

Jev paused in the entrance. "You *didn't* tell. Captain Cham and her magical rock found out on their own."

The boy looked at the front of Zenia's dress but only shook his head, tears welling in his eyes.

"If anyone asks," Jev added, "just say a zyndar made you tell. If anyone threatens you, you come see me at Dharrow Castle. If I'm not there, ask for my cousin Wyleria. She'll take you in and give you Dharrow protection. You've got my word on it, all right?"

"What about my sister and mum?"

"They can come too. We'll take care of them."

The boy hesitated, then nodded shakily.

"Coming, my lady Captain?" Jev offered his arm to Zenia, as if he meant to escort her into a ballroom rather than a dingy tunnel with a damp mildew scent drifting out of it.

"Of course." Zenia looked toward the windows to make sure nobody was peering in to witness any of this—and possibly blame the boy— then joined Jev in the tunnel. Since Jev's arm was still out in offering, she laid her hand on it, though she felt silly doing so.

Sashan seemed slightly less distraught after Jev's promise, but he made a point of picking up his tools and turning his back to them. Clearly not wanting anything to do with them.

Zenia and Jev had only taken three steps into the tunnel when the door rumbled shut again of its own accord. Zenia glanced back uneasily as darkness fell over them. She didn't think the dragon tear had done that.

"Hm," Jev said. "It's possible I should have asked the kid for a couple of lanterns before striding into a dark tunnel."

Before Zenia could form a silent request, her dragon tear flared, its blue illumination shining through her dress. She pulled it out on its thong, letting it lie on top of the fabric. The light was sufficient to brighten the sides of the tunnel and more than ten feet ahead of them.

"That's handy." Jev patted her hand, his calloused palm warm against her skin, and she grew aware of the firm muscles of his arm beneath her fingers. "Maybe I *should* let Targyon lend me a dragon tear."

"So you would never need a lantern again?"

"Precisely." He smiled and winked. "Think how useful that would be when going to the latrine in the middle of the night."

Zenia snorted. "You say the most romantic things when we're alone together."

His smile grew lopsided, and he lowered his arm. She winced inwardly, realizing she shouldn't allude to being romantic with him, however much a joke it had been.

"If latrine talk isn't to your tastes," he said, "perhaps we can go back to discussing beard hair."

"Or we could see where this tunnel goes."

"Wise."

Jev stuck his hands in his pockets, and they walked down the passage, side-by-side but no longer with linked arms. Zenia wished she hadn't made the joke and that her hand was still on his arm.

She heard water running in the distance and made herself focus on the task at hand. They might run into trouble in here, especially if it turned out to be a back door into the Night Travelers' lair. She wondered what had led Cutter to that guild. Had he wanted their assistance? Or had he suspected them of having Grindmor's diamond tools?

Zenia believed Iridium of the Fifth Dragon guild had originally taken them, but she had either moved them before Grindmor located them, or someone else had taken them. A rival guild?

It was also possible Cutter had sought out the Night Travelers for information. They were known to be procurers of such as well as deliverers of messages—Zenia well remembered the Night Traveler agent who'd delivered a threat to her and Jev out at Nhole Castle. The guild also fielded assassins, though from what little Zenia knew of Cutter, she couldn't imagine him hiring an assassin to deal with his problems. Dwarves, in general, were honorable and had independent streaks.

"Even floor," Jev said as they continued, the water growing louder. "Definitely carved by man. Or dwarf, I suppose." He moved to one of the walls. They were as smooth as the floor and ceiling, the whole tunnel having a circular shape. "A dwarf with a giant steam-powered tunnel-boring machine, perhaps?"

"Such as Master Grindmor used to get us out of Iridium's lair?"

"Maybe. I suppose she could have been responsible for this, but why would she be working with the Night Travelers? She seemed coerced into working with Iridium and only because she wanted a lead on her tools." Jev started walking again but dragged his fingers along the wall, then rubbed them together and held them closer to Zenia's light. "I'm trying to tell if there's dust on the walls. It's hard to gauge if a tunnel is a week old or a hundred years old."

"I don't think dust collects on vertical surfaces." Zenia waved at the ceiling. "You would expect rock to settle over time, though, and cracks to appear, the occasional bit of rubble to fall. This is still seamless."

Jev nodded. "It's surprising how many tunnels are under the city that I had no idea about. You wouldn't think you'd find so many, if only because Korvann is right on the ocean. Wouldn't tunnels below sea level naturally fill with water? If they weren't pumped out regularly?"

"I think so, but only the half mile around the docks is truly that low. The Air and Earth quarters are well up the ridge toward the castle. I'm sure we're a couple hundred feet above the water here. Iridium's tunnels would have been too. They were…" Zenia paused, attempting to imagine a map of the city in her head. "We may not be far from them, actually. I don't know where the outer borders were, but I got the impression her hideout was large."

"It is."

He sounded certain. Zenia looked curiously at him. She didn't think he had seen more of it than she had. Unless he'd been back since the night they had been kidnapped.

"Lornysh was helping Cutter fill in a map the other day," Jev explained. "I didn't look that closely—now, I wish I had—but the tunnels were extensive. I suppose they didn't *all* belong to her guild, but I don't know."

"How did Lornysh know so much about them?"

As they continued forward, Zenia imagined Iridium adding notches to her bedpost that signified elven lovers.

"I don't know exactly, but he mentioned having to find hidden ways to navigate the city," Jev said. "People find him suspicious for walking around in late spring with a cloak and a raised hood."

"What's keeping him here?"

The walls grew green with a mildew carpet as the water noise increased. The dragon tear's blue light didn't flatter the fuzzy growth, and Zenia wrinkled her nose at its pungent scent.

"I'm not entirely sure," Jev said. "I'd say it was my charisma and innate appeal, but I've been so busy that we haven't done much together. I barely knew—he was the one to tell me Cutter is missing."

"Oh? And is he above suspicion?"

"Yes," Jev said firmly and without hesitation.

Zenia eyed him but didn't argue. Jev knew the elf a lot better than she did, though she couldn't help but wonder why Lornysh had sided with the kingdom army against his own people.

"Is that a pond? Or a river?" Jev pointed ahead, toward the edge of the gem's influence.

"Both?"

The tunnel they followed led straight to a stony bank with a pool blocking their route, water tumbling into it from a fall at one end. It must have exited underwater through some hole on the far side. The area appeared more natural than the drilled tunnel, with limestone walls and jagged boulders jumbled around the pool.

"This must be the Little Jade River," Jev said. "It goes underground a couple of miles outside of the city, and I'd heard that it empties into the Jade just before it reaches the sea."

"The tunnel doesn't go on." Zenia pointed to the lumpy rock wall opposite the pool from them.

"That's surprising. If this Morash passes through that clock shop regularly, there must be a *through* to pass to. This is a lovely spot, but I can't believe he comes here to meditate."

Zenia spotted a brown cylinder on the ground between two rocks and reached for it. It turned out to be the remains of a cigar. "How about to smoke?"

"You think his wife kicks him out of the house and he has to come here to do that? Do members of criminal organizations have wives and houses?"

"If he's like Teitor the Trafficker, whom I helped arrest a year ago, he could have wives and houses in multiple kingdoms."

"That sounds like a lot of work." Jev leaned out of the tunnel to peer to either side of it.

There wasn't a path, but he stepped into the pool and headed toward the waterfall. It wasn't that shallow, even along the stone wall.

"Careful," Zenia said, watching the water churning around Jev's thighs. "There might be crocodiles in there."

He jumped, looking down in alarm, then glared over his shoulder at her.

"Sorry." She lifted an apologetic hand, remembering that he was less than fond of the creatures. "I'm sure there aren't. There wouldn't be anything for them to hunt."

"Except nosy agents," Jev grumbled, his voice barely audible over the waterfall.

Zenia leaned out and turned her chest toward the fall, trying to provide more light for him. She wasn't yet ready to jump in after him. The spray droplets reaching her cheeks were icy cold. The Jade and Little Jade flowed straight from the snow-capped peaks of the towering Erlek Mountains.

Jev found a gap between the waterfall and the stone wall, stuck his head inside, and then climbed up into it. Zenia blinked as he disappeared from sight.

Assuming it was some tiny niche behind the waterfall, she waited for him to reappear. But long seconds passed, and he did not. Did a new tunnel start up back there? Could he see without her dragon tear?

Reluctantly, she removed her shoes and stockings, hiked up her dress, and eased one foot into the water. She gasped at the icy water and how strong of a current whipped past her bare legs. Rocks slick with underwater growth licked at the bottoms of her feet, and she bared her teeth. Maybe taking her shoes off hadn't been a good idea.

Still, she made herself continue on, the frigid water rising almost to her waist. The spray from the fall grew stronger, and she gave up on holding her dress above the pool. The hem ballooned out around her on the rippling surface of the water.

By the time she reached the spot where Jev had disappeared, her legs were numb. She patted about on the slick rocks, looking for a way to pull herself up as spray spattered the side of her face.

A hand extended from the dark niche, and she almost lost her footing. Jev lunged and caught her under the shoulder. Before she could thank him, he gripped her other armpit and hoisted her into the air. She squawked and grabbed his shoulders. He lifted her easily, carrying her behind the curtain of water before setting her down.

"Thanks," she said, her teeth almost chattering. "I think."

"You're not sure?"

"If I should thank you for disappearing and forcing me to follow you through an icy pool?"

"I'm sure I didn't *force* you." Jev smiled, his dark hair plastered to his head. He lowered his arms to her waist but didn't let go, as if he feared she would topple over if he released his support.

But she was fine. The rough rock floor was relatively even back here and wet but not slick like the bottom of the pond. She didn't step away from him for she could feel the warmth of his hands through her wet dress. They were the only warm thing around, and she wanted to press herself closer rather than pulling away.

"Are you all right?" His brow creased, and he looked down at her.

"Yes." She realized she was still gripping his shoulders and could once again feel hard muscle beneath his clothing. She ought to let go.

Instead, she made the mistake of looking down. His hair wasn't the only thing plastered down by water. Her dragon tear continued to glow, and she could see every muscle of his chest through his thin wet shirt. Her mind jumped back to the night in Iridium's lair when she'd seen him naked—*all* of him naked. Odd how she could barely remember the faces of the men who'd held them prisoner, but she remembered his every contour.

Blushing, she jerked her gaze up, certain he'd noticed her gaping at his chest. But his gaze was still cast downward, toward *her* chest. She was almost as soaked as he, and her dress clung to her breasts and hips, leaving little to the imagination.

Maybe he felt her gaze upon his face, for he lifted his eyes. He didn't appear embarrassed at having been caught looking. When his eyes met hers, a zing of energy seemed to leap between them, and she no longer felt the cold. His look smoldered with heat, and she felt that warmth pour into her. With no conscious thought, she stepped closer until their chests touched.

His gaze shifted to her lips, and she knew with all her heart that she wanted him to kiss her. Wanted him to slip his arms around her.

That would be the right thing, the back of her mind said. She'd been foolish to push him away. He wasn't some cad who would abandon her once they had sex. He was honorable. He wouldn't treat her poorly. There was no reason they couldn't be enjoying each other's company every night. They could be enjoying each other's company right now.

She parted her lips and tilted her head back, inviting him to kiss her. Inviting him to wrap his arms around her, his entire body around her.

Jev blinked, then jerked his gaze from her. He cleared his throat and stepped back, dropping his hands.

As soon as his body separated from hers, icy air swept in, leaving her shivering in her wet dress. Disappointment flooded her as Jev turned his back on her. His shoulders rose as he took a deep breath.

"I'm glad you came," he said, still not looking at her. "I could use your light."

He pointed toward the far side of the small cave Zenia had barely noticed after he'd pulled her inside. She made herself peer around now. It was more of a shelf than a cave and didn't extend far behind the waterfall, only about six feet before slanting down to meet the ground. He stepped up to the damp rock on the far side and waved for her to join him.

"You might want to make the glow softer if you can," he added, leaning his head against the wall.

No, she realized. He was looking at something. *Into* something.

She had to stand shoulder to shoulder with him to see what. A horizontal gap a couple of feet long and three or four inches high ran through the wall. Jev glanced at her shoulder, then shifted sideways so she could see. And so they weren't touching.

Zenia peered into the gap, surprised to see light on the far side. Not a lot of it, perhaps only the illumination of a single lantern. The rock wall was only a few inches thick here, and she could make out a large room carved into the stone beyond it. A wood door stood closed on the far side.

"What—" she started to ask, but the door opened, and she shut her mouth.

Two men walked into view. She recognized the face of one before they came closer to the crack—to this conveniently placed peep hole—cutting down the view to only their chests. It was one of Iridium's guards, one of the ones who'd escorted Zenia to that cell.

Two more people stepped into view from the side, both carrying crates. Zenia thought she heard voices but barely. With the waterfall roaring in her ears, she couldn't make out words.

She wrapped her fingers around her dragon tear, both to dull its glow and in the hope that it could augment her hearing somehow.

"Put them over there," she instantly heard one of the men say. "The boss'll want to inspect this shipment firsthand before we fence anything or store it in the vault."

"No kidding, brains. Get out of my way."

When the men stepped out of their limited view, Jev leaned back—he probably couldn't hear anything. Zenia lifted a hand toward him as she willed the dragon tear to show her the room, just as it had the tunnel.

Its earlier eagerness had faded, and a sense of boredom came from it. Were people carrying boxes around uninteresting? Or did it believe she wouldn't get anything useful out of the spying?

She added a hint of sternness to her mien as she once again envisioned it showing her what lay beyond the wall. This time, the gem did so, and she grew aware of a large room used for storage with boxes, barrels, and bolts of silk stacked along one wall. But that wasn't all. The room opened up into a cavern that appeared natural, long ago carved out by the Little Jade River flowing through it.

Two longboats had been dragged to a stone bank. Zenia's vision changed as the dragon tear zipped past the boats, out into the water, and down a winding underground channel. Light came from ahead, an opening with dozens of roots dangling down over it. Someone had cut just enough of them away for a narrow boat to access the open water of the Jade River, a mile inland from its delta.

Jev touched her shoulder, and she was vaguely aware of him asking if she could hear him. She struggled to pull back her consciousness. The gem had almost seemed to want to sweep her down the river and out to sea to soar over the waves. She shook her head. That was her imagination, she was certain.

"I'm fine," she whispered, growing more aware of her own body again and also of Jev standing next to her.

When she was once again viewing the world through her own eyes, she couldn't see the people through the horizontal gap anymore. Nor, she realized, could the dragon tear sense them in the room. They'd stored their boxes—goods pilfered from some innocent person, no doubt—and disappeared through the doorway. That door was closed again, but she did sense tunnels behind it. The tunnels to Fifth Dragon's lair? Was Iridium the "boss" to whom the men had referred? Zenia believed so based on her brief stay in Iridium's tunnels. This was the same part of the city.

"You must be finding that crack a lot more interesting than I did," Jev observed. "Aren't you cold?"

He rubbed his own arms. She kept herself from looking at them or his chest again, merely stepping back from the crack.

"Yes." And she was. She hadn't been aware of the cold when she'd been swept up in the magic, but her teeth chattered after she spoke.

"I think that's Iridium's lair and someone—that Morash, I suppose—comes back here to spy on it."

Jev nodded. "I assume so." He glanced at her, though he shifted his gaze away quickly. Maybe he was trying not to look at her chest too. "I'm sorry I don't have a dry cloak to chivalrously offer you."

"I think I'd rather have a towel, chivalrously acquired or pilfered from a laundry basket." Zenia pointed toward Iridium's room. "It's attached to a waterway that leads to the river. They're able to row their stolen goods in from that way. I wouldn't be surprised if they took things off ships docked in the harbor, then disappeared up the Jade and into the caverns." She gritted her teeth at the notion of such blatant thievery. "I'm going to tell the watch about this."

"Not a bad idea, but maybe it should wait. Although it was interesting to learn that the Night Travelers spy on Iridium's people, it's a dead-end as far as finding Cutter and Grindmor. We may need to ask Iridium for a favor."

"I'm not asking that woman for anything."

"Then *I* might need to ask her for a favor."

"I can guess what she would want in return." Zenia felt a flare of repulsion as she imagined Iridium stepping close to a naked Jev and running a hand over his chest. Or maybe that was... possessiveness? No, she simply didn't want some snake of a woman manipulating him.

"That wouldn't be on the table as an offering," Jev said coolly.

Zenia looked into his eyes, worried she had offended him. "I just meant that it's what she'll want. You told me about her bedpost, remember? She may not be willing to trade information for a lesser offering."

"Once, you couldn't imagine a woman wanting me at all," Jev said, his tone turning dry. If he'd been irritated at the unintended slight to his honor, he got over it quickly. "I'm glad you see me as a greater offering now."

"Well, you were scruffy at the time."

He looked down at his sodden form. Zenia perchance did, too, and immediately regretted it. He might be bedraggled at the moment, but she would definitely insert the word sexy for scruffy.

He looked up, and she jerked her gaze back to his face. Damn it, why couldn't she feel normal around him? Not awkward and stupid?

"And you still are scruffy," Zenia said, trying to cover her discombobulation with a joke. "That woman has odd tastes."

"Yes, no doubt. Come. We both need dry clothes, and it's probably almost dark out by now. Let's go back to the castle and call it a day."

He offered a hand to help her down from the waterfall shelf and through the pool, but she waved him back. She could manage on her own. Besides, touching him stirred up too many temptations.

CHAPTER 6

W HEN JEV HEADED DOWN TO the Crown Agents office in Alderoth Castle, after a short stop in his room to change into dry clothes, he found Zenia standing outside the door talking to Rhi.

Back at that waterfall, he'd suggested they both call it a day, but he'd felt he should check his desk for new reports that might have come in. He wasn't surprised that Zenia must have had similar thoughts. He *was* surprised she'd changed more quickly than he had and beaten him down here.

So much for the notion that women took forever when it came to clothing and getting ready. Not that Zenia was a typical woman. The only time he'd seen her wear makeup had been for their brief date, and she usually pulled her hair back into a ponytail or simple braid. Not that the simple attire detracted from her beauty. She didn't *need* makeup to pique his interest, as that foolish moment behind the waterfall attested.

He'd been so close to kissing her, to *more* than kissing her. And he'd been certain she wanted it. The way she'd stepped close to him, her soft, full breasts touching his chest, her hands gripping his shoulders, her face tipping up toward his, her lips parting. He'd been a hair's breadth from capturing that mouth with his own when he'd remembered her words from the other night, her confession of the promise she'd made to herself not to have sex until she married.

For a selfish and dishonorable moment, he'd thought he might be able to convince her to break that promise, that she might find him so irresistible that she would gladly do so. Thank the founders, he'd been able to flog that notion out of his brain before he acted upon it. Convincing Zenia to break her word would be as bad as breaking his own.

But why did she have to be so sexy? And he so… lonely, damn it.

He hated to think he needed a woman to be happy, but he admitted that he dearly longed to blow off some sexual steam. Not, he thought firmly, with any zyndari woman his father wanted him to marry. But maybe he should wander out into the city and try to find someone to date. Someone to take his mind off—

Rhi and Zenia stopped talking and turned to look at him as he approached.

Jev strove to wipe any thoughts about sex off his face and give them a venerable and regal nod. He also made sure not to slip on the spot where Garlok had fallen earlier. It was hard to be regal while resting on one's backside on the floor.

"I'll let you know if I find out anything around the dinner table," Rhi said, finishing her conversation with Zenia. "I got invited to eat in the castle by that handsome steward Korik who thinks I'll be good company." She winked, then waved and headed up the hallway, nodding at Jev. "Good evening, Zyndar."

"Rhi." He nodded back and stepped aside so she could pass.

She seemed to sway her hips more than usual and offered him a flirtatious smile. He supposed he wouldn't have to look too far to find someone willing to go to bed with him, though on the chance it would disturb Zenia, he wouldn't consider her friend. Even if she *was* willing.

Rhi had taken to wearing loose gray and green trousers and a tunic that she could punch and kick in as easily as she had in her gi. At least, he thought they were gray and green, rather than two shades of gray. Colors were always muted in his eyes, and there were shades of blue and green he only recognized as such because people had told them they weren't gray. He was positive Zenia's eyes were green, but he wondered if they were more vibrant to others than they were to him. He found them perfectly appealing as they were, but he remembered being startled as a boy when one of his cousins had promised him the grass around the pond was a vivid green. Unfortunately, there weren't many colors he saw as vivid. He decided Zenia's eyes must be vivid. The rest of her was memorable, so why wouldn't they be?

"Heading in too?" Zenia nodded to him and reached for the knob.

Jev snorted to himself, realizing it would be hard to find another woman to fall for if he was busy contemplating Zenia's vividness.

"Yes, I want to see if any reports from foreign agents have come in while I've been gone." Since meeting with Targyon that afternoon, Jev had a heightened interest in the goings on in other nations, especially the dwarven nation of Preskabroto. For the last ten years, he hadn't worried about more than Taziira, other than to watch for possible allies from other kingdoms coming to reinforce the elves. He would have to spend time researching how other nations—elven, dwarven, and human—currently felt about Kor.

"Me too." Zenia opened the door. "Though my reports would be from agents from around the kingdom. Maybe it's possible Master Grindmor was taken out of the capital. She—"

Zenia halted, and Jev, walking in behind her, immediately saw why. The work day had ended an hour ago, and there was only one agent left sitting at a desk in the office, but it was the irksome Zyndar Garlok.

Jev stepped up to Zenia's shoulder, prepared to defend her if Garlok launched snide comments at her. Or maybe *support* her was the better word, since she'd proven that morning she was capable of launching snide comments right back.

"Nice of you to come in to work today," Garlok drawled, clasping his hands behind his head and leaning back in his chair. "Do you remember where your desks are? I can show you if you've forgotten."

Jev had no idea why the man hadn't followed Targyon's suggestion of retirement. It was obvious he didn't like working for Jev or Zenia.

"No need, Zyndar," Zenia said, heading for their two desks in the back of the office. Maybe she didn't intend to launch comments, snide or otherwise, at Garlok this evening.

Too bad. Jev enjoyed seeing her in defying-zyndar-pomposity mode.

"Dharrow," Garlok said, "it may have escaped your notice, but you and your girlfriend are in charge of the office. That means you're supposed to spend your days *in* the office where people can deliver reports to you and ask questions."

"Thanks for the tip, but *Captain* Cham and I are aware of our duties. We read the handbook you were good enough to revamp for us." Jev smiled icily, far more annoyed at the man's dismissal of Zenia than any suggestion that he was slacking at his job.

Garlok scowled down at his papercut-laden fingers. "I'll be shocked if you've read it already. Or if you intend to at all. I don't know why you took this job, war hero, but it requires more than poking enemies with swords."

Since Jev had never described himself as a war hero, he assumed someone else had described him thus to Garlok. Or maybe Garlok had decided to adopt the term for his own sarcastic needs. It did surprise him that Garlok seemed to think he'd merely been an infantry officer out there. Even if he was still finding his way into this job, and dearly needed to get up-to-date on all foreign and internal affairs, he didn't think himself unqualified, not after leading the intelligence company in the army. Granted, he'd commanded the smart men who'd done most of the footwork and didn't claim any brilliance himself, but wasn't that similar to what he was now doing here? He thought so.

"You're not a field agent here," Garlok went on, and Jev wished he hadn't paused to reflect. It must have given Garlok time to ramp himself up for more. "You *have* field agents. You should spend your days in the office, doing paperwork. Unless you find the paperwork too daunting. Maybe you could *become* a field agent and let me have my old job back." Garlok's eyes glinted, and Jev had no doubt the man would love to zyndar over him and send him off on idiotic errands. Maybe he was even contemplating some way to make that come about.

"The fact that you believe paperwork is more daunting than going into battle with men trying to kill you tells me you did nothing but sit on your ass for the ten years I was fighting for the king in enemy territory." Maybe Jev should have asked Zenia to launch snide comments for him. He didn't seem to be as good at it.

"I can do more from my ass while eating a sandwich and drinking a beer than you ever will from your feet," Garlok said.

"Once you two decide who has the bigger penis, can you come back here, Jev?" Zenia asked.

He grunted, happy for the excuse to end the infantile conversation, and headed past Garlok to where Zenia stood behind her desk, a desk buried in mounds of folders. His own desk was even more covered. Or was the word *smothered*? They'd only brought that desk in for him a few days ago. How could it have acquired so many folders so quickly?

Garlok's face grew a few shades redder, and he lurched to his feet.

Jev thought he might launch a physical attack, but the man merely strode toward the coatrack by the door.

Jev stopped in front of his desk, keeping his back to Garlok so the man wouldn't see his reaction to the towering stacks of folders. Granted, he hadn't been in here much in the last couple of days, but this was ridiculous. Zenia's was piled almost as high, and she *had* been here. Maybe not much today, but in the previous days, she had been. Jev didn't see how so much could have accumulated unless...

He turned, squinting at Garlok. The man was standing with his hand on the doorknob, smirking.

"You sure you don't find that daunting?" Garlok asked.

Had he somehow encouraged all the agents to turn in extra work?

"Not at all," Zenia answered for Jev. "I'm disappointed the stacks are so small. I'll be done with these in an hour, and then what will I do? Help Steward Korik catalog the king's wine cellar?"

Garlok grunted and strode out, slamming the door behind him.

"It's possible that man doesn't like me," Zenia said.

"He just doesn't like that we were promoted and he was demoted. He'll get over it."

Or he would hatch a dastardly plot that they would have to deal with instead of focusing on finding Grindmor. Jev grimaced.

"This is a quarterly weather phenomenon report for the regions around the kingdom," Zenia observed, looking into one folder. "Turned in two months early."

"I'm wagering there's some fluff in these piles."

She opened a folder on another stack. "Hm, some legitimate reports too."

Jev eyed the mounds on his desk. He'd wanted to see if anything important was going on, but the idea of sorting maintenance reports from useful information gave him a headache. It had already been a long day. Maybe he would save this fun for the morning. Or for after they completed their mission.

Jev snorted at himself, disgusted to admit that Garlok had been right in that he *did* find mounds of paperwork more daunting than going into battle. He wouldn't mind a fight right now, a way to release some tension. Maybe he could find Lornysh tonight and get him to spar with him. If nothing else, his friend might have some new ideas on Cutter's whereabouts. Lornysh was likely searching for him too.

"Want to leave this for tomorrow and come with me to get some dinner?" Jev asked.

Zenia used her finger to bookmark a file she'd already started looking through and considered him. "Thanks, but I think I'll wait and have dinner later."

Right, dinner dates might lead to other things. Like them groping each other behind a waterfall. Jev sighed and decided it wasn't a bad idea for them to spend some time apart.

"Good night, Zenia."

"Night," she murmured, her focus already back on the report as she slid into her seat.

After dinner, Jev found Lornysh at the elven embassy. Fortunately, Lornysh somehow sensed him standing outside the courtyard wall and came out before Jev had to lob stones at his window from the rooftop of the nearby tavern.

"Any news on Cutter?" Lornysh asked before Jev could ask a similar question.

Jev felt a twinge of disappointment, knowing that meant his friend hadn't found Cutter either. "Not really. We found out he may have been working with, or perhaps paid, a guild called the Night Travelers to provide information on Iridium's guild, the Fifth Dragon. Or to help him spy on them at least. I take it you haven't learned anything new about his whereabouts?"

"No, and I confess I'm growing concerned." Lornysh pushed back the hood he'd worn as he stepped through the gate, and his silver locks spilled to his shoulders as he leaned against the courtyard wall. "I've hunted all over the city and questioned people from the watch and also from your various criminal guilds."

"They would have likely lied to you."

"They did not," Lornysh said with a chilling confidence that reminded Jev that his friend had a cold, deadly streak. He had even assassinated his own kind before. He was capable of forcefully questioning people and not caring a whit about making enemies among the guilds. "Nobody knows anything about Cutter," Lornysh added. "Or about Master Grindmor. I've assumed they're together, but I also asked about her. As far as the city knows, she's disappeared. You've probably already seen it, but there was a front-page article about her disappearance in one of your newspapers today."

Jev grimaced. He *hadn't* seen it, but maybe a copy was among the piles of papers on his desk. He felt guilty anew for leaving without at least skimming through everything and resolved to go in early in the morning. If he arrived before Garlok, maybe the man would keep his yap shut.

"Do you think they may have been taken outside of the city?" Lornysh asked when Jev didn't speak. "I don't know the rest of your kingdom well, I admit. Do you have any new ideas on where to look?"

He sounded more agitated than usual, and Jev sensed his true concern for Cutter. Judging from the way they constantly sniped at each other, it was easy to think their friendship wasn't that deep, but Jev knew better. They had been the two non-humans in Gryphon Company, both isolated from their own kind and not quite fitting in with the human soldiers. They had spent a lot of time together, even though Lornysh had been a scout often out in the woods, and Cutter had usually been back in camp, carving gems and repairing tools and weapons for people. Jev had occasionally noticed them talking quietly in the trees at night, apart from the humans communing around the campfires.

"I wish I had more ideas," Jev said. "I may have to go see Iridium."

"The guild leader Cutter wanted you to have sex with?"

"Er, yes. But not for that reason. I believe she may know who has Master Grindmor's tools—it's possible *she* still has them stashed away somewhere. They're the most likely bait that would have been used if there truly was a kidnapping."

"I've questioned one of her Fifth Dragon men that I caught out alone in those tunnels. He knew nothing."

"I don't think she's the sort to share confidences with underlings." Jev hadn't seen anyone who had seemed like a mate or second-in-command when he had been there. "I doubt anyone in her organization is privy to all her thoughts."

"So we should question her."

"We?" Jev had been thinking of taking Zenia—and her dragon tear—along, not Lornysh.

Admittedly, Zenia didn't want anything to do with Iridium. Understandable, but Jev thought their new knowledge of the spy hole looking into the Fifth Dragon's storage room might be information Iridium would consider valuable enough to trade for.

"I can effectively get answers from people," Lornysh said.

"Without ripping off their fingernails?"

"Are you partial to the woman's fingernails?"

"No, but she might be."

"Irrelevant."

"Look, Lornysh." Jev patted him on the shoulder. "You're a visitor here, so you don't have to worry about repercussions, but the watch and even zyndar tread lightly when dealing with the guilds. They have a lot of power and influence. If I irked Iridium, I could end up with a legion of assassins on my tail." At least he wouldn't have to worry about his father's marriage plans for him if he ended up dead before this mission was completed.

"So, kill her after we learn what we need," Lornysh said. "Her minions will be too busy attempting to claim her territory for themselves to bother you."

"You're a pragmatic soul, aren't you?"

"I am, but it doesn't take pragmatism to realize the folly of allowing assassins to be assigned to hunt you down. Let us go speak with this woman."

"Very well." Jev didn't need much convincing since he had already been considering it. "But let me do the talking. I want to try bartering information before threatening fingernail removal." Especially since they would have to enter Iridium's domain to find her, and she would be well-protected there. As he recalled, she had a dragon tear of her own, one carved with a dagger. It would lend her superhuman ability in combat.

"I know of two entrances into her territory."

Lornysh did not, Jev noticed, make any promises or agreements regarding fingernails.

"Is either of them from the river?" Jev also knew of two entrances, one that started outside the city walls at the beginning of the mangroves and one that entered from an alley just inside the city wall. They were the ones he'd been led through and escaped through when she'd had him kidnapped. He knew both would be guarded since they had been for his previous visit. Master Grindmor had flattened the men guarding the alley entrance, using magic to bring rocks down on them. Now that Jev thought about it, those rocks may have blocked that entrance permanently.

"No."

"Are they guarded?"

"They were the last time I entered the tunnels," Lornysh said. "I dealt with the guards."

Jev decided not to ask if those guards were still alive. "Let's see if we can find the river entrance that Zenia described to me—her dragon tear showed it to her. It probably won't be guarded, and if I come in that way, Iridium should believe me when I say she has a breach in security."

"That sounds more complicated than dealing with guards."

"Are you not up to the challenge?"

"I'll accept any challenge. Let me go get my bow."

Jev offered him an army salute, his hand to the side of his eye, and smiled.

CHAPTER 7

W HAT HAS YOU SO ENGROSSED? Love letters?"
At the familiar voice, Zenia sat up straight in her desk chair.
Her back ached a protest at her choice to sit in the same spot
hunched over for so long.

Rhi was walking down the center aisle toward her, a lantern in her
hand. Most of the lamps in the office had been extinguished long ago.
Not wanting to be wasteful, Zenia had only left the ones on her desk and
Jev's desk burning.

"I had my date with Steward Korik," Rhi said, "in case you were
wondering. I'm heading back to my palatial horse loft room now." Rhi
looked at the desk in front of Zenia, the folders spread open across it.
"It's late. Not as late as Korik would have liked, but he was overly gropy
for my tastes, and I had no qualms about letting him know."

"Gropy?"

"It's a word. It describes a man who thinks he can slide a hand
between a woman's thighs whether she's given him the touch-me look
or not."

"Oh." Zenia did not know why Rhi had returned to the office, but
Zenia was delving into the foreign-agent reports on Jev's desk and
finding them quite interesting, so she wanted to go back to reading. She
hadn't planned to start organizing his mess—it had taken her three hours
to wrangle hers into tidiness—but she'd decided she would help him
by going through a couple of piles. She'd seen that daunted expression
on his face, the one he'd carefully hidden from Garlok, followed by an
almost panicked one. She believed he would appreciate it if he had a
stack or two fewer to deal with in the morning.

"I guess you're not going to ask what a touch-me look is," Rhi said.

"That's correct. I'd assumed you wouldn't give me one, regardless."

"Nah, probably not." Rhi stopped in front of the desk and tapped one of the folders. "You didn't answer my question."

"About what?" Zenia struggled not to let irritation come out in her tone, but she truly wanted to get back to work.

"Love letters. I'm not your swiftest agent yet, but I do know that's Zyndar Dharrow's desk and not yours."

"Yes, I'm helping him organize his reports."

"You're doing his paperwork? Did he ask you to?"

"No, but I'm sure he won't mind."

"I'm sure he won't either. He'll probably kiss you." Rhi tilted her head. "If you'll allow it. I'm still trying to figure out why you won't. I know he's interested in you. I've seen him look at your chest when he doesn't think anyone is looking."

Zenia pressed her lips together and focused on the report before her. "Did you know that our kingdom is in a precarious position when it comes to relations with other nations?"

She didn't truly want to draw Rhi into a conversation about the documents she was perusing, but it would be better than talking about Jev. And Rhi might grow bored more quickly and go home to bed.

"What nations? Drovak or Vilk?"

"No, we're still on speaking terms with our human neighbors. But it seems our choice to make war on the Taziir has alienated us with them and the three lesser elven kingdoms in the world. Also, the dwarves of Preskabroto and Rocknishgar cut off trade and diplomatic relations with us last winter. I didn't realize that. I don't think it was in the newspapers."

"Maybe Prince Dazron thought it would be wise not to let people know we're making enemies of the other sentient races in the world." Rhi shrugged. "Does it matter though? It's been a long time since we traded much with the dwarves and elves. They have those insular tendencies, right?"

"I'm not sure that's true. There used to be a lot of races that came through Korvann, and we traded with everyone. I've heard that before I was born, trolls, orcs, and ogres even came to the docks and traded from their ships."

"Must have been devastating to the city not to get any more of those shrunken ogre heads that their shamans make."

Zenia tapped the report in front of her. "My point is that I understand now why the king is so eager to patch things up with the dwarves. According to reports from agents monitoring the goings on in three different nations, the trolls of Borc'tol have taken note that we're no longer aligned with any dwarves or elves, any peoples at all who can use magic outside of dragon tears. They've been watching our war and waiting."

"Waiting for what?"

"An opportunity. For us to weaken ourselves and deplete our resources." Zenia decided she had better stay in the office all night to get thoroughly caught up with everything on Jev's desk. She had been thinking of that as his domain and domestic affairs as hers, but if trouble came to Kor's shores from without, it would be a problem for both of them. And for the entire kingdom.

"Well, we did that, didn't we?" Rhi asked.

"Yes." Zenia met her eyes, trying to convey the grimness of the reports.

Rhi frowned at her. "Is there more in there than you've told me?"

"Just that enemies we haven't dealt with in generations have been observed gathering resources and making preparations for travel. Or expansion."

"Enemies like orcs and trolls? They don't work together, right? And they're all over on other continents these days. We'd have a lot of warning if they planned to visit Kor. Weeks, at least. It takes a while to sail an army over in ships. Besides, why would they pick on Kor specifically? There are seven human kingdoms and all manner of smaller tribal nations spread throughout the world. Most of them aren't cozying up to elves and dwarves, either, from what I've heard. Everybody got snippy with each other when it got crowded enough for people to run out of fertile land and resources."

"Nice to know you occasionally picked up a book in between meditating and following your monkly vows of celibacy."

"Ha ha."

"You're right about all of that, as far as I know, but I also know Kor is particularly desirable due to the sea access, rivers that make inland travel easy, and its claim on the ore-rich Erlek Mountains."

"There are other mountains in the world."

"Some more resource-rich than others," Zenia said. "If the archaeologists are to be believed, trolls and ogres had a presence in this area ten thousand years ago. Maybe they want to reclaim the land."

"Ten thousand years ago?" Rhi waved a dismissive hand. "I'm sure ancient history is fascinating, Zenia, but aren't you supposed to be focused on finding that dwarf? Both of those dwarves?"

"We can't let the rest of our work pile up while we work on one case." That was a true statement, but Zenia also did not know where to go next with Grindmor's disappearance. She didn't want to ask Iridium for a favor, nor did she want Jev to barter with the odious woman. She wanted to figure out the problem on her own, as she had so often in the past, without help. Unfortunately, she didn't have any ideas at the moment. Maybe if she went for a walk and let her mind mull over things, she would come up with something.

"You're stuck, aren't you?" Rhi asked.

"No."

"You're usually so focused on an assignment that you wouldn't notice if those stacks of folders jumped off the desk and smacked you on the face."

Zenia glared at her. Maybe it had been a mistake to hire someone who knew her so well.

"I'm getting caught up on work, but I haven't forgotten Grindmor," Zenia said. "Sometimes, you get ideas on how to solve a problem when you're working on something completely unrelated. Or maybe all of this *is* related. What if whoever kidnapped Grindmor knew the king's dwarven visitors were coming and intentionally wanted to start an incident? One that might ensure the dwarves of the world severed the rest of their ties with us and wouldn't come to our aid if we were invaded."

"Sounds like a stretch."

Zenia leaned back in the chair and gripped her chin. She'd been half-joking—or half defending her lack of action on Grindmor's case—but now that she considered the words, she didn't know if they were as much of a stretch as Rhi thought. So far, she hadn't read any reports that truly suggested an invasion force was on the way, just that it would be a good idea to keep an eye on the races that had always hated humans because they seemed to be making preparations for something. For all she knew, they planned to invade each other's lands. Still...

"Who would stand to gain if Kor were invaded?" Zenia mused.

"Uh, no one? Or only the invaders."

"That's not true. In every major upheaval, there are people who lose—usually those tied to the old status quo—and people who win. Those who have been waiting for opportunities to jump into the chaos and find them. Some *make* them."

Rhi's face twisted into a skeptical expression. Zenia didn't let that deter her.

"Who stands to gain from an invasion or some kind of upheaval in Kor?" she repeated. "It would depend on what the result was, I suppose. Would invaders pillage and loot? Or overthrow the monarchy and dismantle the kingdom? If that happened, the zyndar class might disappear. At the least, they might not have anyone to back up their claims that certain lands belong to them."

"Most of them have enough people to make armies of their own and defend their castles. Zenia, even if there was an invasion, we'd fight it off. We have lots of people."

"Do we? We sent a *lot* of young men to the war. And a lot of them didn't come back. I haven't looked to see what the latest population census says, but I wager there's a big gap now in the generation of men from twenty to forty."

"Then the women will fight off the invaders." Rhi yawned. "I'll leave you here to your crazy mullings. Do get some sleep though, eh? It'll be midnight soon."

Zenia, concerned by the reports and having no plans to go to sleep at all, offered a noncommittal wave of her fingers as Rhi headed for the door. She had a niggling feeling she was close to an answer, or at least a lead, and she intended to keep reading files until she found it.

By the time he and Lornysh borrowed a rowboat from the watch and located Iridium's river entrance, Jev was yawning so widely he scared fish away with the creaking of his jaw. Even with Lornysh's nature-attuned elven magic, it had been difficult to find the low opening in the side of the riverbank that marked the spot. Mangroves grew thick along the shoreline, and dozens of their long roots dangled into the water. Had they been relying on the light from Jev's lantern alone, they never would have found the spot at night, but Lornysh's night vision was far superior to his.

"Are you certain this goes all the way into the city?" Lornysh asked from the bow of the boat as he pushed aside roots.

Jev was in charge of rowing, so he had to twist his neck to see into the dark hole they were entering. The *low* dark hole. Lornysh knelt and bent his head as they passed into it. Roots brushed Jev's hair even though he sat on the bench.

In a couple of spots, the roots had been cut back. Others appeared to have been cut below the surface so they could be pushed aside, then fall back into place like a curtain.

"No," Jev said. "Zenia's dragon tear didn't include me in whatever vision it relayed to her. It's a rude little gem."

Lornysh, peering into the pitch darkness ahead of the boat, did not comment. Night had long since fallen by the time they'd started their trek out to the river, so no light seeped into the area from outside. Only the weak lantern sitting on the bench opposite Jev provided a hint of illumination. It wasn't enough to reach the sides of the passage they had entered, though he could see the dirt ceiling above them, roots dangling from it.

"You better row harder," Lornysh said. "The current is strong."

"I noticed." Jev faced the rear again and put his whole body into the rowing motion. "Can your magical elven senses tell how far back it goes?" He was a little surprised Lornysh couldn't simply sniff the air or wiggle an ear—whatever he did to call upon his innate magic—and sense if the passage led into the city.

"A ways."

"Your accuracy would impress a geometry teacher."

When Lornysh didn't respond to the quip, Jev fell silent and rowed, trusting his friend would direct him as needed. He hoped the river didn't twist and turn for miles before ending up in Iridium's lair, because his back already felt the strain of rowing against the current.

He reminded himself to ask Lornysh to spar later and spend more time exercising in general. It had been a regular part of army life, but now that he had a desk job, he would have to be careful not to let himself grow pudgy. That would make it more difficult to get Zenia to ogle his chest. To get *women* to ogle his chest, he corrected himself firmly.

Something moved in the water at the edge of the lamplight, and Jev almost dropped his oar. He tightened his grip and peered into the gloom. The light reflected off a pair of large beady eyes staring at him.

A long tail swished, stirring the water at the surface, and he identified the long body of a crocodile. He released an oar to drop his hand to his pistol. Or would the short sword be a better choice if it attacked? He'd gotten out of the habit of carrying weapons in the city, but he'd known he might need them if he walked into Iridium's stronghold, so he'd gone back for them. Now, he was glad.

The crocodile swished its tail again and swam with the current downstream, toward the river and the exit. He wondered what it had been doing way back in here.

"As long as it's gone now," he muttered to himself.

Lornysh glanced back at him. His gaze flicked dismissively in the direction the crocodile had gone, then back to Jev. No doubt, he'd sensed it and known it was no threat to his ferocious warrior might.

"Is the elven ambassador talking to you since we arrested his wayward scientist?" Jev asked, hoping to head off any discussion about his unreasonable fear of crocodiles. Also, hoping the sound of voices would keep any other crocodiles away and drive back the oppressive silence. Aside from the trickle of water, there was nothing to hint they were now rowing under a city full of people. The branches and dirt above them had transitioned to solid rock. They could be rowing into the center of the world.

"Seldom."

"But he hasn't kicked you out of the tower, right? That seems promising."

"He didn't kick Yilnesh out of the tower, either, and he'd murdered royalty."

"So, standards for guests are low, huh?"

"He did give me an odd warning this morning," Lornysh said. "He suggested I get out of the city."

"Are you sure that wasn't his subtle way of saying he wanted you out of his tower? Do you think I should come in and apologize for my part in burning the courtyard?" Jev felt guilty about that. He'd ridden by the tower during the day and looked through the gate long enough to see all the burned trees and foliage.

"I don't think he wants your apology. And no, he wasn't simply trying to get me to leave. He implied that trouble was coming to the city, and he said he'd written the king—the Taziir king—asking permission to abandon the embassy."

"Really?" Jev squinted back over his shoulder, but Lornysh was peering into the darkness ahead and didn't notice. "That's an extreme move, isn't it?"

"Perhaps. The dwarves left their embassy in your city long ago."

"I didn't know that. I wonder if they'll return now that Targyon has made his overture."

"Overture?" Lornysh glanced back.

Jev considered if Targyon would mind him sharing the information with more than Zenia. Normally, he wouldn't blab, but Targyon knew Lornysh, and Jev didn't think he would object, especially since Lornysh was helping with the hunt for the missing dwarves.

"Five hundred dwarves are on their way to Korvann," Jev said and summarized the rest. At the end, he joked, "Maybe that's why your ambassador wants to leave."

"No, he wouldn't object to dwarves coming."

"Would he object to someone *else* coming?" Jev asked.

During their meeting, Targyon hadn't mentioned extending his offer to any other races. Long ago, the elves might have accepted, but those days were long past now. Targyon certainly wouldn't have invited orcs or trolls, or any of the other races that had warred with humans—frequently and with great passion—in previous centuries. He might have invited the neutral unicorns, if he thought they would come, but Dr. Oligonite was the only one Jev had ever seen. His understanding was that the hoofed people preferred to avoid politics and conflicts, no matter what race was at the heart of it.

"Possibly, but he didn't say anyone in particular was coming," Lornysh said. "He only said that trouble was coming. I'm not positive if it was something that would target me specifically or if he meant trouble for your city."

"You specifically? I know you wouldn't have left any assassins alive on your trail."

Lornysh snorted softly. "No."

"If he's thinking of leaving, that suggests he believes the trouble could affect the city and present a danger to him, right? Either that, or he's mortally offended about his garden and feels he can't stand being among humans any longer."

Jev meant the latter as a joke—at least, he hoped it was a joke—but Lornysh did not respond. Worried he had offended his friend, Jev craned his neck around. Lornysh was peering off into the darkness again. Jev was about to ask if he'd seen or sensed something when Lornysh spoke.

"We may have trouble *here*."

"Oh?" Jev almost stopped rowing, but if he did, the current would carry them backward. The passage had widened, and he could no longer see the ceiling. He hadn't been able to see the sides earlier and still couldn't, but he had the sense of them being farther away now, the river being slower, shallower, and wider. A few stalactites hung down from above, his light barely brushing their tips.

"There's something magical ahead of us."

"Like a dragon tear?" Jev knew Lornysh could sense those.

"No. We may want to turn—"

A loud splash came from the darkness ahead, and Lornysh did not finish the sentence.

Jev stopped rowing. Whatever had made that splash, it sounded heavy. Heavier than a crocodile.

"Take us out," Lornysh ordered as another loud splash erupted.

Whatever made it was closer now.

Jev cursed and rowed with only his right arm to spin the boat around. He didn't want to leave—they would have wasted hours if they couldn't get in this way—but he trusted that the usually dauntless Lornysh wouldn't give the order if it wasn't warranted.

"What is it?" Jev asked.

"A magical creature. A water golem, I believe."

"Founders' hells, who in the city would be able to conjure up one of those?"

"I believe it was set here to act as a permanent sentinel and a magical alarm."

"That doesn't answer my—"

This time, Jev saw the splash. A huge one. He'd turned the boat enough that he now faced the way they'd been going before, and as a hulking dark figure moved toward them, he decided that was not a good thing. It was a strange blend of shadow and water that reflected the lantern light.

Jev rowed hard, but the indistinct creature surged toward their boat.

"Lornysh," Jev blurted, rising to his feet and yanking his pistol free.

The boat rocked alarmingly, but he kept his balance. He pointed the weapon and fired, though he feared it would have no effect on a magical creature. And how the hells had Iridium come to possess a magical creature? He knew Grindmor had made those rock golems. Could a kidnapped dwarf have been convinced to conjure this? Could dwarves even use their magic on water?

The bullet disappeared into the amorphous watery form and did nothing.

Lornysh sprang past Jev, landing lightly in the back of the boat, his bow drawn. The creature rose fully from the water, spreading blob-like arms. It had no eyes or even a distinct head and appeared to be made entirely from water. Lornysh fired at it, one arrow after the other, his movements barely stirring the boat. The arrows disappeared into the creature's watery body the same way Jev's bullet had and didn't appear to do anything.

Jev leaned around Lornysh and fired again. Nothing. The creature grew in size, the top of it reaching the shadowy ceiling high above. It was gathering more and more water, Jev realized. To throw at them?

Lornysh dropped his bow and yanked out a longsword. He barked a command in Elvish. "*Syrisha!*" Fire, the word meant. His sword glowed with orange, almost as if flames ran along the length of its metal blade.

Jev jammed his pistol into its holster and reached for his own sword. He had no magical commands to give it and feared the steel would be as useless as his bullets.

"Row," Lornysh commanded. "Get us out of here."

Jev forced himself to sit again and reach for the oars, but the golem had gathered enough water. It surged at them like a tidal wave.

Lornysh sprang at it an instant before it slammed into the boat. It didn't matter. The water still hit. Jev ducked his head, but the massive power hurled him backward, as if he'd been struck by a boulder.

He heard wood snapping even as he flew out of the boat. The lantern went out, all light disappearing, as water completely encompassed Jev.

He was hurled head over feet more times than he could count. His back slammed into stone, and the air in his lungs whooshed out.

Jev tried to claw his way toward the surface, wherever that was, but the current continued to smother him, battering him like a boxer pummeling a bag. No, it wasn't just the current, he realized as he failed again and again to push away from the rock. It was some sentient being that would hold him under the water until he drowned.

Terror filled him. He tried not to panic, but he could almost feel watery fingers gripping his shoulders, pushing him farther down.

Not knowing what else to do, he yanked his sword out. He stabbed at the water around him. It was strangely dense, far more so than normal water, and his blade met resistance. But did it do anything to harm the creature? He couldn't tell.

A distant yell, muted by the water, reached his ears. An elven war cry.

Wherever Lornysh was, he was still alive and battling the golem. That gave Jev extra inspiration to fight. But how?

He didn't think his sword strikes were doing anything. The creature was intentionally pressing down from above, keeping him from rising to the surface. Was it possible he could slip out underneath it? Do what the golem didn't expect?

His lungs starting to burn, Jev pushed upward again, his boots jammed against the rock wall. Once again, watery fingers forced him down. He fumbled his sword back into its sheath and then abruptly switched the angle of his push. As if he faced some physical obstacle he could swim under, he tried to dive under the creature.

For the first time, he was able to get away from the rock wall. He stroked as hard as he could, his knees and belly scraping the bottom of the river.

Currents stirred behind him. The golem turning to give chase? He stroked harder.

Several long seconds passed, his lungs crying out for him to rise to the surface. It was utterly dark, and he couldn't see a damn thing. Had he escaped the creature? Maybe Lornysh had distracted it.

Jev reached forward for another stroke, and his knuckles slammed into hard rock. He lacked the air to curse, or he would have shouted his frustration. Instead, assuming he'd reached the far side of the river and run out of room, he pushed off the bottom. He almost choked as his lungs spasmed, trying desperately to suck in the air he hadn't yet reached.

Finally, his head broke the surface. He gasped in air so quickly it burned his throat.

It was almost as dark above the surface as below, but a faint orange glow came from one side. Lornysh's sword. He wasn't holding it. It lay by itself on a rocky bank twenty feet away.

Thunderous splashes came from the other direction, followed by a distressed cry. Lornysh.

Jev almost swam straight toward him, but he didn't have a weapon that would be useful on the golem. He turned and swam for the sword. His knee banged another rock, and he had the air for a curse this time. A virulent one.

He scrambled up a bank, the outline of a longboat nearby. Had they reached Iridium's secret dock? It didn't matter now.

He snatched up the glowing sword, hoping the magic wouldn't reject him. If anything, it burned more brightly. Its heat flared, warming Jev's hand. Were those *real* flames? A question for another time.

Jev couldn't see the golem, but he heard the massive splashes. The creature had to be pummeling Lornysh, just as it had done to him.

Swimming as quickly as he could one-handed, Jev fought against the waves their fight created. They slammed into his face, but he glimpsed the pulsating water monster, and that gave him the motivation to push on. But he *didn't* see Lornysh. Had he been forced under?

"Over here, ugly," Jev shouted, the water filling his mouth garbling the words.

The creature spun toward him. He hoped that didn't mean Lornysh was finished.

Massive watery arms reached for Jev. He treaded water, pushing his body as high as he could, and used both hands to swing the blade with all his strength. It lopped through one of those blobby appendages. Water sprayed him in the face, reminding him disturbingly of blood.

That didn't make him pause. He slashed again. He connected, creating another spray, and the creature made some weird indistinct moan like air blowing over an open bottle.

A wave came out of nowhere and slammed into the back of Jev's head. He tried to keep his grip on the sword as he was forced under, but a current like a battering ram slammed against his wrist. Pain erupted, and he couldn't keep from dropping the weapon.

The orange glow spiraled downward, and he would have cursed again, but he was stuck under the water once more. A heavy pressure leaned against his back, pushing him farther down, and Jev knew he was within the creature's grasp again.

He shifted his angle, letting it push him toward the bottom and even trying to swim in that direction. The sword, only visible due to its glow, had stopped moving. It must have hit the bottom.

Jev drew near and reached for the sword, the oppressive weight still on his back. He realized he wasn't close enough to touch the blade. He kicked furiously, but he only got farther away from the orange glow. The golem knew what Jev wanted and was shoving him the other way, damn it.

With his lungs burning again, Jev feared he'd have to give up and rush to the surface. If the creature would let him. He gave one last valiant effort, twisting and kicking, hoping to evade the golem. It smashed him into the bottom, and rocks gouged his chest through his clothing.

The orange glow of the sword moved. For a horrified second, Jev thought the creature was knocking it farther away from him. As if it needed to. But then he saw Lornysh's face outlined by the light of the sword, his pale blue eyes reflecting its orange light. With the weapon in hand, he lunged toward the water above Jev.

The force pressing down on Jev disappeared. He twisted, looking up as he groped for the bottom with his feet so he could push off. The orange glow highlighted the sword as Lornysh whipped it back and forth, hardly impeded by the water.

Jev wanted to stay and help, but he no longer had a weapon that could hurt the creature. And his lungs were on the verge of spasming again. The last thing Lornysh needed was to worry about hauling Jev's drowning body up from the bottom.

Jev pushed away from the fight and toward the surface. Once he made it, he gasped in air and turned, hoping to see Lornysh up and the creature defeated. The water churned, and he realized his friend still battled the golem. He might be injured and running low on air.

"Need something to help," Jev panted and spun back toward the bank again.

It was dark, no hint of a lantern anywhere, but if that was the room where people had been unloading crates earlier, maybe some of them were still stacked against the walls. He swam for shore, hoping to find something useful—and matches he could light so he could see.

Jev tripped over the longboat as he climbed out of the water. He growled and started past it, annoyed he hadn't remembered it was there, but paused. Maybe there were matches in *it*.

A huge splash sounded out in the water. Orange flashed above the surface, and for a second, Jev glimpsed Lornysh flying toward the ceiling. He stopped shy of crashing into it, gravity carrying him downward again. The light of his sword revealed the golem rising up from the water again, still alive. Lornysh gave another battle cry and angled his sword downward as he tumbled toward the creature.

That battle could go on forever. Jev leaned over the side of the longboat, patting around and hoping to chance across a safety kit, but his knuckles bashed against wood first. A crate? No, a keg of something. Alcohol? He envisioned lighting alcohol on fire and hurling it into the water. Could that help?

Jev felt around. The longboat was loaded with kegs. Had Iridium's people just stolen them or were they preparing to take them somewhere? To sell? Or use as a bribe? Who could be bribed with alcohol?

He leaned close and sniffed one of the kegs, expecting to smell brandy or whiskey, but he jerked back.

"Not alcohol, you fool. Black powder." He knew the scent well.

As more splashes sounded in the water, Lornysh and his sword disappearing beneath the surface again, Jev went back to hunting for matches. He brushed against a rope—a *fuse*. He didn't know who or what Iridium planned to blow up, but if he could light one of those kegs and throw it, maybe the explosion would be enough to kill the golem.

Iridium and the entire city would know he was in this cave if Jev caused an explosion, but he doubted it mattered now. Lornysh had called the golem an alarm as well as a sentinel.

"Jev!" came a weak cry from the water.

Lornysh. He sounded tired, maybe injured.

"Lure it over here," Jev yelled. "I found land. And something else." A fit of inspiration struck. "Bring your *sword*."

Preferably with the flame still dancing along its surface. He didn't say the words out loud, having no idea if a golem could understand human words.

The orange glow came into view again. Jev expected to see Lornysh swimming toward him, but he was *flying* toward him. The golem had thrown him again.

Lornysh hurtled through the air, arms flailing. Somehow, he managed to retain a grip on that sword.

"Drop it here," Jev yelled as he ducked so Lornysh wouldn't smash into him.

A splash sounded less than twenty feet away. The golem was following him. Could it come up on land?

Lornysh waited until he landed, somehow spinning like a cat and coming down on his feet, but then he obeyed Jev. He tossed the sword, hilt first.

Jev snatched it out of the air, the flames brightening the longboat and confirming what he'd felt. More than a dozen kegs of black powder, at least two of them with fuses trailing out.

Aware of the creature closing in, rising higher and higher as the water grew shallower, Jev used the flaming blade to light the closest fuse. He considered leaving the keg in the boat to blow up the eleven others with it but feared he would bring down the ceiling—and maybe the city above it—with an explosion that large.

He tossed the sword aside, gripped the barrel, and staggered as he hefted it over his shoulder. It was heavier than he'd anticipated, and he wouldn't be able to throw it that far. Not that he needed to. The golem was only ten feet away.

He glanced at the fuse, making himself wait until it burned down. If he threw the keg in the water before it exploded, it would just go out.

Eight feet.

"Throw it, Jev," Lornysh said from behind him, bent over, gripping his knees. "I'll make sure the timing is right."

Jev had no idea how he would do that, but he couldn't dally any longer, anyway. The golem's arms, reformed from the water once again, stretched toward him.

Jev hurled the keg with all the strength he had left. It wasn't enough.

The keg dipped, and he knew it would splash out in front of the golem, the fuse extinguishing in the water. But then, a gust of wind battered him from behind. Somehow, it caught the keg and hurled it farther.

An instant before it would have slammed into the golem's watery torso, the black powder exploded with a cacophonous roar.

Jev staggered back, jerking his arm up to protect his face as brilliant light burned his eyes and lit every crevice in the cavern. The force of the explosion knocked him onto his butt. Pieces of wood from the keg slammed onto the bank all around him. He twisted, burying his head in his arms.

The light faded. Wood continued to patter down, and rocks fell into the water. Jev cringed, hoping the entire ceiling wouldn't come down.

Fortunately, silence soon fell.

Jev lifted his head, risking a look at the water. Once again, only the orange light of Lornysh's blade, resting on the rocky bank where Jev had left it, illuminated the cavern. The water had grown still.

Lornysh still gripped his knees as he stared in the same direction.

"Please tell me it's dead," Jev said.

"I believe it's gone quiescent."

"Is that the same as dead?" Jev asked hopefully.

"Not exactly. It means it's entered a period of dormancy while it regenerates."

"Does that by chance take a couple thousand years?"

"No. It could only be hours. Maybe days. But either way, I suggest we find one of the other exits."

"I agree."

A throat cleared behind them, lantern light entering the cavern.

"My, my, what has the tide brought in?"

CHAPTER 8

B UTTERFLIES CAVORTED IN ZENIA'S BELLY as she took the stairs toward the floor of the castle that held the king's suite and office. She had been up there before and spoken to Targyon a few times but never without Jev being present. She'd stopped at Jev's room and knocked on his door on the way up, thinking it would be easier to get a meeting with the king if he came, but he hadn't answered. Since she hadn't heard any snores or thumps, she'd assumed he was already out for the morning—or that he hadn't come back the night before. Where he'd gone, she didn't know. Not down to the office to start on his paperwork. She knew because she'd been there all night. She hadn't slept, and after all she'd sifted through, she didn't know if she would any time soon.

As she passed a window, dawn's light barely brightening the gardens in the courtyard below, Zenia wondered if it was too early to knock on Targyon's door. Did he sleep late? She'd made herself wait until dawn, but she'd been antsy for hours, waiting to talk to him.

She checked his secretary's office first, but it was locked, nobody answering. Apparently, secretaries didn't start work at dawn. After waffling about whether she should bother Targyon in his suite, she made herself continue to the door. Two armed bodyguards stood outside, both looking tired, as if the night shift hadn't ended yet, but both watched her approach with sharp eyes.

Zenia lifted her chin and did her best to appear confident, like someone who belonged there and had the right to ask them to roust the king from bed.

"Captain Cham of the Crown Agents to see the king, please," she said. "It's important."

She recognized the men and assumed they recognized her, but she wasn't surprised when they hesitated, sharing long looks with each other.

"Zyndar Dharrow usually comes up to see the king," one said. "And not before dawn."

"It *is* dawn, not before it, and Zyndar Dharrow is busy elsewhere." Zenia hoped he hadn't gone to see Iridium. The idea of him being gone all night with *her* alarmed her for more reasons than one. "Will you ask him if he'll see me, please?"

The guards exchanged long looks again, then turned mulish expressions toward her. Would she have to use the dragon tear to add magical power to her request? She doubted Targyon had intended her to use the gem on his own people when he'd given it to her, but this was important. She would go mad if she had to pace for another hour and ponder the questions that had been batting around in her mind all night. She couldn't rest until she knew more, and she hoped Targyon had information beyond what was in those reports on Jev's desk.

"His breakfast is usually delivered in an hour," the guard said. "Wait until then, and then I'll ask—

"You will ask him now," Zenia said, imploring the dragon tear to add coercion to her words. "Or stand aside so *I* can ask him if he'll see me."

"I'll ask him now," the guards said at the same time, their voices having gone monotone.

As they turned toward the door together, almost bumping into each other, Zenia shivered at how easy this particular dragon tear made it to manipulate people. Already, she doubted her choice to employ it. These weren't criminals she needed to interrogate for the safety of the kingdom.

The two guards walked inside together. She hadn't meant for both of them to go but didn't want to risk losing her chance if she tried to alter the command.

Thank you, she told the dragon tear silently, following the men inside.

It vibrated with a pleased sensation. Zenia doubted *it* felt qualms about manipulating people.

"What?" came Targyon's startled voice from the bedroom.

Both guards had entered, and Zenia winced, imagining him waking in alarm to the hulking men standing next to his bed.

They spoke together, their words tumbling into each other. Zenia stepped up to the door, wanting to explain and not wanting Targyon to realize she'd brainwashed, however temporarily, his bodyguards.

"Sire? It's Captain Cham, Sire." She didn't presume to step in farther than the threshold, and she had to peer past the guards to glimpse Targyon. "I'm sorry it's so early, but I really need to talk to you. I've been up all night going over reports from your foreign agents."

Targyon sat up in bed and shooed the bodyguards back a few steps. The men blinked a few times, opening their mouths and looking around as if they didn't know how they had gotten there. She hoped they would leave without questioning her.

"Reports from the foreign agents?" Targyon pushed a hand through his rumpled pale brown hair. "Isn't that Jev's domain?"

Zenia held back a grimace, hoping he wouldn't think she had been presumptuous for looking at the reports on his desk. Was it possible Targyon didn't *want* her knowing what was going on overseas? That he'd assigned that particular aspect of the job to Jev because he trusted Jev implicitly and she was still an uncertainty to him?

"Yes, Sire," she said carefully. "I finished going through the paperwork on my desk and wanted to help him organize his last night. It was hard to organize without reading things, and I didn't think there would be any problem with me seeing the reports."

The guards shifted farther back, and Zenia realized Targyon was naked, or at least shirtless, in bed, the blanket and sheets around his waist. She flushed with embarrassment, thinking of the conversation he'd had with Jev about the royal pajamas being too silky against his... nether regions.

"Last night?" Targyon looked her up and down.

She wondered if she was even more rumpled than he and if he could tell she hadn't slept. Or changed clothes since yesterday. By the founders, what had she been thinking? She should have washed her face and put on fresh clothing before presuming to ask him for a meeting.

Oh well. She'd make the best of it and ask before she lost her courage—or he dismissed her.

"Yes, Sire. There was a lot to do. I couldn't sleep, so I worked on organizing both our desks. I'm not sure where he is this morning, or I would have discussed this with him, but, Sire, I have questions for you about foreign affairs. Do you have a few minutes? I can be quick. I just need to know if you know what I now know. And what you think about it. Or if you know *more* than what I know, it would be extremely useful if you could tell me about it. So I know too." Damn, had that sounded as inane to him as it had to her? She'd intended to be vague rather than speaking plainly in front of the men, but…

"What'd she say?" one guard muttered to the other.

Targyon looked blearily at her, like a man who also hadn't slept much. And who might need coffee before he could decipher her vagueness.

"All right," he finally said. "Give me a minute to dress. Jolf, will you find someone to send up breakfast early? And coffee. Two cups. And a large pot."

"Yes, Sire."

Jolf hurried away. The second man hesitated, looking from Targyon to Zenia.

"I'll wait out here," Zenia said—almost blurted—as Targyon shifted the blanket aside.

She turned her back and rushed out before she could find out if Targyon was entirely naked. The idea of seeing her king walking around nude mortified her.

The bodyguard walked through the sitting room, frowning at her as he passed, but he didn't do anything more threatening, nor did he accuse her of manipulating him magically, though he must have suspected it.

Zenia perched on the edge of a chair to wait. When Targyon came out dressed in a loose tunic and suede trousers, she lurched to her feet and curtsied. She realized she hadn't when he'd been in bed.

"Relax," Targyon said and waved her toward a table with two chairs by the window. "If you're capable of it." He offered a half smile as he headed for one of the chairs.

She didn't know how to take that but decided it probably wasn't an insult. "Yes, Sire. May I ask my questions?"

"Before the coffee has come? Are you sure you want to risk it?"

"Risk it, Sire?"

"My answers might not be that coherent in a pre-caffeinated state."

"Oh."

He issued the half smile again, and she realized he was joking with her. Maybe her reaction was the wrong one, for his smile faded.

"I speak more quickly when I'm caffeinated, Sire," she said, attempting to respond to his humor in kind, however belatedly. "You may not find it calming."

"Little about my new job is calming. Go ahead." He waved his hand. "You said foreign affairs reports? Not anything about Master Grindmor?" Was that disappointment in his eyes?

"Yes, but I believe there may be a link."

"Oh?"

"You're aware of reports of orcs, ogres, and trolls making preparations for something?"

"Yes."

She blew out a relieved breath, glad he already knew about the reports. How long had they been coming in? Had Jev known and not said anything to her?

"The trolls of Borc'tol appear to be spearheading it," Targyon added.

Zenia nodded. The reports hadn't said that specifically, but there had been mentions of troll emissaries spotted in the main orc and ogre cities.

"I was thinking that Kor may be a potential target if they align with each other and seek to extend the boundaries of their kingdoms."

She waited to see if Targyon would express skepticism similar to Rhi's.

But Targyon nodded. "We have a lot to attract would-be conquerors, trollish and otherwise. Invasion attempts have happened often in past centuries, and potential enemies may see us as weak right now."

"Yes." Zenia sagged with relief, so glad he was on the same level with her. "Do you think that's likely? Is that why you invited dwarves to come to the city?"

"It is. I want to establish alliances that have frayed in the last couple of generations. We've offended the dwarves the least with our isolationist ways of the last twenty years, so I reached out to them first. I've also sent messages to the Taziir, but I'm not surprised they haven't responded. The war is too recent, the deaths too fresh. They may have dropped my messages straight into the fire without reading them." Targyon tilted his head. "I discussed some of this with Jev, but he didn't mention— You think there's a link to Master Grindmor's kidnapping?"

"It's just a hunch right now, I admit, but it seems like someone who had something to gain from an upheaval in the kingdom may have wanted to ensure relations remained strained between the dwarves and us."

Targyon glanced to the door as a servant walked in with a coffee tray.

"Stuffed gort leaves, boiled eggs, and warmed flat bread are on the way, Sire," the servant said. He poured two mugs of coffee and backed out of the room while bowing.

"It's an interesting idea," Targyon said, "though my understanding of the situation thus far is that the guilds—the Fifth Dragon, in particular—originally stole Grindmor's tools and may be behind the kidnapping."

"That's still possible, Sire. The guilds may believe they have something to gain from an upheaval in Kor."

"True. Do you have a list of people you believe have the most to gain?"

Should she have? She'd just come up with her idea. And she'd been organizing Jev's desk. Damn, maybe she should have come up with more than her rambling thoughts before approaching Targyon.

"Not yet," she reluctantly admitted, "but I could work on a list today."

"You could also sleep today." He smiled faintly.

She *did* look tired and rumpled, didn't she? "Isn't time imperative? The dwarves are on their way, right?"

"They are. I just don't want my new Crown Agent captains to burn themselves out their first month on the job."

"I'll be fine, Sire. I'll work on the list and then get some rest. I just wanted to see—well, you seem at least as well informed as Jev and I."

"Do I? Does that mean I'm impressive or that you two need to work harder?"

"Er." She had been about to ask him if he knew anything more, but now, she was reluctant to admit to their ignorance. Did he already see her work as substandard? Because she'd only now realized what was going on overseas?

"Sorry." Targyon winced and held up a hand. "I was trying to be, ah… delightfully humorous. Charming, even. It comes so easily for Jev. I, on the other hand, always get flustered around women."

"Oh." It hadn't occurred to Zenia that Targyon, even if he'd only recently been appointed to this supreme office, might have such feelings of inadequacy. He was only twenty-two, she reminded herself, and as far as being charming with the opposite sex... she could empathize. She hadn't the foggiest idea how to do it. If she actually wanted to find someone to marry and father her children, she might have to put some effort into learning. Jev had been... well, he'd instigated everything, all the charm, while she'd been busy trying to arrest him.

"I didn't mean to imply you weren't good at your job," Targyon added. "Or that I'm impressive. Hm, I usually save this for Jev. He was my commanding officer, you know. He was used to molding insecure and waffly young officers."

"Waffly, Sire?"

"It's a word. An adjective based on waffle. To speak equivocally about. I know words, just not women." He smiled tentatively. "Do you think I can find a woman that likes that?"

"I'll be flabbergasted if you can't find a woman, Sire," Zenia said carefully, perplexed as to how the conversation had drifted to this subject.

"Because I'm king now or because of my passion for words?"

"Uhm."

"That's what I'm afraid of." Targyon sipped from his coffee mug, then cleared his throat. "All right. A list, Captain. Bring me a list of people and organizations who have something significant to gain by the kingdom being distracted with a war on its shores. Or by the possible reform that could result if we were able to repel an invasion attempt." He frowned and shook his head. "As for whether I know more than you know, I'm afraid not. All of my intelligence comes out of your office. I keep waiting for the spirit of the Fire Founder—I was born under the Fire Dragon's stars, you see—to send me visions during the night, but all I've experienced in bed so far is learning to sleep in fancy pajamas with a fabric canopy dangling over my head."

"Yes, Sire." Already thinking of the list she had to make, and where she would go to do research to make it, she only half heard the words about a vision.

She pushed herself away from the table and headed for the door, determined to have a list for Targyon by the end of the day. She paused with her hand on the knob, realizing he hadn't dismissed her. Targyon didn't seem to have noticed. He was studying his coffee mug with his legs folded cross-legged in his chair. He looked forlorn and maybe a little lost, and she felt a twinge of sympathy. He was far too young for this job. Finding a word-loving woman should be all he needed to worry about at this age.

She almost said something, but she didn't know what words of assurance wouldn't sound like a lecture or mothering. He might be young, but he was the king. Even if that was new, he'd been zyndar all his life, and he wouldn't want to be advised by some common woman.

Soundlessly, she curtsied and slipped out to do her duty.

Jev stood up as Lornysh rolled, grabbed his glowing sword, and jumped to his feet, turning to face the newcomers. Jev knew he was injured and exhausted after battling the golem, but Lornysh didn't let any sign of it show.

"Hello, Iridium," Jev said, also striving not to let his soggy weariness show.

The Fifth Dragon leader strolled into the storage cavern, flanked by six armed men. She wore deep blue silks that could have been a dress or a nightgown. Given the late—or was it now considered *early?*—hour, the latter seemed more likely.

"Did I wake you? My apologies." He groped for a way to take control of the situation. He had intended to sneak into her inner sanctum in a position of power, or at least with the advantage of surprise. But now, she had the advantage, her men all leveling pistols or rifles in Jev's direction.

Actually, most of them were pointed in *Lornysh's* direction. He crouched, glaring at the men as he held his flaming orange sword aloft.

"Jevlain Dharrow," Iridium drawled, touching her lush, dark hair and smiling, though it appeared strained. Her gaze flicked past his shoulder and toward the water. Looking for her magical sentinel?

Jev wondered who she'd managed to get to conjure the golem. Lornysh hadn't mentioned what kind of mage might be capable of it. An elf?

"Your visit was unexpected," Iridium said. "And am I right in assuming you deprived me of a keg of black powder? And a golem?"

"Actually, my elven friend says the golem is likely only being quiet now."

"Quiescent," Lornysh corrected without taking his eyes from the guards.

"Quietly," Jev said, offering a smile of his own for Iridium. He'd come to ask her for a favor—no, to barter information—so he had better use as much charisma as he could muster. "As for the keg, we assumed you'd want to test your black powder before deploying it to… where is it going? Did you mention it?"

One of her elegant eyebrows rose. "I did not."

"Huh. Well, it's convenient that you came out here to see us, as you're the reason I'm here. I wish to speak with you."

"You've reconsidered my offer?"

"Which offer was that? To sleep with you and give you several of my family's dragon tears? That offer wasn't overly palatable to me at the time."

"But you've reconsidered?" Iridium kept smiling at him, but she also sent a few speculative looks at Lornysh.

Jev couldn't tell if she thought him someone she should hire for her guild or someone she should invite to bed. Or both.

"I haven't," Jev said. "But I have some information you may be interested in. And I believe you have information *I* may be interested in. I came to propose a trade." He wondered if there was any way he could glean where Grindmor was *and* what Iridium planned to do with those kegs. Blow her way into some zyndar's castle to steal *his* dragon tears?

"You propose a trade? My dear zyndar, you're in a rather disadvantaged position to propose anything." She waved at his clothing, which was dripping a small lake onto the rocky bank at his feet. "I could simply have you tortured to learn everything you know."

"A disadvantage? My lady, do you not recognize a deadly elven warden when you see one?" Jev extended a hand toward Lornysh, pleased that he was indeed oozing deadliness. Somehow, the water his clothes dripped wasn't that noticeable, perhaps because of the glowing sword. "He singlehandedly quiescent-ed your unsanctioned-in-the-city water golem."

"If I give you the elven word for that term," Lornysh muttered out of the side of his mouth, "will you quit mangling it?"

"Unlikely," Jev murmured back. He raised his voice for Iridium and added, "Do you truly think six puny humans will be a match for him?"

The puny humans, all over six feet tall and well-muscled, grumbled among themselves.

Iridium's smile didn't fade, but she did consider Lornysh again, her gaze lingering this time.

Jev didn't truly know if Lornysh could, with his modest help, get the jump on those men and defeat them before they could shoot him, but he was betting on Iridium not knowing that either. Even before the war had started, the Taziir had earned a reputation of being extremely difficult to kill, and Jev was positive stories of their mages and wardens had floated back across the Anchor Sea. Few of Kor's inhabitants would question their deadliness.

"What do you propose, Jev dear?" Iridium asked.

"You tell me where Master Grindmor is, and I'll tell you about a hole in your security I found."

"A hole you just made?" she asked dryly, glancing toward the water.

"Another one." He almost added that her rivals might even now be spying on them, but that would be giving too much away too soon. Besides, on the chance she already knew about the gap in the wall, he didn't want to share his information until she shared hers.

Her eyelids drooped, and she regarded him through her lashes. "Your word as zyndar that you honestly believe you have valuable information I'll care about and don't already know?"

Damn, she knew how to pull his strings. Not wanting to be foresworn, Jev chose his words carefully.

"I honestly believe I have information you'll want to know. I think it's *unlikely* you already know it, but I can't read minds."

"No? Perhaps you should have brought your pretty girlfriend with the rock instead of Points over there."

"She doesn't like speaking with you as much as I do." Jev refused to be baited by the girlfriend comment, and he also refused to let the fact that it wasn't true bother him.

"Odd."

"Yes. Are you interested, or shall my friend and I leave and offer my information to some of your rivals?" Not the ones, Jev added to himself, that already knew about the spy hole.

Iridium contemplated Lornysh, contemplated her guards, then thoughtfully tapped the dragon tear hanging from her neck. The lighting was too dim for Jev to see the carving, but if it was the same one she'd worn before, it held a dagger and would enhance her combat abilities. Though she wasn't pointing any weapons at them, she wore a weapons belt around her nightgown, a mace and pistol hanging from it.

Jev mentally added a seventh fighter to the Lornysh equation and decided he would, if she started a fight, go for her, since she probably had the most trick chips in her bag, and leave his friend to deal with the others.

Iridium must not have found the odds as superior as she originally believed, or maybe she was simply curious what Jev knew, for she finally said, "I agree to a trade of information with you: all I know about the dwarf gem cutter for all you know about… whatever it is you think I'll care about." She smirked. "But you will share your information first."

"No."

"No?" She genuinely seemed surprised by the rejection.

"You have my word as zyndar that I'll tell you what I know after you tell me what you know. I haven't yet seen anything to show me how good your word is, so we do it my way."

Her smirk turned into a sneer. "I see. Because you were born in a castle, you think your word is better than mine."

"*I* have proven I honor my word over and over all of my life and, if memory serves, even to you by not attacking you in your bedroom. You've never given your word to me to demonstrate its worth."

"By the founders," Lornysh growled, "quit piddling around like infants and make a deal." He glared both at Iridium and at Jev.

The outburst surprised him until he remembered his friend was likely injured. His dark green and wet clothing could be hiding a lot of blood.

Even more surprising, Iridium appeared abashed. The emotion disappeared quickly—Jev couldn't imagine her ever blushing—but she nodded and faced him.

"I don't know where the dwarf is. Either of the dwarves you're missing." Her eyes narrowed slightly, and Jev suspected she was making a point to let him know how much she knew of his problems.

"But you were originally the one to take Grindmor's diamond tools and coerce her into doing favors for you under the pretext of helping her search for them."

"You make it sound so ignoble."

He took that as confirmation. "Did you move the tools before she recovered them or did someone else take them?"

Iridium spread her arms. "I didn't move them, and I have no idea who took them. I will say that I was irritated when I found out they were gone. I had some of my people flogged, since there were few who knew they were in that pump house in the first place. I discovered I had someone selling information to outsiders. That person no longer works for me." She issued a vulpine smile.

Jev had a feeling that person no longer worked for anyone. "Do you know who he sold information about the tools' whereabouts to?"

"A number of people, apparently. Other guilds, mostly. I don't know who took the tools, nor do I know where in the city they are, if they're in the city at all. My resources say they're not."

"Resources? People who can sense magic?" Jev remembered Lornysh suggesting that Cutter might not be in the city any longer since he couldn't sense or find him.

"I don't believe I'm honor bound to answer that question, Jevlain, dear. It has nothing to do with Grindmor's whereabouts."

"But you don't know Grindmor's whereabouts, do you?"

"I do not."

"Perhaps, to be equitable, you should offer me some other information. Such as whose vault door you're planning to blow up today." Jev tipped his head toward the longboat and the remaining kegs.

"I've been perfectly equitable, considering you've shared nothing with me thus far." She gave him a pointed look.

He couldn't deny it was true, and he wouldn't feel honorable if he continued to hold out.

"There's a hole in the wall over there." Jev pointed toward the crack he and Zenia had peered through. He was relieved when Iridium's eyes widened and she spun to look. That meant she hadn't known and he truly had valuable information for her. "People can stand behind a waterfall over there and observe the goings on in this storage area. They can and they do. A man named Morash from the Night Travelers guild is a frequent spy. He enters through a tunnel accessible via a clock shop in the quarry square."

Jev made a mental note to order that apprentice and his family to Dharrow Castle so he would be protected from any fallout that might come about if Iridium lashed out at the Night Travelers over this.

"Go check." Iridium waved four of her men toward the stone wall, then turned back to Jev. "How did you find out about this, Crown Agent?"

He didn't know why she'd switched her title for him. To imply Crown Agents ought to be above snooping through tunnels and finding peepholes?

Jev shrugged. "I discovered it in my search for Master Grindmor and my friend."

"There's a crack over here, Boss," one of the men called, his nose to the stone.

Jev nodded, believing he was in the right spot.

"Maybe I can hear a waterfall? I'm not sure. It's real muffled. It's too dark to see through the crack. I can't tell if it goes anywhere."

"Mark the place," Iridium said. "We'll cover it later. After our guests have left." She waved at Jev and Lornysh, then extended a hand toward the water. Inviting them to go out the way they had come? "Unless you two want to stay and entertain me. I believe dawn is approaching, but I'm not opposed to staying in bed late. With entertainment."

Jev almost choked. He had no idea if she truly wanted both of them to join her, but his mind stuttered at the mere suggestion.

"No," he said, "but we lost our boat, so we would appreciate it if you let us use one of your back doors."

"Do zyndar boys and elven wardens not learn how to swim in their youth?"

Thinking of Lornysh's injury, quiescent golems, and crocodiles, Jev said, "Show us the door, Iridium. We've given you more than you've given us."

"While destroying my guard golem and blowing up a valuable keg of powder," she said, irritation in her tone.

Jev suspected most of that was a result of learning her rivals were spying on her, but he didn't try to stop her when she ordered her men to follow her and headed for the door. He was tired of dealing with her and tired of this night in general. He wanted to get Lornysh to a healer and rest.

Her party left with all the lanterns, and the door thudded shut. A clang sounded as a bar was dropped to further lock it.

"Do you think you can swim out?" Jev stepped closer to Lornysh and the boat, wondering if his friend needed an arm for support.

"No, but I can sit in this boat while you row it out." Lornysh lowered the tip of his sword to the ground and leaned on it like a cane.

Jev was surprised he would treat the weapon so but supposed a magical blade wouldn't be scratched or dulled by a few rocks.

"We could dump the black powder in the water and make her day worse," Lornysh added.

Jev rubbed the back of his neck. He found the idea of taking the boat questionable—it was theft, after all—but reasoned he could leave it tied up when they reached the Jade River. Her people would find it. He could even argue that she must have known he would take the boat when she'd left him here with it. But the explosives... If they destroyed them, she would doubtless see it as a hostile sign and consider him an enemy after that. Even if her information hadn't been that useful, other than confirming that she neither had the dwarves nor had the tools anymore, he thought he could, as things stood now, come to her again to trade information. That might be useful in the future.

Of course, all this assumed he could believe what she'd told him today. Could he?

"Does your brain hurt when you spend that much time thinking?" Lornysh asked into his long silence.

"It does today." Jev grabbed one of the kegs and set it on dry land instead of chucking it into the water. "Settle yourself in while I unload these. I'll row us out."

"You're sure you shouldn't destroy them? What if she's planning a crime against the crown? Something that harms people in your city?"

"Then I'll have regrets that I made this choice, no doubt. But I can't condemn her before she commits a crime. With luck, she's going to blow up the Night Travelers' headquarters."

"Unlikely, since she prepared this boat before she knew about the spies."

"Just... let it go, Lornysh," Jev said as he continued to unload kegs. "She could be a valuable informant in the future."

Lornysh grunted but didn't object further. As Jev pushed the boat into the water, leaving the full kegs of powder behind them, he hoped he wasn't making a big mistake.

CHAPTER 9

J EV HELPED LORNYSH TO THE elven embassy—he refused to be taken to a hospital, claiming he could find a healer inside the tower—before heading out of the city and up the hill to the castle. Bright sun blazed down on his shoulders, helping to dry his clothing, but it did little to keep him from yawning. Unfortunately, after his night's adventure, he didn't have any more of a clue where to find Cutter and Grindmor than before. All he knew was that Iridium, if her word could be believed, hadn't taken them.

He was inclined to believe her, less because of her word and more because he couldn't imagine why she would have orchestrated the kidnapping. Before, when Iridium had been coercing Grindmor into doing favors for her, her motives had made sense. But unless she thought she could sell the grumpy dwarf master to someone, he couldn't see why she would have done this.

The gate guards waved Jev in without commenting on his bedraggled appearance. He thought about the mounds of files suffocating his desk and almost detoured to his room to wash, change clothing, and sleep for ten hours, but Garlok's words from the day before made him feel he should at least check in before tending to personal needs. He probably shouldn't take time to tend to them at all. There might be something to what the undeniably experienced Garlok had said, that Jev should remain in the office, going over reports from agents and informants, rather than traipsing around the city himself. He hated to admit it though. Mostly because it sounded boring. He dreaded the hours he would have to spend to sort through those files.

Fortunately, when Jev entered the office, Garlok wasn't among the agents at their desks. Several men offered polite greetings of, "Good morning, Zyndar Dharrow," to him. He voiced appropriate responses on the way through, but his attention quickly focused on the back of the room.

Perplexingly, his desk was empty of all the folders from the previous day. A single folder to one side was all that remained, no more than a few papers inside it. Dare he hope that someone had stolen the others? That would be a shame.

Zenia sat at her desk, clad in the same clothing from the day before. Her folders were gone, too, though they had been replaced by books and far too many newspapers to represent the day's offerings. She was bent over them intently, circling things.

"Zenia?" Jev came to stand beside her and peer down at her work after giving his clean desk another puzzled glance. "Have you been here all night? Because if you had planned to stay up all night, you should have come with me, so we could have stayed up all night together."

That had sounded more amusing in his head. He was tired. He caught Agents Torson and Brokko looking his way and decided to lower his voice. And not do anything that might be mistaken for flirting.

"Aside from a brief meeting with the king, yes," Zenia said.

Targyon had called her up to his office? Had he been looking for Jev too?

Zenia circled something else without looking up. Maybe he should leave her to her research. He assumed it was related to Grindmor in some way. He looked at his desk again.

"Did you notice a folder thief come in and steal everything out of my area?" he asked.

"I consolidated the reports and filed them for you."

"You… did my paperwork for me? *All* of it? And it's in there?" He pointed to the single folder.

"The maintenance reports went to Khomas—they should have gone there in the first place. The foreign agents' reports had a lot of repetition. You'll find all the pertinent information in that folder. I assure you I was thorough."

She looked up at him earnestly, and Jev realized she might have thought he doubted her thoroughness. No, he was busy being shocked she'd done all his odious work for him. In one night. He was positive it would have taken him a week to wade through that.

"Zenia." Jev reached down and took her hands. Though a puzzled furrow creased her brow, she allowed him to lift her to her feet. He promptly enveloped her in a hug. "I can't believe you organized everything for me. You're wonderful."

"I—oh." She sounded startled, and it took her a moment to react and return the hug.

Maybe he shouldn't hug her in front of all the other agents, but they ought to understand how delighted he was. They all had hoards of paperwork of their own to deal with.

"*Thank* you." Jev forced himself to step back, especially since he'd already noticed her lovely curves pressed against him and the faint scent of her shampoo.

Someone giggled. It was not a manly giggle.

Zenia blushed. "You're welcome."

When Jev checked, he found most of the agents looking their way, some smirking, some rolling their eyes. Both groups straightened their faces as soon as he looked at them.

"She did my *paperwork*," Jev said to explain the hug, though he shouldn't have to explain himself to any of them.

"If I hugged her, would she do mine?" Brokko muttered.

Jev, having noticed the man's tendency to glance at Zenia's chest, said, "She'd be more likely to do your paperwork if you *didn't* hug her."

That elicited a few more snickers. Brokko glared around at the offenders.

Jev waved at all of them, a gesture he hoped implied they should get back to work.

"Can I help *you* with anything, Zenia?" Jev decided offering her a foot rub or a massage wouldn't be appropriate with the agents looking on. Sadly, it probably wouldn't be appropriate even in private.

"Uhm." She considered her newspapers. "I'm brainstorming."

"Would my brain be helpful? Wait, don't answer that. If the answer is negative, it'll crush my ego."

"Somehow, I doubt your ego is so fragile." Her eyes twinkled a bit as she waved for him to drag over his chair, but she mostly looked tired. He wondered, were he to use his zyndar status and attempt to command her to go to bed, if she would go. He doubted it.

"The king has me making a list of people who would stand to gain from an upheaval in the city, possibly caused by an invasion or other hostile actions from our enemies."

Jev thought of his meeting with Targyon. He hadn't realized trouble might be so imminent. "Did he suggest it or did you?"

"I don't remember, but I brought up my musings to him, things inspired by your reports." She waved toward the now-empty desk.

"Is that somehow related to Grindmor being missing?"

"I don't know, but..." Zenia tapped a finger on the topmost newspaper on her stack. She'd circled an article about the number of wealthy, non-zyndar individuals attending the symphony going up. "I have a hunch that everything is tied together."

"I understand about hunches." Jev often relied upon them.

"I think it's coming from the fact that Grindmor's disappearance coincides with the launch of that ship full of dwarves the king invited to settle in the city. I got the estimated date of their arrival and calculated how long the journey from their homeland should take, and determined the kidnapping had to have happened at the same time as they left their homeland." Zenia pulled a list of names out from under the newspaper. "I don't have any evidence linking these people to any crimes. I'm just making a list of prominent subjects who have been mentioned in the newspapers over the last few years. Some of them I'm aware of, as they've financed the building of new structures in the city and occasionally donated large sums of money to the temples. They get plaques and a lot of publicity when they do that, so I wouldn't assume they're simply good-hearted and altruistic. Some make deals with the archmages, as well, for leniency or favor from the founders."

Jev looked over the list. There were eight names on it so far. He only recognized one of them, an explorer, cartographer, and philanthropist who'd reputedly made his money finding diamond mines in unclaimed parts of the world. He had to be eighty years old. He'd been legendary for his exploits even when Jev had been a boy.

"It wouldn't take more than a day or two to go talk to these people with the help of your dragon tear," Jev said, though he didn't feel that optimistic about such chats resulting in anything. He understood hunches, but this seemed a roundabout way to find Grindmor's kidnapper since no motives had yet been identified. Admittedly, they had little else to go on.

"I'm still collecting names. There may be more."

"Why is it you believe the wealthy would be the ones who would gain from upheaval?"

"They have the resources to act if an opportunity presents itself."

"None of your names are zyndar," Jev observed, still working to understand her thinking. "If you add wealthy zyndar, your list would grow exponentially."

"I know, but your people are already rewarded significantly by the status quo. I would expect them *not* to want to rock the boat."

"Possibly, but a lot of zyndar families want more and better lands closer to the major cities. If the current system were disrupted by a war or the king were overthrown, they would have the men to raise armies and invade neighbors. Well—" Jev scraped his fingers through his beard, "—perhaps not. Almost all zyndar families were tasked with forming a company to add to the king's army for the war. A lot of those men didn't come back, as I well know." Fewer than a hundred of the two hundred and fifty men Jev had recruited from Dharrow lands had made it back, something that he felt guilt over, even if he'd been transferred to Gryphon Company years ago and his uncle had taken over leadership of the company.

"Land," Zenia murmured, her eyes growing thoughtful. "Land?"

"Yes, it's the stuff we stand on. If you need a better definition, I can get a dictionary. Or maybe Targyon will come down and provide one. He's *like* a dictionary, but his answers tend to go more in depth. I guess that makes him like an encyclopedia."

Zenia didn't seem to be paying attention to his blather. Her eyes were focused—actually, they were unfocused—past his shoulder. "Until recently, only zyndar families have been able to own land."

"Yes." Jev still had no idea where she was going, but he tried to be helpful. "Long ago, the kings of old cut up the kingdom and gave large swaths of land to warriors who proved themselves by great deeds. They became the first zyndar. Of course, the land wasn't given free and clear. The zyndar were expected to put it to use and create income so taxes could be collected for the king's coffers. They took on tenant farmers and craftsmen to help toward that end, offering protection in exchange for those people giving a portion of their earnings to the zyndar who could then send it along to the king. Eventually, there wasn't any land left for the king to give, though for a couple of centuries, we expanded eastward and southward to claim more, so he could reward more men, but it's been a while since anyone new was made zyndar. It grew dangerous to attempt to expand further, and the borders have remained unchanged for the last two hundred years."

That probably hadn't been that helpful. Zenia was nodding impatiently, like she'd already known all that.

"Right," she said, "and there's little chance for a common man or woman, no matter how wealthy they become through industry or trade, to acquire land of their own. Not *everybody* wants to be some tenant to a zyndar. Commoners dream of having the ultimate freedom and stability of land of their own."

Jev thought about pointing out that being zyndar didn't involve much freedom, at least not for the heir to a prime. It was a big responsibility to have so many tenants and so many obligations to everyone. But he sensed Zenia was going another route and wasn't worried about the details.

"Technically, commoners can buy land now," Jev pointed out. "Abdor's daddy, King Ebonon signed that law into existence. Under pressure from the Orders, if I remember my history lessons."

"Orders bribed by the new commoner wealth, yes. But there's been a problem. There just hasn't been that much land for sale. Zyndar families—and their holdings—never go anywhere. Your families are so old at this point that there's always an heir somewhere, even if the zyndar prime's children all die to disease or war."

Jev thought of his dead brother and grimaced. "Yes. If I died, my father would name one of his brothers or nephews."

"If there was an invasion, Korvann could be a place where battles were fought," Zenia said. "We've got the harbor, and as the home of the king, it's considered the most important city in the kingdom."

"Possibly. If I were leading an army, I'd go ashore somewhere less populated rather than making a direct assault, but I won't deny that fighting would likely come to the city eventually. I—" Jev lurched to his feet, a realization smacking him like a wet towel.

"What?"

"I just realized the elven ambassador must know something about this. Maybe more than we do. He warned Lornysh to get out of the city and told him he was thinking of leaving too." For the first time, fear blossomed in Jev's chest. Real fear. Earlier, talk of enemies taking advantage had been academic, something that might happen eventually if Kor didn't solidify some alliances. But was it possible this threat loomed far closer than he'd realized? By the founders, the last thing he wanted was to fight another war. And one on home soil that threatened his family and the Dharrow tenants? He groaned.

Zenia was watching his face. "Maybe we should talk to him again."

"Again? We didn't succeed in talking to him the first time. And he's not going to want to see us now. I— Wait." Another idea smacked him. "I wonder if that would work." He drummed his fingers on his thigh.

"Are you going to tell me or keep me in suspense?"

"I don't know. So far, you've only been teasing me with what's in *your* mind."

"I've been thinking out loud, not teasing you. I was about to suggest that wealthy commoners might finally get their chance to acquire valuable land along the coast, maybe right here in the city, if a war started. Your people would hunker down in their castles or lead armies across the countryside. The city might be damaged. Or if there was fighting, buildings destroyed. If zyndar castles or other buildings were damaged, they might be willing to sell some of their land in order to pay for rebuilding. Land that's never been available to buy could suddenly be for sale cheap."

"Assuming people wanted to buy land in a war zone."

"A war wouldn't last forever. Presumably, we would fight off invaders eventually. Unless we were conquered, and then our conquerors would own all the land." Zenia frowned.

"Your would-be land buyer would be taking quite a gamble that all this would turn out in his favor."

"True, but I believe I'll go down to the property office and see if I can dig up anything interesting. Maybe someone has made purchase offers lately and had them turned down. If so, the clerk might remember that."

"All right. You do that. I'm going to ask Targyon if I can make a most generous offer to supply dirt, plants, and workers to help the elven ambassador reconstruct the extensive gardens that my helpers so thoughtlessly burned down the night we were after Yilnesh."

"Dirt? A ruse to get close to him and ask questions?"

"Exactly, though not entirely a ruse. I *was* responsible for that and do feel guilty. Maybe I'll leave out the king and make the offer myself. Either way, it should provide an opportunity to speak with him. If I offer an apology, maybe he won't shoo me away."

"Or set his guard creature on you? It's still alive, isn't it?"

"They. I think there were two. And yes, still alive."

"Maybe I should go with you. Even if he agrees to talk to you, he may lie, and you wouldn't be able to detect it without a dragon tear."

"You don't think I can tell when an uppity elf is lying to me? I've been friends with Lornysh for years, you know."

"Does he lie regularly to you?"

"No, that's Cutter. He cheats terribly at chips." Jev smiled, but a twinge of nostalgia and worry tainted the gesture as he remembered the last time they had played, on the ship sailing back home to Kor. He realized that if there was anything to Zenia's musings, if someone wanted to ensure the dwarven nation remained indifferent to Kor—or even declared Kor to be an enemy—then what he'd assumed had been a kidnapping might have been a murder. What if they found Grindmor and Cutter but too late? What if only their bodies remained? Murdered in a ghastly way to ensure dwarven hatred.

"Jev?"

He shook his head, pushing away the grisly thoughts. "If I don't make any headway with him, I'll come back and get you, but I think you should follow your hunch and finish your list for Targyon."

"All right." She sounded reluctant to let him go off on his own. Was she worried about him or just didn't think he could get answers without her dragon tear? Maybe she just liked his company, and *that* was why she wanted to go with him.

Wishful thinking, Jev, he told himself. "Whatever the ambassador knows, I don't think it's going to have anything to do with who took Grindmor. It sounds like it's more important than ever that we find her."

Grimly, he realized that finding her wouldn't stop an invasion if one was coming. All it would do was keep relations between Preskabroto and Kor from deteriorating. That was a good thing, but he didn't see how it could stop a war if one had already been set in motion.

"All right," Zenia said. "I'll finish my list and head to the property office."

"Good. I'll forgo the nap I was fantasizing about and visit the embassy."

"Change your clothes first, Jev. You smell like a swamp."

Jev plucked at his still-damp garb from the night before. "Technically, it was a river, but I see your point. One shouldn't look overly bedraggled when calling upon a foreign dignitary."

He took a step but paused when Zenia spoke again.

"Did you learn anything from Iridium?" she asked casually. She'd picked up her pen and was once again bent over the newspaper.

His heart gave a guilty lurch. He hadn't told her where he'd gone, and while she hadn't attempted to forbid him from visiting Iridium, he knew she'd been against it.

"Only that she originally took the master's tools and doesn't know where they are now. She punished someone in her organization who leaked the information about their location but doesn't know who all the information went to. She says she doesn't know where Grindmor or the tools are now."

"Ah."

"I also suspect she wants to add Lornysh to her bedpost notch collection."

"I didn't think elves could be zyndar," Zenia said, not looking up. She didn't sound fazed by any of the information, but Jev couldn't tell if she was irked with him for going to see Iridium.

"Lornysh definitely is not zyndar, but she could be expanding her tastes. Let me know if you find anything at the property office, will you?"

"Of course. Let me know if you need help with the ambassador."

Jev hesitated before heading off, feeling he should say something more, some apology for running off to have adventures without her, or seeing a woman she disliked. Maybe he just wasn't ready to leave her for the day.

Clingy, Jev, he admonished himself. Time to get over her and move on.

Still, he spoke again, having the urge to tease a smile out of her. "Thank you, again, for doing my paperwork." Maybe, once he found Cutter, he would take Cutter up on his offer to help him make Zenia a gift. Even if they weren't dating, one could give a thank-you gift to a colleague, right? "I'm incredibly relieved that you're my co-captain instead of Garlok."

Zenia lifted her head and gave him a semblance of an army salute. "You're welcome."

"You're relieved I'm *your* co-captain, too, right?"

"Of course. If I didn't have a co-captain, all the reports would get stacked on a single desk, and it would collapse under the weight. That would be burdensome." Her eyes twinkled.

It wasn't quite a smile, but it would do.

Jev bowed low. "I'm pleased that my desk and I are here to accept some of your burden."

He headed off to change clothes and plan what he would say to the elven ambassador—or the minions who guarded the door.

CHAPTER 10

ZENIA MADE IT ALL THE way out to the bright sunlight of
the castle gardens before she realized she was wearing shoes that
didn't match. She only had three pairs of shoes. How, when she'd
gone up to wash and change her clothes, had she managed to leave with
two distinctly different shades of brown?

"Because you're tired and need a nap," she grumbled to herself,
stepping off the main path to sit on a stone bench nestled between two
small lemon trees.

A fountain gurgled nearby, the same one Lunis Drem had lain
slumped against the night she'd tangled with the rogue elven scientist.
Lunis had become involved with that fiasco before Zenia ever met
her, but Zenia felt she'd failed the younger woman somehow. That she
should have been able to help her and prevent her from being exiled.

Zenia sat on the bench, pondering her shoes and whether she had the energy
to go all the way back up to her room to change. Would whatever clerk worked
in the kingdom property office care about her footwear? Or even notice?

She drew out the list of twelve names she'd made from select
newspaper articles and journals printed in the last few years. After
staying up all night, she was so tired she doubted whether any of her
hypotheses about Grindmor's kidnapping made sense. Was it truly
likely some wealthy commoner would be behind the event?

She remembered the note she'd received a couple of days earlier, the
warning to 'ware the wealthy. She wished she could question the person
who'd sent it, especially since he or she had also sent a warning about
Drem. The person clearly had some knowledge of what was going on in

the castle and the city. If Zenia took the warning as credible, she might be on the right path.

A noisy yawn escaped her mouth. As tired as she was, would she learn anything from visiting the property office now? Maybe she should wait until tomorrow. But, no. Jev hadn't slept the night before, either, and he'd gone off to question the ambassador. She could make it through another day and wait to sleep that night. She refused to let him work harder or longer hours than she.

As she pushed herself to her feet, voices kept her from stepping straight out onto the main walkway.

"I don't care if it's uncouth to talk about," a woman said, coming up the broad walkway toward the castle. "The whole situation is absolutely ridiculous. That the Orders would have chosen *him* over my Rolgon. He's barely out of his teenage years."

Another woman issued a delicate snort. "You're just irked that you're not queen right now."

"Ladies," another female voice said. "While I understand being upset over the dubious choice of Targyon, I don't think you should speak of it here. There are certainly spies in the castle, and you know how such people like to jump on anything that might be considered treasonous and make accusations."

The three women came into sight, ladies in their twenties and thirties, their dark hair bound back in sophisticated twists and braids that must have taken an hour each to construct. They wore flowing, pale blue, lavender, and yellow dresses, all trimmed with elegant silver or gold embroidery. Their soft slippers were wholly inappropriate for walking, and Zenia assumed the women had been dropped off by carriages rather than having strolled up the long road to the castle on foot.

Zenia sat back down on the bench, hoping they would pass by without noticing her. She had no interest in their conversation, nor would she waste one of her agents on following them around. Spies, please.

"I don't care who hears me talking," the first one said. "They all know it's true. Rolgon is more experienced in politics. Why, Targyon didn't even grow up in the capital. His parents teach grubby commoners at some university in another city."

One of the women looked toward the fountain, then started when she noticed Zenia. She paused, and the others did too.

Zenia groaned inwardly, anticipating some snide remark about her mismatched shoes if nothing else. She stood up, hoping she could slip past them without incident and return to her errand.

"Is that a gardener?" one asked. "Girl, should you be sitting down instead of working?"

Girl? Zenia lifted her chin. "I'm one of the king's Crown Agents. It's my job to sit in the garden and spy on the conversations of frilly zyndari women with nothing better to do with their lives than complain."

Perhaps that hadn't been the most tactful opening, especially for someone who didn't want to start an incident, but their talk of Targyon being a poor choice irked her.

"A *spy?*" the youngest woman whispered, eyes widening.

The oldest—this Rolgon's wife, presumably—sniffed derisively. "She's nothing but some common worker. Girl, do you not know you're supposed to curtsy for your superiors? And address us as zyndari or *my lady*? Your manner is entirely inexcusable."

"I'm sure it is." Zenia walked toward them since they'd stopped in the way, but she intended to continue right past. She doubted any of them would try to grab her—they might break a nail—but she kept an eye on them.

"What is your name, girl? I will surely report your impudence. Don't think my husband won't see to it you're flogged."

"I'm trembling." Zenia made it past them and strode toward the front gate. She grimaced at the sight of another woman in elegant clothing walking toward the group. A reinforcement?

"If you won't give your name," Rolgon's wife called, "I'll simply provide a description. I'm certain others have noticed your drab dress and mismatched shoes. If you were truly one of the king's spies, you could afford to dress yourself fittingly for the job."

Zenia kept walking, though heat warmed her cheeks. Nobody had questioned her attire when she'd worn her blue inquisitor robe, and even zyndari had shied away from drawing her attention. Worse, she recognized the woman walking toward her. Naysha. What was Jev's ex-fiancée doing up here for a second day in a row? Had she come to see him? If so, *why?*

The woman was carrying something, a rectangular object wrapped in brown paper and a curly blue ribbon. A gift?

"Whatever are you yelling about, Zyndari Dominqua?" Naysha asked, looking curiously at Zenia, but directing the words to the woman behind her.

The shrill one—Dominqua?—had followed her down the walkway, as if she had intended to flog Zenia herself. Or harass her until she got a name.

"That gardener or whatever she is," Dominqua said with another sniff. "She doesn't show proper respect for zyndari. I don't know *what* she's doing in the castle. The staff wear uniforms and don't look so scruffy."

"She claimed to be a *spy*," the youngest one said.

"No spy so disheveled has ever existed, I'm certain," Dominqua said. "She needs to be punished for her impudence."

Zenia wanted to continue to the gate, to bypass all of them, but Naysha stopped directly in front of her. Zenia could have stepped onto the grass to get around her, but she had a feeling Naysha recognized her and might think it odd if a Crown Agent fled ignominiously from some self-important noblewomen.

"This woman is one of King Targyon's agents." Naysha extended a hand toward Zenia. "I imagine she dresses like a commoner so she can go out among them and not attract notice."

Zenia clenched her teeth and didn't point out that she *was* a commoner, that most of the agents were. She didn't want to deal with these people, but since they were all looking at her, she made herself turn enough to face them. That damned Dominqua had stalked right up behind her like a dog on the trail of a rabbit.

"Yes," Zenia said. "As I would have told you if you hadn't jumped to conclusions, I'm Captain Cham of the king's Crown Agents."

"She works with Jev," Naysha added, as if they all knew who "Jev" was. Maybe they did. All zyndar seemed to know each other. "I met her yesterday."

"Even if she is a legitimate spy, that doesn't excuse her behavior," Dominqua said. "She walked right past us without curtsying and refused to call us by title."

"I'm sure that made your already taxing day terribly stressful," Naysha said.

Dominqua's brow creased. "Zyndari Naysha, you mock me. That's inappropriate."

"Maybe you can have her flogged too," one of Dominqua's buddies said.

Zenia had no idea if it was a joke or not. She dug into her pocket and pulled out a notepad, seeking to end this idiocy.

"Dominqua... what's her last name?" she asked Naysha.

"Tollestin," Naysha supplied, though she tilted her head curiously.

"Wife of Rolgon Alderoth, one of Targyon's brothers?"

"His oldest brother, yes."

"What are you doing?" Dominqua asked as Zenia wrote down her name.

"Just making a note," Zenia said. "I'll inform the king of your seditious words from earlier."

"Seditious! I was merely saying what everybody knows, that the crown should have gone to one of Abdor's more experienced and older nephews."

"You also spoke poorly of the Orders for their decision." Zenia scribbled another line. "I'll have words with the archmages to let them know you could cause trouble. I used to be an inquisitor, you know. I'm close to the archmages." She almost laughed at her own audacity for making such a claim, but she was positive the foppish women wouldn't know who she was or that she'd been ostracized.

"Why, I—are you threatening me?" Dominqua spun to her friends. "Is she *threatening* me?"

"I have to go," the youngest blurted, the one who'd first warned Dominqua about the potential for spies.

"I should too," the other one said, following her young friend toward the castle as fast as her slippered feet would take her.

Zenia spotted Rhi walking out of the castle, whistling as she strolled in their direction, her bo balanced on her shoulder. She gave the frilly women a lazy, half-hearted curtsy as they hustled past her.

"What was her name, Zyndari Naysha?" Dominqua asked, sadly not so easy to scare off. "Captain Something?"

"Captain Zenia Cham," Zenia said, indifferent to the woman reporting her. Maybe it was a cavalier attitude, but she doubted Targyon would care if some gossiping zyndari reported her for a lack of decorum. She might be his brother's wife, but Zenia doubted Dominqua bothered playing the role of staunch supporter even in Targyon's presence.

"I shall remember that, *Commoner* Cham," Dominqua said.

"Give your tongue a rest, Dominqua." Naysha made a shooing motion with her hand.

Dominqua squinted at her. "I will remember your impudence, too, Naysha. Your family isn't *that* important, and you married well beneath your station. You should have been loyal to Jevlain Dharrow." She whirled, her dress flapping around her legs, and stalked toward the castle.

"It must be nice not to have children or a job and simply eat, breathe, and take up space all day," Naysha said, speaking loudly enough for the departing Dominqua to hear.

Zenia didn't know what to say. The reference to Jev surprised her, mostly because she wouldn't have assumed it common knowledge that he'd been engaged and Naysha had broken it off. Maybe ten years ago it would have been, but how odd that someone outside of their families would remember it.

Rhi must have been close enough to hear the last few sentences. She was still whistling, but she had lowered her bo and was using it as a walking stick. She made a deeper, more elaborate curtsy as Dominqua passed her and, seemingly accidentally, stuck her bo out and almost tripped the woman. Sadly, Dominqua jumped over it and didn't fall.

"Oh, terribly sorry, Zyndari. Forgive my clumsiness."

Dominqua threw an exasperated look over her shoulder but must have been too flustered to issue more threats of flogging.

"Don't worry," Naysha said quietly to Zenia. "Nobody likes her. Even if I don't quite understand why the Orders chose Targyon, I can understand why they *didn't* choose his brother. Rolgon left home young to attend school in the capital and spent ten years currying favor and trying to get an important position in the castle. The rest of Targyon's brothers are far more palatable."

"Thank you," Zenia said, feeling she should express some gratitude toward Naysha for coming to her defense. There was something surreal about thanking the woman who'd abandoned Jev all those years ago, who hadn't waited for him. Even though Zenia didn't want him to be married, she felt indignation on his behalf.

"Do you know if Jev is in your office today?" Naysha asked Zenia as Rhi stopped near them.

When Naysha looked at her, Rhi curtsied—without whacking her with her bo—and offered a polite, "Zyndari," though she also glanced at Zenia as if to ask if she should go on the attack. The day before, Rhi had seemed more offended than Zenia at seeing Naysha holding Jev's hands.

Zenia shook her head slightly, then answered Naysha. "I believe he already left on an errand. I'm not sure how long it will take."

"Ah, that's unfortunate. I wished to give him something." Naysha lifted the wrapped box Zenia had noticed before. "I suppose there's no need for me to see him in person. I'm certain Grift would find it improper if I did so two days in a row."

Naysha's mouth twisted with an emotion Zenia struggled to identify. She almost called upon her dragon tear but reminded herself that Naysha wasn't a suspect to be questioned. Besides, if she was having... feelings toward Jev, Zenia didn't want to know about—

Thoughts flooded her mind, a scattering of memories involving a younger version of Jev, his form rangier, his face without the beard. With a woman—Naysha—at his side. In a room full of laughing people in a castle. At a garden party with candles floating on lily pads in a pool. On a moonlit beach by the sea, where they walked hand in hand and shared a kiss. A sense of regret and sadness tinged all the memories. Questions of what might have been if she had merely waited, if she hadn't felt so lonely when he'd gone, if she hadn't needed someone else to make her feel happy, to give her life purpose. *Naysha's* life.

I said I didn't *want to know,* Zenia thought toward the dragon tear, attempting to shove the other woman's memories out of her mind.

A sense of apology came from the dragon tear. It seemed genuine, and she thought the gem might have misinterpreted her desire. Or maybe it had read something in her subconscious that conflicted with her conscious thoughts.

Zenia frowned at herself.

"Yes," Naysha said to herself, giving no sign that she knew Zenia's dragon tear had rooted around in her mind. "Better that I don't see him, but I did wish to give him this. It's far too late to make amends, I know, and it's more about assuaging my guilt than anything else, I suppose, but—" She had been looking down at the gift, but now she lifted her gaze toward Zenia and Rhi. Her cheeks colored faintly. "Never mind. Nothing you need to worry about, but would you give this to him for me, Captain?"

Rhi's eyebrows rose, but she didn't say anything.

Zenia hadn't planned to go back into the castle, but she supposed she could go change her shoes in case she ran into anymore snobby zyndari on the way to the property office.

"I can leave it on his desk." Zenia accepted the gift.

"Good. Thank you." Naysha nodded, then hurried toward the gate, her pace oddly quick.

Zenia didn't want to spend too much time contemplating the woman or her motivations, but she couldn't help but wonder if Naysha would leave her husband if Jev were to show an interest in renewing their romance. Naysha didn't seem as happy in her life as maybe she thought she should be.

What would Zenia do if that happened?

Nothing, she told herself firmly. She and Jev were not a couple, nor could they ever be. Not unless he was willing to marry a commoner, and he hadn't indicated he was. Of course, she hadn't professed her love for him and asked him if he'd consider it...

But she didn't love him. It had only been a couple of weeks, and she barely knew him. Besides, even if she thought she did love him, she wouldn't ask him to give up his lands and everything he'd been born to for her.

"Can we open it?" Rhi peered over her shoulder.

"Of course not."

"Can we shake it?"

"No."

"Don't tell me you aren't dying to know what she's giving him," Rhi said. "And why she's giving him things. Do you think she wants him back? Isn't she married? Do you think she wants to have an affair?"

"Whatever she wants is none of our business," Zenia said firmly and headed back toward the castle, glad there was no sign of the three zyndari women.

"Are you sure?" Rhi matched her pace.

"Yes."

"Because for a while, it seemed like you'd like him to be your business."

"He's zyndar and I'm not. There can't ever be business between us." Zenia looked at Rhi. "What are you doing out here?" She hadn't seen Rhi in the office that morning.

"That odious Garlok had me running errands all morning. Is he allowed to do that? Aren't you and Jev my superiors, and that's it? Anyway, he came into the office, so I scurried out. I heard you'd just left and thought you might be going somewhere exciting and where you would desperately need my help."

"After I set this on Jev's desk and change my shoes, I'm going to see the kingdom property office clerk."

Rhi wrinkled her nose. "Any chance that'll be more exciting than it sounds?"

"I don't think so. But you're welcome to come along and help." Zenia wouldn't mind company to keep her mind from wandering down paths it shouldn't take. Or dwell on Naysha's all-too-vivid memories. Something about seeing Jev, even a young and different Jev, kissing another woman bothered her far more than she wanted to admit.

As Jev rode toward the city gate, he spotted a familiar figure coming out of it, one that was also on horseback.

"Good evening, Zyndar Dharrow," Hydal said formally, glancing toward the stoic watchmen standing guard beside the gate.

"Zyndar Hydal," Jev said. He hadn't seen Hydal since the morning at his castle and had started to wonder if his former officer would indeed come up to the Crown Agents office to be assigned work. "You weren't, by chance, on your way up to Alderoth Castle, were you?"

"I was, but perhaps I won't go now. The weather looks like it'll be inclement this afternoon." Hydal pointed his chin toward a few dark clouds meandering down from the mountains.

"Could be." Jev nodded toward the gate, figuring Hydal wanted to be out of earshot of the watchmen before speaking openly. Did he have some scintillating gossip that hadn't hit the streets yet?

Once they left the watchmen behind to ride down the street, steam-wagon drivers and messengers on bicycles paying them no mind, Hydal spoke more freely.

"I was coming up to see you, Jev. You've saved me time by coming to me."

"I aim to make people's lives easier."

"It occurred to me that I would be a more effective secret agent—" Hydal's lips quirked up as if the idea tickled him, "—if people didn't have a reason to associate me with your job or your office."

"I had the same thought. Actually, Targyon did, and I agreed with it."

"Ah, good."

"Perhaps nobody would think it strange if a few old army buddies got together a couple of times a month for a game of chips or cards," Jev suggested.

"Indeed, indeed. We can get Tuoark or another neutral party to host them. I'm sure he'd be willing if we brought alcohol."

"The way to men's hearts, as always."

"We ought to be able to round up a few other regulars we can trust to be discreet."

"I know Cutter would enjoy playing. Once we find him." Feeling wistful, Jev looked at Hydal, wondering if his new secret agent might have heard anything about the missing dwarves. He doubted it, and it wasn't the news Jev had suggested Hydal seek out, but he kept hoping helpful clues would fall in his lap.

"If he comes, I'll be sure to bring extra krons. And a friend with keen eyes. I'm positive that dwarf cheats."

"Oh, he does," Jev said. "Nobody suspects him of anything nefarious since dwarves are supposed to be honest."

"I think it's more the hook. You think he can't do any sleight of hand with the chips using his hook, so you don't pay much attention when the bag gets passed to him. You forget that he's a gem carver and has deft hands. *Hand.*"

"Quite true." Jev turned his horse at an intersection.

"Where are you headed?" Hydal asked.

"The elven embassy."

"Ah, not far. I'll get to the point then." Hydal scratched his jaw as he casually looked around, ensuring nobody was nearby or paying too much attention to them.

Jev nudged his horse closer to Hydal's. "Fresh gossip?" he asked just loudly enough to be heard over their hoofbeats and the street noise.

"Some new, some old. Zyndar with too much time on their hands continue to speculate that you're pulling Targyon's strings, though Targyon hasn't stirred up any trouble in this last week, so I don't think anyone is terribly worried at the moment. There is talk that his brother, Rolgon, at his wife's suggestion, may be documenting some of Targyon's choices in the hope of convincing the archmages to declare him unfit for the throne."

"I'll keep an eye on them." Jev knew Rolgon and his wife lived in the castle, Rolgon holding some minor position overseeing alcohol taxes and production in the kingdom. "I suppose our zyndar brethren wouldn't have any news about foreign matters." He was far more interested in enemies of the kingdom and kidnapped dwarves than the usual gossip around the throne and other zyndar right now.

"Foreign matters?" Hydal lifted his eyebrows. "I'm not aware of anything, and I don't believe I've heard mention of our neighbors in Drovak or Vilk. Should I be listening for such?"

"No." Jev decided not to mention the talk of the orcs, trolls, and ogres. He trusted Hydal but wasn't sure if he should make his new agent a confidant yet, especially since he'd brought Hydal on to keep an eye on domestic zyndar affairs.

"There are also some zyndari women scheming to get your hand in marriage. That information comes via the mouths of their brothers and uncles, you understand. I was at a chips game, as it so happens, sampling fine cigars from Harbold's estate."

"*Scheming?*"

"Several people used the word. It seemed apt, so I appropriated it."

"How so? Like they're going to approach my father?" Curse the founders' scaled hides, Jev didn't want to have to worry about this now. He hoped he didn't *need* to worry about it. His father had given him through the summer to find someone appropriate.

"Mm, not yet. Perhaps some other zyndari might, but the ones I heard about, sisters Hemia and Fremia Bludnor, believe there's an obstacle."

"Sisters?" He had only a vague idea who those women were and didn't think they were old enough to worry about marriage yet. Or were they? They hadn't been when he'd left, but that had been longer ago than he cared to admit. "Wait, obstacle? What obstacle?"

"An attractive co-worker of yours. There's a rumor going around that you and she are mating like overly libidinous orcs."

"What?" Jev didn't fall off his horse, but only because it was a placid mare with a broad, steady back. "Who's been saying that?"

Hydal eyed him curiously. "It's true?"

"No, of course not."

"Ah. Your reaction surprised me."

"I'm just affronted on Ze—Captain Cham's behalf."

"Not your own? You're the one under scrutiny. Nobody would think anything of a common woman luring a zyndar man into her clutches."

"She's not common. And she's not luring anyone." Jev almost missed the turn to take them the last half mile to the tower. Cursing, he guided his horse down a less busy street. "I mean, she's technically of common blood—though her father is an asshole of a zyndar who didn't acknowledge her or help her mother when she needed it—but she's not a common individual. She's unique. And she would never lure or use a zyndar. She doesn't even like zyndar. She doesn't *dislike* me, I mean, but she doesn't care about my social status. I've convinced her I'm a charming and honorable man."

Jev realized he was babbling and clamped his mouth shut. It wasn't as if Hydal was arguing with him. No, he was gazing extremely blandly at Jev.

"Never mind." Jev wanted to drop it, but if Hydal had brought this up, it had to have some significance. "What do you mean I'm under *scrutiny?*"

First, he was being accused of planting himself in a position to manipulate Targyon, and now, someone believed... what? That he wouldn't marry a zyndari woman because he was having a torrid love affair with Zenia? Even if he wouldn't have minded the latter being true, he resented having so many people watching him and making assumptions. It hadn't been like this when he'd been younger, had it? Or had he simply forgotten in the years he'd been away what the zyndar social circles were like?

"Just that those two women are spreading rumors, and their brother believed they might take the rumors to your father. Or have their mother do it, casually mentioning to him that you're sleeping with a com—a woman of common blood."

"You're giving me a headache, Hydal."

"Sorry, sir."

"Jev."

"Sorry, Jev. Will it help if I let you win at our first chips game?"

"Only if Cutter is there at my side cheating at the same time. I don't suppose you've heard any news related to his kidnapping?"

"I haven't, I'm afraid. Honestly, none of the zyndar or zyndari care a whit about the missing dwarves. I think someone mentioned it was tedious that Grindmor is gone because she wants a new clasp made for her favorite piece of jewelry and everyone knows the dwarf master is the best craftsman—woman—in the city."

"Tedious, right. Do you ever get tired of—"

A thunderous boom sounded in the distance, the cobblestones trembling under them. Jev's placid mare squealed and sidestepped, her eyes bulging. Hydal's horse reared up, almost throwing him. Up and down the street, other people's mounts reacted similarly. Only the steam vehicles were unaffected, though the drivers all stared down the road behind Jev.

He got his mare under control enough to turn her so he could peer in that direction. A great cloud of gray smoke rose into the air above the buildings.

"I need to check on that," Jev called over the complaints of Hydal's horse. "Will you be all right?"

Hydal finally coerced the horse into staying on all four hooves. "Yes. Do you want me to come with you?"

"No, secret agents don't accompany their employers to public explosions."

"Understood, sir. Be careful. And don't forget to introduce me to that lady friend of yours, eh?"

"I'll invite her to our chips game too," Jev called over his shoulder as he urged his horse to race down the street. What had been hit? Some public building? A water tower? Was it sabotage from the very non-human enemies that they feared were targeting the kingdom? Some kind of preemptive attack? Or—Jev cursed as the memory of Iridium's kegs of black powder came to mind—had one of the guilds struck a public target for some reason?

As he made his way through the city toward the smoke, he passed people riding the other way.

"What happened?" a watchman on foot yelled to the passersby. He was heading toward the smoke too.

"The Water Order Temple was attacked," a rider yelled back.

Zenia's old temple? Who would dare attack the domain of one of the religious Orders? Iridium? To what end?

Then Jev remembered some rumors from several days before that he'd almost forgotten, suggestions that the Water Order archmage—Zenia's former boss—had made threats about cleaning up the criminal guild infestations and putting bounties on the heads of the leaders. Could this be related?

He rounded a whitewashed building, and the temple came into view, its white marble walls and columns still standing, at least in the front where a dragon fountain watched over it from its square. But the smoke came from the back, and as Jev rode closer, he spotted a crowd gathering at the rear corner of the structure. The *collapsed* rear corner. Several rooms must have been lost, and judging by the snaps and cracks still coming from the temple, the roof might soon fall in other places.

Jev rode as close as he could and dismounted. The gray and white uniforms of watchmen and women were among the crowd, the law enforcers trying to keep people back. Monks and mages dressed in blue assisted, but most of them were frantically pushing aside rubble.

Jev left his horse and pushed his way through the crowd. He didn't know what help he could offer that the watchmen weren't already giving, but his stomach churned at the memory of those kegs. Kegs he could have thrown into the river and ruined. Not that Iridium couldn't have acquired more, but he had worried she meant to use them for some ill and hadn't done anything about it. If people had been killed...

"I'm Zyndar Dharrow," Jev barked when watchmen tried to stop him. He pushed past them and lunged to the edge of the rubble.

The busy monks and mages didn't look at him. One mage stood with his fingers wrapped around a dragon tear and his other hand thrust out. A huge piece of marble floated out above the heads of his colleagues. They gave it a few nervous glances but continued with what they were doing. Digging someone out of the rubble.

"Who's under there?" Jev asked. "Do you need help?"

"You've helped the Water Order enough," a woman's cool voice came from his side.

He recognized the inquisitor who'd interrogated him, and fear struck him like a splash of icy water to the face. What was her name? Zenia had said it. Marlyna.

Memories sprang into his mind of her standing outside his cell and raking mental daggers through his brain. Of how ineffective he'd been at guarding his thoughts. Of how much it had hurt when he tried. She'd elicited pain he couldn't fight off, pain so intense he hadn't been able to keep from screaming.

Jev straightened his spine and composed his face, not wanting her to know she'd had a lasting impact on him.

Marlyna curled a lip, maybe poking into his mind right then, but soon turned her attention to the rubble. Two burly monks had succeeded in digging a robed woman out, and they were pulling her back to safety.

Dust coated the woman's robe and face, but Jev recognized her. His other tormentor and the person who had treated Zenia so poorly. Archmage Sazshen.

"Was anyone else in there?" one of the mages asked as his comrade floated more rubble out of the building.

The clanging of one of the Fire Order steam vehicles sounded in the distance. Nothing appeared to be burning, so they were making the trip for nothing.

"I don't sense anyone else under the rubble," Inquisitor Marlyna said. "Those are the archmage's quarters. Someone knew just where to strike."

"Who?" someone shouted. "Who knew where to strike?"

"I didn't see anyone," a mage said.

"Neither did I," another said.

Jev thought of Iridium and looked around for signs that those kegs had been used. It was possible someone else might have been responsible for the explosion. Maybe she'd had nothing to do with this.

Archmage Sazshen groaned, her eyes squinted shut, her face twisted with pain.

"Someone get a healer," one of the mages ordered.

Jev spotted a few slivers of wood in the rubble. Might they have come from those kegs? It would be impossible to prove unless someone had seen a known Fifth Dragon operative placing the explosives, but Jev's gut told him the guild had been responsible. Ballsy of Iridium to order this attack during daylight. Why hadn't she done it at night when the explosion would have been more likely to find the archmage asleep in bed, and it would have been easier to plant the kegs without being noticed? Maybe Iridium had worried Jev would tell the watch about her plans. Or maybe she had a spy in the temple, someone who could tell her when the archmage went to her quarters.

Nurses with stretchers arrived, and the monks placed Sazshen on one. She groaned again. Bloodied and in pain but alive. That was good. Jev didn't like any of these people, but he would have felt even more guilt if someone had died after he chose not to destroy those kegs.

"You know," Marlyna growled from his side, disbelief and suspicion in her voice.

"What?" Jev asked.

"You know who did this."

"It's just a guess. I don't know how we would prove it."

"The Fifth Dragon," Marlyna said, peering into his eyes.

An uncomfortably familiar scraping sensation raked down the back of his brain. He recognized her icy probe right away and knew she was reading his thoughts. Painfully.

He winced and grabbed her wrist. Her eyes flared with indignation.

"I am not your prisoner now," Jev said, squeezing her wrist just enough to distract her from hurting him. "Stay out of my mind."

"You cavort with the criminal guilds." The sneer returned, conveying righteousness along with her distaste and indignation. "You knew this would happen, and you let it."

"I did not know. If you saw my thoughts, you know that's the truth." At least, he *hoped* she could discern the truth. Since he'd been thinking about those kegs, maybe that was all she'd seen in his mind. Or maybe she would see what she wanted to see, no matter what the truth was.

"You cavort with criminals," Marlyna repeated. "And they say you control the king."

She tried to jerk her arm away from him. Surprised by the accusation, Jev loosened his grip and let her step back. He didn't know *why* he was surprised. If the zyndar could come up with that idea, there was no reason the Orders couldn't.

For a bleak, distressed moment, he wished he was back on the front, back fighting elves in Taziira. He didn't believe he'd been doing the right thing then, but life had been much simpler.

"I don't control anyone," he said firmly and willed her to see the truth.

But she took another step back, still sneering. "Leave this place, Zyndar Dharrow. You are not welcome here. You may control the king, but you do not control the Water Order. Or any of the other Orders, and we have religious sway over the people. Never forget that."

Jev shook his head in disgust. He couldn't reason with her. There was no point in staying, so he headed to the elven embassy.

CHAPTER 11

T WILIGHT SHADOWED THE STREETS BY the time
Zenia stepped out of the property office on Abacus Street. She
yawned ferociously, and her stomach growled like a dragon fresh
out of hibernation. She vowed to eat something, then sleep for a very
long time.

She looked at the bench outside the office, wondering if Rhi was
waiting there—she'd grown bored and gone outside hours earlier. To
her surprise, Jev sat slumped on it, staring toward an intersection where
a pair of marble combatants poured water into the fountain at their feet.

"Jev?" Zenia asked uncertainly.

She headed toward him, wondering if she'd mistaken someone else
for him. It was dark, and his usually tidy hair was tousled.

"Yes." He turned, offering her a quick smile, but it didn't last. "Good
evening, my lady Captain."

The shadows hid his eyes, so it was likely only her imagination that
he seemed haunted. He was just tired, she decided. The same as she.

"How long have you been here?" Zenia stopped beside his bench.
"Why didn't you come in?"

He hesitated but soon flashed his smile again. "I was afraid you'd
put me to work. I thought I'd wait out here and take a nap."

"Does napping upright with your eyes open work well?"

"Not as well as in bed with a friendly woman snuggled in your
arms." He grimaced, seeming to find the words a mistake. "If memory
serves. It's been a long time since I experienced that."

Zenia thought of Naysha's memories, wishing again that she could
un-see them. "Iridium wasn't willing?"

"She doesn't seem like a snuggler. More like someone you wouldn't want to turn your back to." His voice lowered almost to a mumble. "I'm tired of always having to watch my back."

Maybe her first instinct had been right, and more than weariness plagued him.

She moved around to sit on the bench beside him. "Did something happen today?"

"Someone blew a hole in the Water Order Temple—nobody was killed, but your old archmage was injured. I don't have proof, but I think it might have been Iridium. That dragons-cursed inquisitor Marlyna scraped through my thoughts and saw me thinking that. She accused me of colluding with the criminal guilds and promised she'd be watching me. She also believes I'm controlling Targyon. That's a common belief, apparently, with lots of zyndar thinking it too. It seems that because we served together, people think I somehow made the Orders pick Targyon for the throne and then set myself up in an office in the castle so I could pull his strings. Oh, some women are apparently thinking of telling my father that you and I have been having a torrid relationship, too, no doubt so the old man will put an end to it by swiftly arranging my marriage to an appropriate zyndari woman. One of them, no doubt."

Jev rubbed his face, let his head drop back, almost clunking it on the bench, and stared up at the darkening sky. The street was quiet, with the offices closed for the day, and there wasn't anyone except Zenia around to hear his words. She didn't know what to think of everything, but he sounded so weary and distressed that she wanted to hug him. Badly.

"I'm sorry." He looked at her and smiled again—it was definitely a forced smile. "I didn't mean to blurt all that out. It's been a trying day. I'm feeling ganged up on and pitying myself. I'll deal with it. Sleep will help."

Zenia shifted closer, wrapped her arms around him, and rested her face against his shoulder.

"That might help too," he said. It didn't sound like as much of a joke as he might have meant it to be.

"I'm sorry the world is bullying you," Zenia said. "Especially my former colleagues."

He slipped his arm around her waist and returned the hug, dropping his forehead to the top of her head. She closed her eyes, wishing she could use her dragon tear's magic to make him feel better. But she didn't think magic worked that way. She also doubted she could use it to brainwash all those idiots who were making accusations into shutting their maws.

What could they stand to gain from slandering him? Well, marriage, she supposed, in the case of whatever women wanted to talk to his father. Idiots. As if they would enjoy being a part of a marriage they maneuvered the man into joining.

"Thanks," Jev murmured. He kissed the top of her head, then withdrew his arm.

Zenia missed it immediately. With reluctance, she withdrew her own arms and lifted her face from his shoulder, though she gazed at his profile for a few seconds before shifting to look at the dark street. She didn't know who had started rumors about them having torrid relationships, but she thought of their hug that morning in the office. She couldn't imagine having rejected it, but maybe she should have. They should be careful not to give the appearance of impropriety. The last thing she wanted was for Jev's father to be pressured into making a swift decision regarding his son's marital future. Even if she and Jev could never be more than friends, she wanted to see her friends happy, not manipulated into misery.

They were still sitting close enough for Jev to nudge her shoulder with his. "Were you in that office all afternoon? Did you learn anything helpful?"

She made herself shift her focus from wanting to comfort him back to their work, though she was aware of the warmth of his shoulder against hers and let herself lean against him. "Not what I expected."

"But something you didn't expect?"

"Yes. I wanted to know if anyone had tried to buy desirable land in the city and been denied. What I found is that someone very recently purchased a huge swath of land five miles up the Jade River."

"Isn't that the area that's so swampy and wet that all past attempts to drain it and turn it to farmland failed?"

Zenia nodded. "That's most of the Jade River near the city. It's nothing but swamp and mangroves. Most places, those trees grow about a half mile inland from the river, but three streams drain into the Jade in this section of land, so the mangroves extend almost ten miles inland there. Previously, the Nhole family owned it." Zenia had been surprised to find the transaction involved someone she'd met, though she assumed the zyndar prime—Dr. Ghara Nhole's father—had been the one responsible, not Ghara or her mother. Their estate had been old and rundown when Zenia and Jev visited—especially that dilapidated leaky cottage—so maybe it made sense that they would accept an offer to sell relatively useless land.

"Previously? Who owns it now?"

"A man named Tildar Braksnoth. He's on the list I made of wealthy commoners. I haven't had a chance to research him extensively yet, but from what I've heard of the man, he grew up poor and on the streets and built his fortune from scratch."

"Fortune in what?" Jev asked. "Logging?"

Zenia had wondered that same thing when she'd been reading about the transaction, since cutting down the mangrove trees for lumber was the only use she could imagine for that land. "He manufactures steam carriages and wagons, and he's funding experiments on a steam vehicle that would run on rails. I don't remember what it's called. One of the newspapers spoke of it and him, but as I said, I'll have to do more research."

"Unless he wants to drive his vehicles through a swamp, I'm puzzled as to why he would want that land. Did he spend a lot?"

"Yes. The Nholes refused his first two offers."

"Were those offers all this year?"

"All in the last month."

"Interesting," Jev said.

"I thought so. I got his address from the clerk. He rents a townhouse in the city in an exclusive neighborhood. It's on the other side of town, and I'm exhausted, so I think we should wait until tomorrow to visit him, but we should definitely visit him."

"Most definitely," Jev said. "He rents it, you say? He doesn't own it?"

"A zyndar family owns that whole strip of town. Your people own *most* of the city."

"I feel I should be offended every time you call the zyndar *my* people." His tone sounded more dry than offended.

Zenia considered her use of the term. She hadn't consciously thought about it—hadn't even been aware she was doing so—and she realized her prejudices were showing. She was thinking of the zyndar as if they were some alien race, something inhuman. Which—she remembered her run-in with the dunderheads that morning—maybe some of them were. But Jev wasn't. He never had been.

"*Those* people," she corrected, hoping he found it amusing. She made a note to try to stop segregating them into some special category. Not *all* of them were awful and inhuman.

Jev chuckled and wrapped an arm around her shoulders. Apology accepted, the gesture seemed to say.

She knew she shouldn't, but she hoped he would leave his arm there this time. She leaned a little more against his side. "Did you learn anything from the elven ambassador?" she asked. "Or did he refuse to see you?"

"He wasn't there, and neither were those two guards who stopped me last time."

"Oh? What about their creatures?"

"I didn't see them. I walked up to the front door and knocked, preparing my speech about offering to help the elves rebuild their garden."

"And?" she prompted when he paused.

"Lornysh answered."

"Did he have an opinion on the gardens?"

Jev snorted. "No. Maybe because he's recovering from injuries he received fighting a water golem last night."

"A water golem? Where?"

"Under the city. Guarding Iridium's lair."

Zenia digested that, shocked that such a creature could exist so close to the city. And that Iridium knew someone who could conjure up such a powerful magical monster. That woman was definitely dangerous. Zenia hoped Jev wouldn't feel compelled to visit her again. Nothing good could come out of dealing with her, as Marlyna's accusations surely proved.

"Lornysh said the ambassador's dresser is empty and his bags are gone. There are only a couple of elves left in the tower, none of the original staff."

"Should we find it ominous that they all felt compelled to leave the city?"

"Probably." Jev squeezed her shoulders and released her. He leaned forward and pushed himself to his feet. "Let's go back and get some rest. We'll visit this Braksnoth's house in the morning and hope the solutions to our problems lie with him."

Zenia found it unlikely that one wealthy businessman could solve *all* their problems, unfortunately, but she *would* hope for a lead. Jev offered her a hand up, and she accepted it, heading into the night with him. Her head ached, and her eyes had sand in them. She definitely needed rest.

His comment about resting in bed snuggled up with a woman came to mind, and as they headed back, she let herself imagine being that woman. Just daydreaming about such a thing couldn't hurt. Though would she be able to have such dreams once he married someone else? She shouldn't. She would have to find someone else to dream about. That notion made her heart ache.

The next morning, Jev woke from a concupiscent dream so full of vigorous activity that he was shocked he wasn't more exhausted than when he'd gone to bed. But he was more stimulated than exhausted, distressingly so. He hoped Zenia's dragon tear didn't tell her about his wayward mind. A man couldn't be held responsible for his *dreams*, surely.

Besides, she was the one who had hugged him the night before. The warmth of her touch had to be what had primed his mind for a night of lurid dreaming. And the fact that someone he hadn't expected to offer condolences or empathy had done so. Granted, she wasn't as hard and aloof as she'd been as an inquisitor. Like him, Zenia seemed to be off kilter as she struggled to find her footing in this new role.

Jev rubbed his face and sat on the edge of his bed. He hadn't meant to blurt out all his problems to her—his father would spit with disgust and tell him real men didn't whine to women—but if he'd known it could elicit hugs, he might have been tempted to try before.

"No," he grumbled. "No eliciting hugs."

He needed to focus on finding Cutter and Grindmor and what was increasingly looking like a threat to the entire city, if not the entire kingdom. And yet...

He looked toward the window. Dawn had come, but he still had an hour until he was due to meet Zenia in the kitchen for breakfast. From there, they would head to the mangrove-buying man's townhouse. Tildar. That was his name.

Jev wondered if he had time to pick flowers or do something nice for Zenia. Hugs and dreams aside, he felt he should give her a thank-you gift for staying up the previous night to do his paperwork. Or he should *make* her a gift. That was what Cutter had suggested.

The fact that he wasn't here to help with that, as he'd offered to do, filled Jev with sadness. So far, he'd tried to keep himself from worrying too much or from dwelling on the idea that the dwarves might have been killed instead of kidnapped, but it was hard not to let such thoughts creep into his mind.

Jev washed and dressed and headed down to the gardens. He still wanted to create a gold or silver chain for Zenia's dragon tear, but he wouldn't know how to do such a thing, so he would wait until he had Cutter's help. For now...

As he strolled the pathways, the flowers and grass damp with morning dew, he considered which ones she might like. Or would she like any of them? She was a practical woman. Maybe she would be puzzled by such a frivolous offering.

Jev grumbled an order to stop doubting himself and plucked a couple of stalks full of elegant floral bells rising to a tapered point. He had no idea what they were called, but they had an appealing smell that reminded him of the shampoo Zenia favored. He was fairly certain they were purple and not gray—someone had once told him there weren't any gray flowers—but he'd never seen purple well. Should he attempt to match them to something or simply take her these two stalks? Or just one? There was no way he could create a whole bouquet, not with colors that went together, so maybe he should choose a single offering. But he'd already removed two from the garden, and it seemed wasteful to discard one.

He stared bleakly around at the myriad flowers lining the path and felt utterly lost. By the founders, he should have purchased something practical for her. He could do practical. For example, maybe she needed a new pistol. He hadn't seen her wearing that one with the ivory handle she'd had when they first met. Had she been forced to return it to the temple, the same as she had her old dragon tear?

Jev felt confident he could pick out an attractive pistol. Maybe a matched set. But would she accept what would be considered a relatively expensive gift from him?

Someone paused at the head of the path, and Jev almost cast his flowers to the side, feeling he'd been caught doing something he shouldn't. But he kept them. On the chance Zenia would like them, he couldn't bring himself to throw away his chosen prizes.

Rhi peered down the pathway at him. She carried her bo and a knapsack and looked to be heading to work for the day.

"I'd ask if you were lost, Zyndar Dharrow, but I'm positive you've been to the castle more times than I have."

"I have, but I don't spend that much time in the gardens." He wasn't sure whether to hide his flowers and shoo her away before she noticed them or ask her opinion. If anyone would know Zenia's taste in flowers—or if she liked them at all—Rhi ought to.

"Hm." Rhi's gaze drifted to his hand. She'd already seen them. "That answers that question, I think."

"What question?"

"Whether it was you or Zenia who decided you two wouldn't continue dating."

Jev wanted to protest since the comment made him sound like a rotten lemon plucked from a tree, found lacking, and cast alongside the road. It hadn't been like that at all.

Rhi walked toward him. "Are you hoping to woo her with flowers? I don't know if any man has given her flowers before. Inquisitors are too daunting for flowers."

"Yes, she's mentioned her dauntingness before."

"You don't find her so? That's funny since you met as she arrested you."

"Tried to arrest me." Jev held up the flowers. "These are purple, right?"

Rhi squinted at him as if she suspected him of making a joke.

"I'm colorblind," he said.

"Ah. I'd say that explains your bland choices in clothing, but Zenia can see fine and picks bland stuff too. You two could be bland together if the flowers work and you win her over."

"I'm not trying to win her over. I want to give her something as a thank-you for doing an insane amount of work for me."

"I thought you thanked her with a hug." Rhi smirked.

She hadn't even been there. What the hells?

"I wouldn't have suspected an office of men would be such a gossip-filled place," Jev muttered, abruptly wondering if the rumors that he and Zenia were sleeping together had started in his own office. With Zyndar Garlok, perhaps? Jev wouldn't have guessed him a gossip, but a griper, yes. He was the only person there who would have likely been invited into meetings with people in the same circles as Hydal.

"Hugs are big news," Rhi said.

"That's pathetic given all the concerns looming on the horizon."

Rhi lifted her eyebrows. Jev decided he would let Zenia explain everything to her if she wanted. Since they didn't yet have true evidence of conquerors on the way, he didn't want to make a formal announcement to the office.

"Would a white flower go well with these?" Jev asked.

"Sure. Maybe something with a large bloom to contrast all those small bells. How about that? Or those?"

Jev stepped over to make a selection. "Do you think Zenia likes flowers?"

"You'll find out if she flings her arms and legs around you for a passionate kiss."

After his dream from the night before, Jev had no trouble imagining how he would respond to that, but he shook his head. "That won't happen."

"Why not?" Rhi genuinely sounded curious.

Jev was surprised Zenia hadn't confided in her. Maybe she had been too busy this past week.

"Zenia doesn't want someone to date. She wants someone to marry." As soon as Jev made the statement, he wondered if it was actually correct. She'd said she wouldn't have sex with someone she wasn't married to, but had she actually implied she wanted to get married? She'd seemed distressed to end things with him, and he'd had the sense from their discussions that she might be interested if he proposed, but… maybe he'd been reading too much into her oblique words.

"Does she? Huh. I didn't know she aspired to that."

"I thought girlfriends always shared such things with each other," he said lightly, though if Zenia had never brought it up with Rhi, that made him doubly doubt whether marriage was truly something she wanted.

"She's private. She doesn't talk much about her love interests. I've wondered from time to time… Well, it's none of my business."

"Nor mine," he said, though he wanted to know *what* exactly Rhi wondered.

"If you propose to her, maybe it could be your business." Rhi grinned.

"I can't," Jev said, though he realized belatedly she hadn't been serious.

"Why not? You don't seem like someone who cares that much about social decorum between the classes."

"It's less about decorum and more about obligations. As my father's heir, it's my duty to marry an appropriate zyndari woman."

"Is that what you *want* to do?"

"It's what I've always known I'll have to do."

"You didn't answer my question."

Jev smiled sadly. "I know, but it's the only answer I've got. I'm my father's only son now. I can't fail him in this. If my brother were still alive, maybe I could have walked away from everything, knowing the estate would be in his hands, but he's not. And I can't claim he would have been a great choice for zyndar prime even if he were."

"No chance your father would accept Zenia as a wife for you? Her father was zyndar. Did you know that?"

"Yes, and I know she loathes her father and wouldn't likely accept it even if he suddenly did the right thing and acknowledged her as his daughter." True, but the thought made Jev wonder for the first time if he could somehow talk Veran Morningfar into acknowledging Zenia and if it would make a difference to his father. He knew his old man wanted him to marry a Kolinsnor or Alderoth or maybe a Stellash… a zyndari woman from one of the truly powerful families with long histories of creating brave and talented war leaders. But maybe if Zenia were at least half zyndar…

"Are you going to pluck that one before the season ends and it withers and dies?"

Jev picked the flower his hand had been hovering over. "Yes."

"Good. I look forward to seeing whether or not they end up in a vase on Zenia's desk." Rhi headed back to the main walkway.

"A vase?" Was he supposed to supply that too?

Rhi waved over her shoulder.

Jev trailed slowly after her, curious whether Rhi would report the details of their conversation to Zenia. It wasn't anything she didn't already know, but he imagined her being hurt to hear his rejection of the marriage idea emphasized again. Maybe not. Maybe he didn't mean that much to her.

But he didn't see her doing paperwork for anyone else.

He sighed and headed for the kitchen. Maybe he was a fool for not considering marriage. He wished Zenia had agreed to a few more dates—and, all right, sex—so he could better know how they would be together. Would they enjoy sleeping together? Living together? If he knew, that would make it easier to decide… What?

"You know exactly what," he muttered.

If it had been only about him, he could have walked away from everything, from his lands, his rights, and even his title if need be. But all the people who lived on Dharrow land needed a good leader to take the reins once his father died, and he'd always known it was his duty to be that person, to responsibly watch over the family and the estate. To choose anything less, no matter what his heart wanted, would be a breach of duty. Of honor.

No, he couldn't walk away from that, and his father had already said he wouldn't accept a commoner for Jev. But wouldn't it be a crime of sorts to give up without even trying? Maybe, one day this summer, Jev would go see Morningfar. Could he talk the man into acknowledging Zenia without punching him for being such an ass to her all those years ago?

CHAPTER 12

ENIA POKED AT HER BOWL of porridge, barely aware of it or the clatter of pots and pans on the other side of the kitchen. She sat at the table in the back with a couple of the castle staff, two women who chatted amiably with each other. She was too busy dwelling on another dream—another *nightmare*—that she'd had.

It had been similar to the one from the other night where she'd been trapped in a cave with a sword-wielding orc approaching. This time, it had gone further, with the orc swinging that sword like an axe, bringing it down on her shoulder. She'd woken with a cry of pain, her body drenched in sweat, the dragon tear glowing on her nightgown. She'd been shocked to find her arm still intact, no evidence of a wound. The nightmare had been disturbingly real and even now, she felt a dull ache in her shoulder.

Was it some kind of sign? Visions sent by the founders? Would orcs be the ones spearheading an attack on Kor? And if so, how did they tie in to the wealthy land-buying Tildar?

Someone set a glass vase of flowers down next to her bowl, and Zenia stirred, her awareness returning to the kitchen.

Jev smiled down at her, his hair combed and his beard freshly trimmed. "Good morning."

Zenia made herself smile, though she wasn't in the mood for it. He appeared far perkier than she. He must have had better dreams.

The two maids stopped chatting and looked over at him. The older one rested her chin on her hands, as if waiting to see what would happen. The younger one gave Jev a long appraising look up and down.

A surge of possessiveness went through Zenia, and she wanted to pull him down and say, "Mine."

But he wasn't.

"Morning, Jev," she said, glancing at the flowers.

"I thought you might like them." He hesitated, his smile faltering. "For your desk in the office. So people can tell it's yours instead of mine." He planted the smile back firmly on his face, but he seemed uncertain.

Was he nervous about giving her flowers? Why would such a small gesture daunt him? Unless he worried she would take it as a sign that he hoped she would change her mind about dating him. And having sex with him.

But she didn't believe he was angling for that. He could have kissed her and more when she'd been standing chest to chest with him behind that waterfall. She would have let him. She'd wanted him, no matter what promises she'd made to herself. But he'd been the one to step back. He knew her vow, and he wouldn't attempt to make her break it. She knew that about him by now. There was no questioning his honor.

"Thank you," she said, realizing she might be making him nervous by not saying anything. "They're lovely. Does that mean I'll get fewer folders dropped on my desk?"

"Probably not."

She lifted the vase, bringing the flowers to her nose. The purple lupines smelled wonderful. They were some of her favorites.

Jev's smile grew more relaxed. "I just need a few minutes to wolf down some food, and we can head off to that townhouse. Want me to refill—oh, never mind. Did you just start?"

"Not exactly." Zenia thought about telling him about her dreams and might have if they had been alone. But they weren't. She frowned at the maid watching Jev's butt as he went to retrieve a bowl.

A back door opened, and one of the pages hustled in, a boy that had been sent to retrieve Jev before. Tamordon, that was his name.

"Captain Cham," he blurted, stopping at her side. "The king wants to see you. In his office."

Jev ambled over with his bowl of porridge.

"The king wants to see you, too, Zyndar," the page said. "In his office."

"Not in his bedroom?"

Zenia almost blushed, thinking he'd heard of how she insisted on seeing Targyon the day before. Early.

"He's in his office, Zyndar," the page said earnestly, looking a little confused by Jev's joke.

"Then we'll definitely go there. Thanks, Tamordon." Jev patted the boy on the shoulder. "Zenia?"

She abandoned her porridge but paused halfway to her feet. Jev might be offended if she likewise abandoned his flowers. What if one of the kitchen staff threw them away? She truly would like to have them on her desk in the office, even though they would wilt quickly down there, given the lack of natural light.

"Captain?" The page was already back at the door, holding it open for them.

"Coming." Zenia grabbed the vase and hustled after Jev. She would feel silly carrying it through the castle, but that was better than leaving the flowers to chance.

She noticed Jev carrying his porridge bowl and spooning in mouthfuls as he ambled after the boy and promptly felt less silly.

"Is that allowed?" she whispered as they followed the page toward the closest stairs.

"Eating? I think most people who live in the castle do it from time to time."

"You know what I mean." She elbowed him.

He grinned at her and took a big bite.

"I'm not going to get a healer if you fall on the stairs and get a spoon lodged in your throat," Zenia said.

"No? What about if it goes up my nose?"

"Definitely not. You would deserve it."

"I can't believe you feel that way." He pointed his porridge-laden spoon at her vase. "You're not going to give my gift to Targyon, are you? I would be devastated."

"No." She almost choked on the idea of strolling into the king's office and handing him flowers. "I didn't want the cooks to throw them away."

"You could have asked one of them to take them to the office for you."

"And give them more work? I'm sure they have plenty." Besides, Zenia didn't think she had the right to order the staff around. In a sense, she was staff too.

Tamordon stopped before the door to the secretary's office and started to open it for them but paused, alarm widening his eyes as he looked at Jev's face.

Zenia leaned around to see what the boy saw, then snorted.

"Is there a problem?" Jev asked.

"Yes," Zenia said. "Young Tamordon here doesn't want to introduce you to the king when there's porridge smeared in your beard."

The boy gave her a relieved look.

"Damn that hoity toity royal decorum," Jev said.

"You're the oddest zyndar I've ever met." Zenia reached up to scrape the gunk off his beard.

He grinned and lowered his face accommodatingly. His eyes were gleaming. She didn't know why he was so cheerful this morning, but the gleam was infectious, and the memory of her nightmare faded from her mind.

She looked down at the porridge in her hand and frowned. What was she supposed to do with it? She didn't have a napkin.

"I'll get it, ma'am." The boy didn't have a napkin either. He scraped it off her palm, considered it, then considered a potted plant near the door. He finally stuck his hand in his pocket and wiped it off in there.

Zenia grimaced, hoping he had plans to launder his trousers soon.

"You're a troublemaker, Jev Dharrow," she whispered as Tamordon pushed open the door.

"Yes, I am." His eyes gleamed some more.

The secretary waved them through without preamble. They found Targyon inside with a man Zenia didn't recognize, but he wore a blue cap identical to the one her informant who worked at the docks had been wearing the other day. She believed it signified a uniform down there.

"Jev, Zenia," Targyon said. "I've just had word from the port authority." He waved to the man who bobbed his head. "A fast clipper arrived this morning. The captain reported passing a massive steamship heading this way, the craft manned by dwarves."

"The ship full of dwarves that you invited, I hope," Jev said, "and not some attack force."

"I'm positive they're the ones I invited. But they're ahead of schedule." Targyon grimaced. "Apparently, that steamship of theirs is fast. They're expected to arrive in port here by dawn tomorrow."

"Maybe tonight, Sire," the dock man said. ˙

Targyon's grimace deepened. "Thank you, Lunt. Dismissed."

The man bowed and let himself out, giving Zenia's vase a curious look as he passed. Targyon seemed to notice it for the first time and also squinted at it in slight confusion.

Zenia held it to her chest, not sure what she would say if asked about it. Should she admit Jev had given the flowers to her? Would the king approve of his two chosen captains exchanging gifts?

The thought jolted her as she realized she hadn't told Jev that his ex-fiancée had brought him a gift the day before. She'd left it on his desk, but she didn't think he had been down to the office since then. Should she say something now? She wasn't obligated to do so, especially not while Targyon was talking to them.

"Please tell me you've got a lead on Master Grindmor." Targyon looked at both of them.

Zenia shoved thoughts of gifts from her mind. "Nothing concrete yet, Sire." Founders' fiery breath, she wished she could, for once, tell him they were close to completing their assignment. "We do have a lead we're going to check out—we were just finishing breakfast before heading out."

She hoped it wasn't disingenuous to call visiting some wealthy man's townhouse a lead. It *could* be a lead. But right now, it was just the purchase of an odd piece of land.

"So, I'm holding you up?" Targyon asked.

"No, Sire," Zenia said as Jev said, "Absolutely, Sire."

She resisted the urge to elbow him again. Not in front of the king.

Targyon frowned at Jev.

"Did you know the elven ambassador fled the city yesterday?" Jev asked.

"He sent a note that he was leaving, yes."

"I hope you have the dock master keeping an eye out for other ships heading to our shores. Ships that would be less welcome than dwarven ones."

Targyon's eyes narrowed. "You believe attackers are on the way?"

"I think there's a reason the elven ambassador and all his staff left the city in a hurry," Jev said. "And that it was more than my rudeness to his garden."

"Hm, I will send word out to all the zyndar families in the area to prepare troops. For good or ill, we have a lot of war veterans now."

"Yes, Sire," Jev said. "Oh, did you hear the news yet about the sabotage to the Water Order Temple?"

"I heard. Guild involvement is suspected." Targyon raised his eyebrows. "A guild you're supposedly aligned with."

Zenia stared at Jev, remembering his comments from the night before.

"I'm not any more involved with Iridium than you are." Jev waved to the desk chair, and for some reason, Targyon's cheeks turned red. "I'll let you know if I decide to let one of the guilds suborn me, but for now, please just know that Inquisitor Marlyna loathes me for some reason, and anything she says about me is likely a lie."

"I'll keep that in mind," Targyon murmured, his face hard to read.

Zenia hoped nothing happened to make him question his trust for Jev. Jev didn't deserve to have his honor questioned. It sounded like he had enough steaming poo being heaped on him right now without Targyon doubting him.

"I won't delay your breakfast further." Targyon waved to the door and looked pointedly at Jev's bowl. He hadn't been shoveling spoonfuls in his mouth during their meeting, but he still held it. "If there's any chance you can find Grindmor today," Targyon added, "I would be extremely grateful."

"We'll try," Jev said.

Zenia nodded, wishing they could promise more than *trying*. But she knew they couldn't.

"I guess breakfast is over," Jev said as they strode out of the office.

"Unless you want to store it in your beard for later, yes."

He grinned at her, then waved to her vase. "If I had a more substantial beard, I'd offer to carry those in it for you too. So your hands don't get tired."

Zenia blushed, though she wasn't sure why. Maybe because his eyes kept gleaming at her.

"I'll hurry down and put them in the office," she said.

"I'll get some horses and meet you out front."

She nodded and strode toward the stairs. Only when she was halfway to the office did she think to wonder if Jev's good mood was due to her accepting his flowers. More than that, she'd been carrying them around. Did he approve?

"Going anywhere interesting?" Rhi asked as Zenia passed through the office.

She was one of only two agents already at a desk. Sort of at a desk. She was standing behind it and exercising her calves as she read a report.

"The townhouse of a wealthy land buyer."

Rhi looked at the flowers in Zenia's hand but didn't seem surprised by them.

"Any chance that will be more interesting than yesterday's visit to the office of boredom?" she asked.

"It's always possible if you want to come."

As Zenia set the vase down on her desk, a desk that had acquired more folders since her last visit, she noticed the wrapped gift resting unopened on Jev's desk. Should she take it to him? No, whatever it was, he didn't likely want to cart it around the city. But she would tell him about it. So it didn't get buried by folders and go unnoticed for weeks. Zenia would be disappointed if she gave a man a gift and that happened to it.

"You sure you don't want to open that?" Rhi asked, her bo in hand, her calf exercises complete. "Or light it on fire and throw it out a window?"

"This office doesn't have any windows."

"Guess we're foiled then."

On a whim—or maybe a hunch—Zenia grabbed her weapons belt with her knife and pistol out of her desk drawer and buckled it on. She didn't know if this Tildar would lead her to Grindmor, but she had a gut feeling that he was up to something—and might not want the king's Crown Agents to know about it.

Thanks to the help of a stable boy, Jev had three horses saddled when Zenia walked out with Rhi. He smiled to himself, pleased he'd guessed right, that Rhi would be in the office and want to come along. Zenia opened her mouth, seeming startled by his assumption. He might have felt silly if she had come out alone, but he merely bowed as they approached and offered the reins.

He was a touch disappointed that Zenia no longer carried the vase—he wasn't sure why, but it had delighted him to see her clutching it close and walking around the castle with his flowers—but it would have been impractical on a horse.

Rhi said nothing about the flowers or her part in advising him. He wondered if she'd told Zenia that she'd helped—and questioned him about marriage.

"I forgot to tell you yesterday," Zenia said after she mounted, "but I ran into Zyndari Naysha in the castle courtyard."

"What?" Jev blurted, his good cheer evaporating.

The idea of Zenia chatting with his ex-fiancée alarmed him—what if they talked all about him? The stupid teenage boy he'd been when Naysha first came to know him? What could possibly have brought her up to the castle two days in a row? Trouble with her husband? For years, he'd imagined that scenario and how he would nobly step in and take her back if she wished it, but now? His father might consider it a reasonable match—and Jev would prefer it to marrying some stranger who manipulated the old man into arranging a marriage—but it wasn't something he daydreamed about anymore. Now, he daydreamed about… someone else. And night-dreamed too.

"She brought a gift for you." Zenia's tone was neutral, and he couldn't tell what she thought of that. "You were out, so she gave it to me to put on your desk in the office. It's there now."

"Huh."

"We didn't open it," Rhi said. "Zenia wanted to."

"Rhi." Zenia glared at her.

Rhi grinned.

"Yes," Jev said, recovering some of his equanimity. "With her bo, no doubt."

"Zenia doesn't have a bo."

"Oh? I must have been thinking of someone else."

Zenia nudged her horse toward the gate, apparently considering the conversation over. Jev would happily do the same, but now, he was curious about the gift and what it signified. Maybe Naysha was still trying to assuage her guilt. It would be foolish of him to think she wanted anything else from him. He nobly resisted the urge to make an excuse and run into the castle to open it.

Jev let the two women take the lead on the way into town while he kept his eyes open for trouble, whether enemy operatives skulking around the city or Iridium's people out setting more explosives. He didn't like that the Water Order inquisitor had complained to Targyon about how Jev was supposedly aligned with the Fifth Dragon. There were enough rumors flying around about him already.

"This is the street," Zenia said, slowing her horse as they turned at an intersection.

Stone townhouses lined either side of the boulevard with wide walkways out front and trees spreading shade over them. The homes reminded Jev of Naysha's townhouse, the one he'd spied on, and he realized they were only three blocks away.

It wasn't surprising. Even though zyndar owned land all over the city, most preferred to reside near others of their social status. His family's city house was nearby too. Sometime, he ought to check in on his cousin who, the last he'd heard, resided in it.

"Mostly zyndar live in these homes, don't they?" Rhi eyed the three- and four-story structures, many with marble steps and columns and carved wyverns or lion heads mounted over the doors, along with other accents to add flair—or maybe pretentiousness.

Jev smiled faintly, knowing that wasn't a word that would have come to mind for him before he'd started spending time with Zenia.

"Yes, they do," Jev said when the women glanced back at him. "Zenia, you said Tildar is a renter, didn't you? Maybe he's trying to buy this property from the current owner too."

"A townhouse would be a good investment," Zenia said. "I'm less certain about a swamp."

"A swamp?" Rhi asked.

Zenia explained her findings from the day before as they rode toward a house even more pretentious than the others. It had gold gutters and drains, and the wyverns and gryphons peering down from the rooftop appeared to be made from solid gold, too, rather than marble. Should thieves with large enough muscles to remove them ever come along, the house would be vandalized promptly.

"Think it came that way?" Jev asked. "Or did he modify it?"

Zenia shrugged. "Maybe the zyndar landlord lives on the other side of the kingdom and hasn't been by recently to object to the modifications."

They halted their horses in front of the yard, and Zenia double-checked the address.

"This is the right spot," she said.

"Nice fountain," Rhi said dryly, pointing her bo to a pair of sculpted stags locked in battle near the walkway up to the house. The sculptor had made them anatomically correct—and well endowed—with the water for the fountain coming out of their nether regions.

"This Tildar either has a disturbing sense of humor," Zenia said, "or he wanted to irk his neighbors."

"Can it be both?" Rhi asked.

"He tried to get appointed to a political office a few years ago. Maybe the reasons he failed had nothing to do with his common birth." Zenia dismounted.

Jev did the same, looking toward the windows and trying to tell if anyone was home. If Tildar was a businessman, he might be out working.

"Did you research him, Zenia?" Jev asked. He couldn't imagine she'd had time, as she'd been as weary as he the night before, but she nodded.

"As much as I could find in the library this morning. He was mentioned in those newspapers I was perusing yesterday. He's been quite busy in the last few years. When his bid for political office didn't work out—zyndar are almost always chosen, and that was the case this time as well—he hosted a few rallies and tried to start some movements among the common people. Jev, you may not have heard, but this was fairly commonplace in the city while the king and so many of the zyndar were gone. People gathering and protesting, trying to get written up in the newspapers and sometimes threatening to quit their jobs en masse if commoners weren't given a voice in government. Tildar was among them, fighting to diminish zyndar power and put power into the hands of the people. That was one of his rally cries. He argued to end the monarchy and start a democracy in which all people had a vote, though from what I was able to gather, he wanted more of a rule-by-the-rich than a rule-by-the-common-man."

"You did *sleep* last night, didn't you?" Jev couldn't believe she'd found time to do so much research.

"Not as much as I wanted to." She touched the front of her dress, the small lump that signified her dragon tear. "I've been having…" She glanced at Rhi, who'd dismounted and was waiting. "Never mind." Zenia lowered her hand.

Rhi frowned.

Jev wanted to pry, but maybe she would tell him later when they were alone. He jogged up the broad marble steps and pulled the gold chain for the gold doorbell.

The sound of footfalls on steps drifted through an open window. Jev's nerves danced a jig in his belly. After hearing all Zenia had researched, he felt more hopeful that this man might be a genuine lead, that he was someone who believed he could indeed gain if the current order were somehow upset.

The door opened, and a woman in a maid's uniform with a very short skirt answered the door, a rag and bottle of silver polish in her hand. "Yes?"

"I'm Zyndar Dharrow." Jev gestured to Rhi and Zenia. "These are friends." He thought he might get further if he didn't announce right off that they were on an investigation for the king. "We need to speak with Tildar Braksnoth."

"He's not here. He's out of town on a business trip."

Jev looked to Zenia. She touched a hand to that lump under her dress, and her eyes grew unfocused.

"Where did he go?" Jev asked.

"Rokvann, he said."

"Do you know when he'll be back?"

"Soon, I think. Perhaps you could try back in a couple of days, Zyndar?" The maid was polite, and Jev didn't sense duplicity from her, but he would wait for Zenia's verdict. "I can bring paper if you would like to leave a message."

"No, thank you. I'll try again later in the week."

The door closed.

"Is it against the Crown Agents Handbook to sneak into people's houses and snoop around?" Rhi asked.

"I don't think we're supposed to do anything criminal in the line of work," Jev said dryly, waving for them to descend the steps. That window was still open.

"What if Zenia uses magic to do the snooping?"

"Oh, I think that's encouraged then." Jev lowered his voice. "Zenia?"

"She was telling the truth," Zenia said. "But she also didn't know much. Her thoughts suggested Tildar is polite enough to her but treats her like the hired help, not a confidant. To her disappointment. He's in his fifties but, in her eyes, still quite handsome. She wears skimpy uniforms, hoping he'll invite her into the bedroom, but he hasn't yet. Apparently, Tildar lost the love of his life to a zyndar man who keeps her as a mistress, and he hasn't been that interested in sex since."

Rhi's mouth drooped open. "Your new rock tells you a lot more than the old one did."

Zenia shifted her weight uneasily. "Well, she thought we were judging her for her short dress and felt defensive. That made her think about her reasons for wearing it. Sometimes, the new dragon tear gives me more than I meant to seek." She still looked uncomfortable.

Jev made a mental note to ask her about that later, to see if anything disturbing was going on. He well remembered Cutter's warning about the significance of an actual dragon being carved on the front.

Hoping to take her mind off her concerns, Jev smiled and touched his chest. "Judging her? Me? Do I look judgmental?"

"A little stern maybe when you're not smiling," Rhi said. "It's the beard."

"Actually, it was more me. I did have the thought that the dress was awfully short, which made me think Tildar might require she wear it because he's the lecherous type to impose himself on the help, but..." Zenia shrugged. "I didn't mean to convey that with my expression. I didn't think I had." She glanced down at her chest—the dragon tear—again, then shook her head and made a dismissive gesture.

Jev would *definitely* ask her about that gem later.

"What next?" Rhi asked. "I hadn't planned to head to Rokvann today."

"Why don't we go out to the man's newly acquired property?" Jev didn't know if they would find any inspiration out there, but he hoped for some luck. The fact that Tildar had a lot of grudges against the zyndar didn't mean he was a criminal mastermind or had anything to do with Cutter's and Grindmor's disappearance, but they didn't have any other leads to follow. The land acquisition *was* odd. Jev just hoped they weren't inadvertently investigating some other, unrelated case that they hadn't even been assigned yet.

Zenia nodded. "I was going to suggest the same thing."

"I wasn't," Rhi said.

"What were you going to suggest?" Jev asked.

"That we go pummel some Fifth Dragon people in revenge for bombing the temple."

"I don't think the Fifth Dragon had anything to do with the dwarves' disappearance," Jev said. "I think Iridium was preemptively striking against Archmage Sazshen, since Sazshen supposedly wanted to put an end to Iridium and her people."

"Supposedly." Rhi prodded her thumb to her chest. "I'm the one who told you that wasn't true, that someone had started a rumor. Sazshen told me that herself before I quit."

"So, who stands to gain if we're distracted by a tiff between the guilds and the Orders?" Jev wondered.

Rhi opened her mouth, but Zenia spoke first, lowering her voice and turning her back to the window. "We're being watched. The maid."

"She's probably wondering why we're skulking out front." Jev took a step toward the street.

"Wait." Zenia slipped her dragon tear out on its leather thong. In broad daylight, it wasn't as obvious when it was glowing, but a few tendrils of blue light emanated from its core. "I know Rhi was joking, but I think I *can* snoop magically. Maybe poke into the man's office. I just need a minute." She wrapped her fingers around her dragon tear and closed her eyes.

The curtain at the front window moved. The maid leaving? Going to get someone else? Or just shifting so she could hear them better?

"What are the odds," Jev said in a louder voice, "that we could talk the king into installing a fountain like that at the castle?"

Rhi looked dubiously at the water streaming out of the stag statues' appendages. "I think he'd fire you if you suggested it."

"He can't fire me; I'm zyndar."

"He'd find some way to get rid of you."

Zenia lowered her hand and nodded toward the street. They collected their horses and moved several houses away before speaking.

"Cutter and Grindmor aren't tied and gagged in any of the closets," she said.

Jev grunted. He hadn't expected *that*, though it would have helped them meet Targyon's deadline.

"And I didn't see anything incredibly condemning," Zenia went on, tapping her chin, "but there *was* a room that was completely filled with swords and firearms. Not a collection someone with too much money mounts on their walls."

"My grandfather had such a collection," Jev said dryly. "It's still in one of the libraries in the castle."

"*One* of the libraries?" Rhi asked.

"My family has lived there for a thousand years. We've purchased a lot of books in that time. We have an armory, too, which is what it sounds like you're describing. But we do have a whole castle to defend. An armory for a townhouse seems excessive. Were there many other people inside?"

"A butler and another maid. An armory, yes," Zenia said. "That's exactly what it seemed like with weapons in racks next to practice dummies and boxes of cleaning kits. I looked in his office, too. I wasn't able to really read through the... vision. It's hard to explain exactly what the dragon tear shows me. I did, however, see that there was a green- and blue-colored map on the desk. It looked like his newly acquired land."

"Land we should definitely visit." Jev nodded to himself, glad he'd grabbed his pistol and short sword on the way out of the castle. He'd noticed that Zenia had also donned her weapons belt before leaving, an unremarkable pistol in the holster. He still mused on getting her a new one, an exquisitely forged one with hand-carved ivory inlays. "Let's grab a few supplies and stop by the elven embassy on the way out of town. I want to see if Lornysh has recovered from his injuries enough to join us. He has a magical sword."

"Are you expecting to run into trouble out on that land?" Rhi leaned forward, thumping her bo on the sidewalk.

"Crocodiles, at the least."

"I'll be disappointed if all we run into are crocodiles," Rhi said.

Jev thought of the water golem he and Lornysh had battled. "I won't."

CHAPTER 13

ENIA SHIFTED HER WEIGHT IN her saddle, alternating between eyeing the noon sun in the sky and the mangroves to the side of the highway. They were the mangroves where she and Jev had tangled with Iridium's men that first night they'd met. Unfortunately, the land they needed to visit today was on the far side of the river, so it was a longer trek from the city. They were almost even with it, but they had to ride another three miles inland, cross the Rapids Bridge, and then travel back downriver on the other side before they would reach Tildar's swath of swamp.

The group had discussed borrowing a boat in the king's name, but it would have taken a lot of effort to paddle it upriver against the current for miles, making it slower than riding. Still, Zenia worried they would end up riding back in the dark again by the time they explored the land and returned on horseback. After her last experience, she felt gun-shy about being out on the highway at night.

"Rhi?" Jev called, trotting up from behind. "Will you switch positions with me?"

He had ridden behind them and beside Lornysh for the first five miles of the trek.

"Are you going to discuss flower preferences with Zenia?" Rhi slowed her horse, though, judging by her glance backward, she wasn't sure she wanted to ride alongside Lornysh.

Zenia still didn't know the taciturn elf well and wouldn't know what to say to him either. He appeared more flint-faced than usual, perhaps because of the injury Jev had mentioned. Whatever it was, his clothing hid it.

"Most definitely," Jev said. "I'm eager to learn if she prefers pink flowers to purple ones."

"Would your colorblind eyes know the difference?" Rhi smirked at him.

"Yes, pink flowers are what I'm more likely to shove up the nose of a sarcastic junior agent."

"So long as they smell good."

Zenia looked at Jev as he brought his horse alongside hers and Rhi fell farther back. She knew he had heavier matters than flower preferences in mind.

"I was wondering how you're doing with the new dragon tear," he said.

Ah. Zenia would rather have discussed flowers. She remembered the way Jev and Rhi had gawked at her when she'd relayed all that information about the maid's sexual interests.

"It's eager to please and sometimes gives me more than I intended to get from people's minds," she explained again.

"Guess I better watch what I think about around you then." Jev smiled, but his eyes seem worried.

"I don't pry into your thoughts." She guessed he didn't like the idea of having his privacy invaded. Who would? "Or the thoughts of any friends." Not intentionally. It was possible the dragon tear would act on some subconscious desire of hers and share something a friend was thinking. After all, Zenia hadn't meant to poke into Naysha's mind.

"That's good. Anything else troubling you? Besides the mission?"

Zenia wondered if he'd caught her staring moodily into her porridge and not eating that morning. He was, she reminded herself, more observant and perceptive than the average man.

Should she tell him about her nightmares? He wouldn't be able to do anything about them, and he might worry. She didn't like that Cutter had thought she shouldn't keep this particular dragon tear. Jev hadn't voiced a similar objection, but she wouldn't be surprised if he silently agreed. She could envision him putting her safety above the benefits the powerful gem gave them.

"Nothing I can't handle," Zenia said, not wanting to outright lie to him.

"Ah, so that's a yes." His tone was light, but he watched her intently. And yes, there was concern in his eyes.

She sensed he wouldn't let the matter drop easily. "I've been having some weird dreams. Variations of the same dream. It's possible it has nothing to do with the dragon tear. Minds are odd."

"They're not dreams about me naked, are they?"

"No," Zenia said. Judging by his smirk, it was a joke, but she wondered what had made him think that. "Why, are you having dreams about *me* naked?"

His smirk faltered before he firmly reaffixed it. "I refuse to answer that question while you're wearing that gem."

Dear founders, did that mean he *was*?

"What are your dreams about?" he asked, and she sensed he wanted to turn the conversation quickly back to her.

A little buzz of warmth came from the dragon tear along with what felt like a question. Was it wondering if she wanted it to poke into his thoughts?

No, she thought at it with emphasis.

"You don't have to tell me," he added when she didn't answer right away. "I just want you to know you can if you want to."

"Thank you. I'll remember that. I would rather focus on our investigation right now. They're just dreams. Not a big deal."

"Hm."

They had reached the Rapids Bridge and guided their horses off the highway and across it. Another well-tended road continued on the far side. Zenia knew it paralleled the coast, a few miles inland, all the way to the border, but she had only traveled about ten miles down it before. Sometimes, she felt her life and her realm of expertise were tiny, since she'd so rarely left the city and had never traveled overseas. Her career had never required it. It had been novel when she'd traveled with Jev to Nhole Castle.

After they had traveled a half mile, Jev pointed to a dirt road, one far less traveled than the main one. It headed back downriver. "That's our turnoff, right? The only way to get to that land, I think, unless you want to go around it and to the coast."

"That's it." The area around the turnoff was clear of trees and occupied by farmhouses with lettuce, gort, and radishes already coming up in the fields behind them. But farther downriver, the dark shadows of mangroves and swamplands darkened the horizon. "I'm glad we're visiting in the middle of the day."

Realizing that made her sound like a scared girl, she chuckled and waved a hand as if it had just been a joke.

But Jev said, "Me too," with feeling.

She looked at him.

"If there are crocodiles waiting, I want to be able to *see* them."

"Of course." Zenia turned her horse down the dirt road, glancing back to check on Rhi and Lornysh. They were still following but not riding together.

That made Zenia feel a little sad even though she didn't think Rhi was deliberately ostracizing the elf. She probably didn't know what to say to him. Still, Zenia decided she would talk to him later and try to get to know him. Even a standoffish elf had to feel lonely from time to time, and Jev had said the other elves in the embassy tower had left.

"Hells," Jev grumbled.

Zenia turned her attention back to the front in time to see the tail end of a crocodile as it waddled across the dirt road and disappeared into a canal alongside. "Maybe Tildar bought the land so he can start a crocodile farm."

"If such a thing exists in the world, I don't want to know about it."

"It can't be much different from owning a farm full of cows. Didn't I see some of those on your land when I visited?" Visited, such a polite way to say she had been there to arrest him.

"We *milk* the cows. And they don't try to eat us while we do it."

"Perhaps some farmers like more of a challenge."

"When I was growing up, we did have a cow that licked my face and nibbled on my hat while I was milking her. It made matters moderately challenging."

Zenia was amused that Jev had actually milked a cow himself. She supposed his father wasn't the kind to shirk work or pawn it all off on the staff. The old man must have deliberately raised his sons to be the same. Even if she didn't care for Heber Dharrow, she did like the result of his influence in Jev.

As the road took them into the mangroves, it grew much darker, the canopy overhead blotting out the sky. The air smelled damper and earthier. Almost immediately, the road, which had been wide enough for them to ride side-by-side, dwindled and turned into a path overrun by thorny vines and tree branches that clawed at their clothing.

Croaking frogs competed with cawing birds, and occasional splashes sounded in stagnant water to the sides of the path. As many crocodiles floated in the murky pools as logs. A huge snake hissed from a tree branch as they rode under it.

Though Jev couldn't be pleased about all the predatory wildlife, he took the lead. Rhi and Lornysh closed the gap, and soon, Zenia could hear the breathing of Rhi's horse right behind hers. It sounded hot and tired—or maybe afraid.

What Zenia had thought was a root in the path moved, shooting into the undergrowth. Her horse shied to the side, almost stepping in the water.

"It may be unwise to take the animals into this," Lornysh announced from the rear.

Jev stopped his horse and looked over their little group.

"They may not be able to travel into the swamp if the path ends or grows too muddy," Lornysh added. "If we're forced to leave them, they'll be targets for the predators in here."

"How much farther is it to Tildar's property?" Jev asked Zenia.

"Still more than a mile to the closest boundary, and then it spans miles in all directions."

"Hm, all right. Dismount, and I'll take the horses back to one of those farmhouses. If I toss my name out, they should be willing to watch them while we're in here. We're not that far from Dharrow land."

"Are you sure you're not just looking for an excuse to escape the crocodiles?" Zenia slid off her horse, careful not to step in the water. The path had definitely gotten narrow. Narrow and muddy. Her boots squished when she landed.

Jev winked as he took her reins. "If I don't come back within twenty minutes, feel free to go on without me."

"I'd pine away with loneliness without your company." Zenia removed the travel pack she'd gone back to collect before they'd left town, then relinquished her horse.

"Lornysh can keep you entertained if Rhi isn't up to it. He's quite charming to the ladies."

Rhi snorted. "Please, I could feel him glaring at me with his icy eyes all the way out here."

"Elven ladies find his glares charming. He's teaching human ladies to feel the same way. He likes a challenge."

Lornysh gave Jev a harder look than any of the crocodiles had.

Jev patted him on the shoulder before taking his and Rhi's reins. "I'll be back soon. Don't go far without me."

Jev rode off with the other horses trailing him. He wasn't able to keep hold of their reins since they had to go single-file, but the horses were content to follow each other. Eager, in fact. One kept trying to gallop and pass Jev. Zenia couldn't blame them for wanting to leave the dark swamp.

"I will go ahead to scout," Lornysh announced.

Without waiting for comment, he jogged down the path deeper into the swamp.

"Did we miss the part where he charmed us?" Rhi asked.

"Possibly."

Rhi peered into the trees to either side of the path. A snake slithered along a nearby branch, flicking its tongue as its eyes focused on them.

"Some men wouldn't leave women alone in snake-infested swamps," Rhi said.

"Yes, but your stick is bigger than theirs. They must assume you can handle yourself."

Rhi grinned and patted her bo. "It is a big stick." She eyed the snake. "And I'm just as adept at whacking reptiles as I am criminals."

"You have experience doing that?"

"I grew up in the stinky armpit of the Earth quarter. I've whacked everything."

Zenia smiled, alternating between looking up and down the path and out into the murky pools of water between the trees. Lornysh had already disappeared from sight.

"Is the hayloft working out for you?" Zenia asked.

"Yes, but it's lonely. Some workers have been rebuilding the farmhouse during the day, but all the old tenants moved out. I'm envious of your room in the castle. You've got staff awake to chat with any time. A hunky zyndar just down the hall if you get cold and need someone to snuggle with."

Zenia ignored that, having already informed Rhi of their lack of snuggling, and said, "Do you miss the temple?"

"Not Miss Snooty Marlyna. Or Sazshen either. But the other monks, yes. I passed Bondokk at the market the other day, and he barely acknowledged me when I waved and called to him. We used to be sparring buddies. And then Makrus, who was with him, told me I should have turned in my bo when I left, that those are weapons for monks only. He's an ass and always has been, but Bondokk nodded in agreement with him. That stung."

"I'm sorry. Your association with me has probably resulted in you being ostracized too."

"Maybe some, but I think my deciding to leave got them frosty with me too. It's a big deal to be accepted into the monk ranks, especially for a woman. I knew some people would be disappointed if I walked away from that, but I didn't realize... I don't know. It's like I denounced the founders and decided to start a new religion. You'd think I was some evil blasphemer."

The snake slithered closer on the branch, revealing its fangs and preparing for an attack.

Zenia reached for her pistol, but Rhi acted first. She whacked the thing flat on the head. It reared up like a horse and snapped at her bo, catching the side. It was enough for the snake's fangs to sink in.

Rhi growled and whipped the bo hard in the opposite direction. The snake's body was coiled tightly around the tree, but Rhi's swing was hard enough to snap the branch. It and the snake whipped across the path, pulled by the bo, and Zenia jumped back, lest she be whacked in the face. The snake lost its grip on the bo as it and the branch flew across a nearby pool of water before splashing down. Rhi sniffed and set the butt of her weapon down. In the water, the snake extricated itself from the branch and slithered away.

"I, for one, am glad you kept your bo," Zenia said.

Rhi winked. "Me too."

"It's a good thing you took care of that snake before I returned," Jev drawled, ambling up the path toward them. "I'm afraid I might not have convinced it to leave in as swift and manly a manner."

"Manly?" Rhi lifted her eyebrows.

"At the least, you displayed great strength."

"I won't argue with that, but it was most assuredly feminine strength."

"But your stick is still larger than mine, right?" Jev asked.

"Oh, absolutely."

"Lornysh scouting?" Jev asked.

"How did you know?" Zenia asked.

"It's what he does. Also, I believe it pains him to have to engage in a conversation with a human for more than three minutes." Jev waved for them to lead the way down the path. Actually, he waved for *Rhi* to lead. With her big stick.

Rhi lifted her chin and went first without complaint. If anything, she appeared pleased to be asked.

"Why is he loitering in Korvann if he doesn't like humans?" she asked over her shoulder.

"I haven't gotten the answer to that question out of him yet," Jev said, "other than that he's enjoying the city's cultural offerings."

"So, he doesn't like talking to humans, but he likes human things?"

"I think he prefers to study humans from a distance. Like a scientist peering into a petri dish."

"What did he do in the army?" Zenia asked as they continued deeper into the marsh, the occasional hoots, chirps, and splashes of wildlife punctuating their conversation. "He worked in your company, didn't he?"

"He was a scout. Occasionally an assassin."

"An assassin of elves?" Zenia glanced over her shoulder at Jev—he had taken up the rear and was carefully watching their surroundings as they walked.

"Yes. I never asked him to go on such missions, but the king found out he was willing and had no qualms about using him."

Zenia remembered the words Lornysh and the elven princess had exchanged at Dharrow Castle, about how he'd made choices to go against his own kind.

She was about to ask *why* Lornysh had turned on his people, but he appeared again on the path ahead of them. She tensed, worried he had found some trouble. But he jogged toward them with the same easy lope he'd used before.

"Find something?" Jev asked.

"Something that may be of interest, yes. I'll show you." Lornysh didn't slow his pace as he turned and led off again, and Zenia had to run to keep up.

She wished she'd worn something less frilly than a dress today—and with more chest support. When they'd left to investigate the townhouse, she hadn't envisioned it leading to runs through swamps. Maybe she would start dressing in trousers and tunics. There wasn't a uniform for the Crown Agents, so presumably whatever was practical was permitted. Maybe if she wore a tunic, Brokko would leer at her chest less often.

The path ended at a patch of grass and tangle of mangrove roots. Lornysh hopped over the roots and continued onward, turning to follow the high ground between two pools of water. Mud squished under their boots, and a crocodile watched their passing from one of the pools. Zenia did not think Rhi was quite strong enough to fling *it* twenty feet if it clamped onto her bo.

Lornysh zigzagged his path, turning here and there, seemingly at random, and Zenia grew nervous about being able to find her way back. She believed they had crossed onto Tildar's property about where the path had ended, but it was hard to judge boundaries out here. Or even tell which direction one was going. The sun's rays couldn't break through the thick canopy, so one could wander in circles for hours. Maybe even days.

Finally, as Zenia was panting and on the verge of begging for a break, Lornysh stopped.

They had reached the largest pool she'd seen yet, almost a lake. An island rose from the middle of the gray water, taken up almost completely by a massive white oak draped in thick curtains of moss. Judging by the trunk's girth, with lower branches thicker than an ogre's waist, the tree had to be several hundred years old.

A rope bridge led out to it, wood planks tied so they hovered an inch or two above the surface. Though the water did not appear that deep, Lornysh headed for the bridge. As Zenia followed him, she saw the reason. Half a dozen crocodiles floated lazily along the surface, a couple of them already eyeing the intruders.

"Uh, Lornysh?" Jev squeezed around Zenia and Rhi to catch his friend before he started across the bridge. "Did you see those?"

Jev pointed not at the crocodiles in the water but at six or seven more resting on the island under the oak.

"Yes," Lornysh said. "I have my sword and my bow, though it's unlikely they will attack a group of warriors."

Zenia doubted anyone would mistake her for a warrior, though with the dragon tear, she might qualify as a mage. She pulled out the gem, intending to leave it atop her dress so she could easily wrap her fingers around it.

To her surprise, it shared a vision with her of its own accord. A wooden platform high in the branches of the huge white oak tree with a spyglass mounted on a tripod up there. A faint magical energy came from the device.

"Before we test that hypothesis," Jev said, "want to tell me *why* this group of warriors would want to visit that tree?"

"There's something magical up there," Zenia said, her eyes blurring as she saw both the platform above and her group. She blinked to refocus, and the vision faded.

Lornysh looked at her, then at her dragon tear. Unlike Cutter, he'd never commented on it. If he thought there was anything extraordinary about it, he hadn't shared it with her.

"Yes," he said simply and faced Jev. "I believe it may be pertinent to your investigation." Lornysh pointed at the oak. "There's a ladder leading up the far side."

Zenia eyed the oak's branches, but from down here, the platform wasn't visible.

"I'll lead," Lornysh said, unsheathing his sword. Maybe he wasn't as certain as he'd sounded that the crocodiles wouldn't attack.

Rhi went second, and Jev, his short sword and pistol in hand, nodded for Zenia to go ahead of him.

"Are you letting me go ahead so you can protect my back?" she asked as they headed across the bridge, the wood planks swaying and creaking underfoot, "or so I'll get eaten before you do?"

"I'm a noble zyndar warrior," he said, eyes narrowing.

She couldn't tell if he was truly offended by her joke or if he was only pretending to be. "Which means you'd risk your life to save mine?"

"I'd *give* my life to save yours," he said, his eyes serious as he looked from her to the crocodiles ahead of them.

"What about if it was my life at risk?" Rhi asked.

"The zyndar code demands a man step in front of danger to any woman," Jev said.

"But you'd be happier about getting impaled by danger to save Zenia?" Rhi smirked back at them.

"This group talks too much," Lornysh announced to no one in particular. The crocodiles, perhaps.

He was almost to the island, and the creatures weren't backing away. The ones in the water drifted closer to the bridge.

Zenia wondered if she could use her dragon tear to mentally coerce them to leave. She could if they were human, but would such power work on an animal?

She was on the verge of trying when Lornysh stepped foot on the island. All seven crocodiles on land raced toward him as one.

"Hells," Jev cursed and rushed past Zenia as Rhi also ran forward to help.

Lornysh shouted a word, and flames appeared along his sword. He leaped past one of the crocodiles, jamming his blade into its head as he went, and landed in front of the tree. He spun toward his attackers and put his back to the thick trunk. Three of the crocodiles lunged for him, jaws snapping. Two others veered toward Rhi and one angled toward Jev.

Terror surged through Zenia's veins as she grabbed her dragon tear with one hand and yanked out her pistol with the other. Jev fired his own pistol, lodging a bullet between one crocodile's eyes. Rhi cracked another in the maw with her bo, but she had to leap into the air to avoid the snapping jaws of one lunging in from behind her.

Zenia almost fired at that one, but her comrades were too close to the creatures. She risked missing and hitting one of them. Better to try to deter the crocodiles with the dragon tear's power.

Before she could focus on drawing upon its magic, movement to the side startled her. She was still out on the bridge, and two of the crocodiles in the water swam toward her at top speed.

She envisioned armor protecting her, and the dragon tear hummed with power. The two crocodiles slammed into an invisible barrier several feet away.

A huge splash came from behind her. Another crocodile. It snapped in the air, trying to bite the invisible shield that blocked it.

Zenia lifted her pistol, aiming between its eyes, but an admonition emanated from her dragon tear, and she paused. Somehow, she understood that she wouldn't be able to fire through the shield it had created around her, just as she wouldn't have been able to fire through a knight's shield of old.

An image came to mind of a crocodile writhing in flames. She couldn't imagine how anything in the water could burn, but she went with the idea, willing a fire to engulf the crocodiles snapping at her shield. More of them had advanced and butted at the invisible barrier. Growling, she envisioned a great ball of fire thrusting out from her on all sides.

Orange light flared so brightly she had to fling an arm up over her eyes. An animal roared in pain. Splashes came from all around her spot on the bridge. The wood creaked and groaned.

Someone cried out. Rhi?

Zenia jerked her mind away from the dragon tear, afraid the flames would spread out too far and hurt her friends.

The orange light disappeared, and she blinked to recover her vision. Charred crocodiles fled in all directions.

"Look out, Zenia!" Jev shouted as he fired at another of the crocodiles on the island.

Zenia spun, fearing another creature was lunging at her from the other direction, but there was nothing behind her. Nothing but flames burning the ropes that held the bridge together. Cursing, she ran toward the island.

The ropes snapped first. The bridge slumped into the water and she lurched, wobbling as she flailed for balance. The wood planks wouldn't support her, and she plunged into the lake. Her boots brushed a muddy bottom four feet down.

Afraid the crocodiles would see she was no longer protected, she swam for the island as quickly as possible. Her arm bumped against something large under the floating planks. A crocodile. She screamed and jerked away, trying to form a shield around herself again, but she was too panicked to focus on calling forth the dragon tear's magic. Until she realized the crocodile wasn't moving. It wasn't even alive. Its entire body was blackened, and the smell of charred hide hung in the air.

A hand gripped her arm. Jev. He'd waded out to her, and he lifted her from the water, gathering her in his arms.

Though she had recovered from her fright of the dead crocodile, Zenia let him carry her without objection. She craned her neck to see if her friends needed help, but their seven crocodiles were also dead, most bleeding from the gashes of Lornysh's sword. His long blade was still shrouded in flames that danced and writhed along the gleaming steel surface. Zenia had heard that elves and dwarves could make magical weapons, but she had never seen one.

"I killed that one," Jev said, pointing at a crocodile with a bullet hole in its eye as he set Zenia down.

He wore a self-deprecating expression rather than a smug one, so Zenia assumed Lornysh had killed most of the others. Or all of them.

"I knocked out at least three," Rhi said.

She stood between two corpses and waved her bo, but those crocodiles also looked to have been slain by a blade. Lornysh gazed blandly at her.

"All right, I *hit* at least three. It's not my fault they have such thick skulls."

"I think Zenia killed six or seven," Jev said, sounding dazed as he looked toward the water where a couple of charred corpses floated.

Zenia shook her head, positive most of them had gotten away. And *she* hadn't done anything. "It was my dragon tear."

"Dragon tears don't act of their own accord," Jev said. "You must have had the idea to use fire. A good choice. Forest animals know to fear flames, and I imagine even those that live around water have a healthy fear of it." He eyed the closest charred corpse. "For good reason."

Zenia, remembering how the idea had popped into her mind from someone else—from the dragon tear itself?—didn't nod in agreement. She caught Lornysh considering her contemplatively.

"What I'd like to know," Zenia said, eager to change the subject, "is why they all attacked en masse. I may be a city girl, but from what I've heard, that's not normal, right? I know wolves do that, but crocodiles aren't pack animals, are they?"

"No," Lornysh said. "I didn't realize it before, but they were activated by a magical command. Coerced to attack as one."

"Activated?" Rhi asked. "Were they not real animals?"

"They were real, but some mage was either controlling them from afar or placed a command in their brains to attack anyone who came close to a specific area." Lornysh gestured toward the island and the tree.

"Is that possible?" Jev gripped his chin. "I've heard of magical artifacts and weapons, but I didn't realize it was possible to leave a command imprinted on an animal."

"Not for most races. It requires an affinity for animals and a great deal of time spent practicing magic on them. Some of my people do it. Dwarves can't. Troll and orc warlocks might be able to. They live close to nature and are proud of their relationships with wild animals, especially predators."

"You said it's also possible someone is out here right now, controlling animals from afar?" Zenia asked.

"It wouldn't be from that far," Lornysh said, "but yes, that's possible. It would be easier than imprinting a command for the long term. Animals have short memories."

"Meaning someone could be watching us right now?"

"Very possibly."

"Fantastic," Rhi muttered.

CHAPTER 14

J EV CAREFULLY CLIMBED UP THE "ladder" running up
the side of the ancient tree. He didn't think the boards nailed to
the trunk qualified for the designation. Nonetheless, he'd stepped
ahead of Lornysh to go first. His ego had been bruised when Zenia made
that comment about him walking last across the bridge.

He *had* intended to watch her back—all of their backs—and he
knew she'd been joking, but he didn't like that the thought had even
come to mind for her. And then Lornysh had been the one to kill most of
the crocodiles, descending upon them like a tornado landing on a pack
of desert jackals. Jev knew the elf was a better warrior than just about
anyone, so that wasn't surprising, but it was hard not to feel twinges of
inadequacy next to him. Something that hadn't bothered Jev back on
Taziira. What was different now? Zenia watching.

He snorted at himself, feeling like a dumb kid for worrying about
such a thing. And for letting it send him first up a tree that Lornysh was
far more qualified to climb than any of them. Still, he wanted to see
what was at the top, what all those crocodiles had been left to guard.

Lornysh was following him up, navigating the boards with ease, no
doubt wondering why they were going so slowly.

The branches thinned as Jev climbed higher and higher. So did the
trunk, but it remained thick enough that it didn't sway under their weight.

Bright sunlight struck the back of Jev's neck as they climbed higher
than the surrounding canopy. He paused to peer around and had an
impressive view in all directions.

He could now see the bottom of a wooden platform above them, so
he kept climbing, soon pulling himself out onto it. Enough branches

supported it that it felt solid, even at this lofty height. He couldn't see the ground through the leaves but guessed they had climbed nearly a hundred feet.

Remembering Zenia's comment about magic, he didn't crawl far out onto the platform. He would let Lornysh, who could sense such things, go first. He noted a log that someone had dragged up the tree for a seat. It rested in front of a tripod with a large spyglass mounted on it. The scope was pointed toward the sea and toward—Jev sucked in a breath—the city.

Even though they were more than five miles upriver, he could make out a couple of the prominent structures that rose above the rooftops, the Obelisk of Tay'Nay'Gor, a war prize more than a thousand years old, and the great silver-topped Dome of the Orders where archmages from all over the kingdom met every two years for deliberation. Or orgies. Those not invited speculated greatly and widely on the goings on. The silver dome gleamed now in the afternoon sun.

"That's the magical item." Lornysh crouched beside him—the branches overhead wouldn't allow them to stand—and pointed at the spyglass.

"Any kind of protection on it?" Jev didn't want to get zapped or knocked out of the tree if he touched it.

"It's hard to tell when the item itself is magical."

"Wonderful."

"If it helps, crocodiles can't climb trees."

"I'd accuse you of making jokes, but I think you're seriously trying to assuage my irrational fear of crocodiles." Jev headed slowly toward the spyglass, his hands outstretched, as if *that* would protect him from being zapped by magic. "Which, now that I've been attacked by six crocodiles at once, no longer seems so irrational."

"I believe only one focused on you."

"It was at least two."

"Six attacked Zenia," Lornysh allowed.

"*More* than six." Jev shuddered, the memory flashing into his mind. He'd been so shocked and horrified when all those crocodiles in the water zeroed in on her that he'd almost let the one facing him bite his leg off.

The huge fireball Zenia had created to destroy all those crocodiles had been even more shocking, but he'd been relieved that she'd been able to do it. For a few seconds, he'd been terrified the creatures would swarm her and kill her before he could get back to her side. If she'd died after he left her out there so he could help the others... Founders, he didn't know if he could have lived with that. He had made a lot of mistakes in his life, but that would have trumped them all.

Shuddering, Jev reached out and touched the end of the spyglass. Nothing happened.

"Her dragon tear is extremely powerful," Lornysh said.

"So I've been told."

"Cutter advised you—and her—on the possible significance of a dragon carved into the front?"

"He said that when sentient creatures are carved into the gems, the magic can create a link to an actual creature out there. I'm not sure I understand. Zenia has said... Well, she hasn't said that much about it, but I don't get the sense she feels any hungry malevolence emanating from it."

"Dragons aren't necessarily malevolent. They're predators, like wolves and tigers. But smart enough to have a language and be extremely dangerous. Fortunately, they're as lazy as lions and would rather sleep in a sunbeam or a cozy cave than hunt constantly."

"Good to know." Jev scooted closer so he could peer through the spyglass. The silver Dome of the Orders was visible in such intricate detail that he could make out the decorative dragon shapes etched in some of the silver roof tiles. He'd never seen a spyglass with such powerful magnification. Was it the magic that amplified it?

"You may want to keep an eye on her. It's a powerful artifact for a human to have. Many humans who have in the past gained access to such power have made poor decisions with it."

"As an inquisitor, she wore a dragon tear that gave her power and didn't abuse it, if that's what you're suggesting."

"This is a very different kind of power. It's palpable, not granted by social delusion."

Jev snorted at that description for the sway the Orders had over the populace.

"She's experimenting now and learning what the dragon tear can do," Lornysh continued. "That's apparent. When she more fully realizes its capabilities... Just be wary and watch her."

"I'm not her keeper." Jev moved the spyglass, wondering what else he could see from this distant perch and how hard it would be to zero in on desirable targets, but it refocused of its own accord. Somehow, it found Alderoth Castle, choosing a magnification that allowed Jev to see the ramparts, with the guards walking along them, and also the front gate and the road leading up to it. "That's disturbing."

"We are no longer talking about the dragon tear, I assume." Lornysh had moved closer and was examining the tripod and outside of the spyglass.

Jev shifted so he could look through the eyepiece.

"Interesting." Lornysh touched the side.

Jev noticed the spyglass itself didn't move—he didn't think it had moved when he tried to adjust it either—but Lornysh kept touching the spot, so he assumed the image at the other end was changing.

"Your army barracks. A popular market. I believe that is the watch headquarters building. Your Fire Order Temple. Someone has been observing your city."

"Tildar?"

Lornysh hesitated before saying, "Perhaps."

He didn't sound convinced. Jev remembered his comment about trolls and orcs having warlocks that specialized in animal magic. What about in making sight-enhancing artifacts?

"Jev." Lornysh leaned away from the spyglass and waved for him to look.

Warily, Jev leaned in. The view had shifted from the city to the ocean, to a great steamship with two bronze smokestacks, each the size of small buildings. The ship itself was massive, the crewmen working on the deck appearing like ants in comparison. Bearded ants.

"Is that the dwarven ship?" Jev asked, awed by all the metal on the vessel.

Bronze and iron gleamed in the sunlight all over the ship. Was there a single wooden spar?

The steamboats that paddled up and down the Jade River were made mostly from wood. Jev had seen a couple of ocean-going steamships being built in the shipyard in the harbor, but they still had wooden masts and cloth sails, the craft not relying entirely on steam. He didn't see evidence of either on the dwarven vessel.

"Yes."

"Any way to tell how far out it is?" Jev couldn't see anything but water around the ship, deep blue water. He touched the spyglass, but it shifted back to the view of the dome.

"Not far is my guess. I haven't heard of an artifact like this augmenting sight for more than twenty miles."

Jev hadn't heard of an artifact like this at all. He shook his head and turned for the ladder. "We better find this Tildar if he's out here. I have questions for him."

Such as why a man who had a townhouse *in* Korvann had to come out here to spy on the city. And why this special spyglass had been set to watch for the approach of that ship.

"I don't think *he* was the one up here," Lornysh said, an odd note in his tone.

Jev paused, a hand on the tree trunk. Lornysh held up something small, matted, bloody, and dark gray.

"What is that?" Did Jev want to know?

"A rat's head."

"Uh, what happened to the rest of it?"

"Judging by the teeth marks, it was eaten."

"As some bird's snack?" Jev looked up, though the oak's leaves blocked the sky directly above. He hadn't heard any eagles or falcons screeching, but he was sure they were around.

"I think by someone sitting and watching through the spyglass," Lornysh said. "Ogres don't usually stoop to eating rodentia, nor would one have been able to climb that ladder, but orcs and trolls are lighter weight and will eat almost anything that moves."

Including humans, if the stories were true.

Jev had occasionally seen and interacted with orcs and trolls in Taziira—the elves claimed the territory around their woodland cities, but they had never striven to keep the entire continent free of other races—but he'd never sat down for meals with them. Nor had he ever wanted to. He didn't like the idea of them sitting out here and munching on a snack while spying on his city, not one bit.

Zenia slogged through the swamp, her wet dress sticking to her body and mud trying to suck her soggy boots off her feet. Her thighs chafed, and the skin of her palms was wrinkled from pushing aside damp foliage that wanted to slap her in the face. There hadn't been a trail for what seemed like hours, and she hadn't the faintest idea where they were in relation to the river and the path back out.

She didn't complain out loud and did her best to stoically tell herself she was doing her duty, that her misery was for the good of the kingdom, but she couldn't help but look forward to escaping this sodden adventure and visiting the steamy bathroom in the castle.

She didn't think Jev, Rhi, or Lornysh, who was leading them to who knew where, could be as uncomfortable as she, since they'd had the wisdom to stay on land instead of burning the bridge they stood on, but nobody was talking much, so maybe they were. Nobody's boots or trousers were dry anymore.

Lornysh stopped abruptly, his head turning to the side.

Zenia, worried another batch of crocodiles might attack, touched her dragon tear and willed it to let her know what creatures were around them. She was almost overwhelmed by the sensation of tremendous life on all sides. The dragon tear made her aware of each insect, reptile, rodent, and bird and where they were in relation to her.

"You all right?" Jev touched her shoulder.

Had she gasped? She must have.

"Yes. Give me a second."

Zenia tried to lessen the intensity of the mental map of life she was receiving. The dragon tear understood and complied, and she was able to sort through it. There weren't any crocodiles or large predators around. Huh. What had made Lornysh pause?

"Just figuring out what my dragon tear can do," she added since Jev was looking at her with concern. She flicked her fingers to wave away the moment.

His concern didn't go away. If anything, his brow furrowed deeper. He'd been staying close since they left the island. What had he thought of the fire she—her dragon tear—had created?

"Now, where are we going?" Rhi mumbled.

Lornysh had turned off in the direction he'd been looking.

"I didn't know where we were going *before*." Jev lowered his hand from Zenia's shoulder.

"You didn't either?" Zenia joked, hoping to distract him from his concerns. "Aren't you and I supposed to be the wise captains leading the troops?"

"Wisdom is required for this job? Targyon got the wrong people then."

She wanted to object but wasn't sure she could. At her old job, she'd felt wise, or at least experienced. She was still adjusting to her new job.

"Just what a junior agent wants to hear about her employers," Rhi said.

"Technically, the king is your employer," Jev said. "We're just the taskmasters cracking the whip at your backside."

"Can someone crack a whip at that elf's backside?" Rhi pointed after Lornysh, who didn't seem to care if they followed or not.

"I would," Jev said, "but it's narrow and bony. Not much of a target."

Lornysh's pointed ears turned back toward him, as if he'd heard that comment, but all he said was, "Come, Jev. You'll want to see this."

"Another magical artifact?" Jev slogged after his friend.

"Among other things."

Rhi looked at Zenia. "He didn't say *we'd* want to see it. Does that mean we can stay here?"

"Maybe, but here isn't that appealing of a place." Zenia looked toward a snake dangling from a branch. It wasn't as big and threatening as the one that had attacked earlier, but she didn't want to take a rest stop under its perch.

"True. This is making me long for a blanket under an umbrella at the beach."

"I've got a small umbrella in my pack." Zenia had added it after that rainstorm they'd run through at Nhole Castle.

"I don't think that alone is going to give this place the correct ambiance."

"I have a blanket too." She didn't mention that the contents of her pack were likely as wet as the rest of her.

"Oh good. We can drape it over that mossy log with the toadstools growing all over it and oozing brown pus. Then it'll be just like we're at the beach."

Not wanting a close view of the pus-oozing toadstools, Zenia hurried to catch up to Jev.

Rhi came after her, grumbling about beaches and waiters from the waterfront taverns bringing food trays around. The group *did* have food and fresh water with them, but Zenia's hands were so dirty—*all* of her was dirty—that she hadn't wanted to pull out anything to eat. That bacteria that had killed Targyon's cousins was on her mind as they traveled through the brackish water, and she didn't want to risk getting anything here in her mouth.

Up ahead, Lornysh paused at the edge of a wide pool surrounded by densely growing mangroves. He looked back and held a finger to his lips, then crouched down behind a clump of raised roots.

Zenia hoped there wasn't another crocodile-infested island in the middle of the pool.

Jev also crouched as he moved the last few feet to join Lornysh in looking across the water. Though Zenia couldn't see anything except trees yet, she emulated the men, staying low and stepping carefully as she approached. Neither of them was speaking. Just looking.

Zenia glimpsed firelight on the other side of the pool along with grimy canvas sheets strung between the trees. No, those were tents. They had found someone's encampment. A *large* encampment. There had to be ten or twelve tents, each large enough to hold several people.

Or maybe not people. Not *human* people.

Zenia stopped and stared when she glimpsed a tall, gangly figure with white hair and blue-gray skin. He was heading into the camp and issued a few hisses and clucks. Was that a language? Or a sign of indigestion?

She remembered seeing a couple of trolls in cages at the waterfront when she had been young, but she had never witnessed one walking free with sheathed knives, axes, and pistols thrust though loops in a multi-pocketed vest that was the only thing the troll wore on its upper body. A black garment similar to a skirt or maybe a kilt hung down to its knees.

Jev reached out and pulled her down beside him where the roots would hide them. Zenia realized she'd been gawking—and crouching out in the open. If they were spotted by the trolls, trolls who likely did not want to be discovered by Korvann's inhabitants, they could end up chased through the swamp for miles. And killed, she added grimly to herself. Judging by the number of tents, her little team was sorely outnumbered.

Rhi hunkered down beside her, careful not to knock her bo against the roots. Her expression was grim, too, and she likely wasn't thinking of beaches any longer.

"There's a cabin behind the tents," Jev breathed, his voice barely audible.

Zenia leaned closer, her shoulder brushing his, to hear him. Lornysh nodded from his other side, his ears not having trouble hearing whispers. It took a moment for Zenia to pick out the cabin since it was the same drab gray-brown as the rest of the swamp, and moss carpeted its log walls. Maybe it had been a hunting cabin for the Nholes once. Zenia knew zyndar went on safaris in exotic lands to hunt ferocious predators. She didn't know about five miles up the river from the city to tangle with crocodiles.

Lornysh tapped Jev's shoulder and pointed back the way they had come. Their group carefully backtracked until they could no longer see the pool or the tents.

"A scouting party," Lornysh said, watching their surroundings as he spoke. "A large one. It's hard to tell how long they've been here, but the tents sagged, as if they've been up in the damp weather for many days."

Jev stroked his beard. "We'll have to go back to town and get help to deal with them. If Krox is around, he can round up some experienced soldiers."

"I believe there are twenty or thirty trolls in camp right now. We can deal with them."

"We?" Jev pointed at his chest, then Lornysh's. He didn't include Zenia and Rhi.

Rhi's eyes narrowed.

Since "deal with them," likely meant kill them, Zenia didn't object to being left out. Even though those trolls had come to spy on Korvann, if not lead an attack on it, she would have a hard time sneaking up on them and shooting to kill. That had never been her duty as an inquisitor. She questioned people and arrested them, leaving the execution of justice to the city's headsmen.

"It will be dark soon," Lornysh said. "It'll be easier to sneak up on them and strike without others noticing and raising an alarm."

Jev grimaced. Zenia didn't know if it was because he disliked the idea of playing the role of assassin or if he was skeptical they could kill that many by themselves. Zenia would be.

"Aren't you still injured?" Jev waved to his friend's abdomen.

"Nothing that will impede me. As you saw with the crocodiles."

"Maybe we could capture one to question first," Zenia said.

"Troll isn't a language I speak," Jev said.

Lornysh didn't comment. Did he understand their language? Maybe he did but didn't *want* to question them. Did elves have a vendetta against trolls? Or maybe he did personally.

"I think I could grasp some of their thoughts without understanding the language." Zenia touched her dragon tear.

"I assure you, you already know why they're here," Lornysh said.

"It would be useful to learn about their plans," Jev said. "How many are here and how many more are coming. And if our dwarven friends are out in this swamp somewhere. Admittedly, it's hard to imagine that a pack of trolls sneaked into the city to kidnap Grindmor. They're distinctive."

"If we can capture one, I won't object, but it may be easier to pick them off from afar." Lornysh removed his bow from his back. "Before they realize we're out here and raise an alarm."

"When have you ever chosen the easy way, my friend?" Jev smiled, though he looked worried.

Zenia didn't like the idea of Jev and Lornysh going in to fight the trolls alone. "It wouldn't take that long to go back to town and gather reinforcements. Better to have equal or better numbers than theirs, right?"

"It took us hours to travel out here. We may not have that much time." Lornysh looked at Jev. "Remember, the dwarven ship is close."

Zenia was about to point out that they had taken a circuitous route to this point and hadn't been pushing their horses on the ride out, but it *was* getting darker. Under the dense canopy, she couldn't see the sun, but twilight couldn't be that far off. Even if they found reinforcements, leading them back to this spot in the dark would be a challenge. And tomorrow might be too late.

Jev lowered his hand and nodded, a decision made. "Let's deal with them. Zenia, will you and Rhi stay here? If we can draw one away from the others, we'll bring him for you to question."

"We can help fight," Rhi said.

"We're going to kill them, not concuss them," Lornysh said bluntly.

"Stay here," Jev told her more gently. "Zenia would be lonely without any company."

"Maybe she wants to fight too," Rhi said mulishly.

"Do you?" Jev raised his eyebrows toward Zenia.

"I would have a hard time killing strangers," Zenia admitted.

"You annihilated strange crocodiles," Rhi pointed out.

Zenia grimaced, not wanting to be reminded of the incident since she'd also foolishly destroyed the bridge she'd been standing on.

"We'll be back as soon as possible," Jev said. "Stay behind that log and out of trouble, eh?"

Zenia eyed the log. It was the same one Rhi had pointed to earlier, moss and fungus blanketing it. It looked like she would indeed get a better view of the pus-oozing toadstools.

CHAPTER 15

JEV LET LORNYSH TAKE THE lead, knowing his friend could see well in the dark and move silently, even through mud and water, but he was more than ready to fight. The fact that these trolls were here spying on the city from only a handful of miles away from Dharrow land made him furious. There could be no innocent explanation for this. He hoped the scouts hadn't been roaming the countryside, stealing animals and attacking people they found out by themselves. What if some were even now skulking around on Dharrow land?

His fingers tightened around his pistol grip. He held his short sword in his other hand.

Just ahead of him, Lornysh paused and fired his bow twice. Then he burst into motion, running forward and slinging the bow over his back as he yanked out his sword.

Jev couldn't yet see what he'd fired at, but he ran after to help.

Lornysh jumped over a dark figure sprawled in the mud, then sprang behind a tree. A grunt sounded, followed by a gasp of pain. Jev paused when he reached the figure, a dead troll with an arrow sticking out of each eye.

As Jev stepped over the body, Lornysh pulled a second troll out from behind the tree. Though Lornysh wasn't as tall as his blue-skinned adversary, he had no trouble keeping a dagger to the troll's throat and a hand over his mouth. Long-fingered hands with yellow nails whipped up and grabbed Lornysh's arm, trying to dislodge it, but his grip might as well have been made of steel.

He pushed the troll ahead of him, and Jev stepped aside, realizing Lornysh wanted to get his prisoner out of hearing range from camp. A couple of times, the troll's arms flexed, and he kicked behind him, but Lornysh evaded the attacks like a dancer, barely missing a step. He sank his dagger deeper, and his prisoner stopped struggling.

"What questions do you have for him?" Lornysh asked when they were farther from the camp. He stopped and turned his prisoner to face Jev.

"That was Zenia who wanted to chat with him." Jev did have questions, but he doubted the troll would answer them without magical coercion. Or even understand them. "Do you speak his language?"

"Enough of it."

"How many trolls are here scouting?" Jev asked. "And how many more are coming?"

The troll glared at Jev with black eyes, the irises and pupils the same inky shade, and both equally filled with loathing. Blue lips curled, and the troll spat. Then he spoke.

"This land was ours long ago, and it will be again. Your people are weak and even your own kind will betray you for power. Trolls are strong, and the entire world knows this and accepts it. Many wish to ally with us. Your kind will fall, and these marshes and mountains will be ours again." He turned his gaze toward the trees and the muddy pools, perhaps seeing them better in the dark than Jev did. Though his lips remained curled, his dark eyes seemed loving as he gazed upon vines dangling from branches.

Jev was surprised the troll had not only answered but was speaking in the coastal trade language—most of the words were similar to the Kingdom tongue, though his accent was different and especially harsh. Lornysh's eyes were slitted in concentration. Maybe he had some magic that could convince a prisoner to speak.

"You said one of my people betrayed his own kind," Jev said. "Who was it? Tildar Braksnoth?"

"It does not matter now. We did not need him. The dwarves will not help you. The elves will not help you. We will slay your males and take your ugly females for our slaves and boil your children and eat them."

"Big talk for a troll with a dagger to his throat," Jev said, showing only defiance and not fear, though he couldn't help but think again about how close this scouting party was to his family's lands. His kin who lived in the castle wouldn't be stolen away in the night, but what about those living in the villages around the estate? The villages weren't walled and protected by night guards. His father's unclaimed children—little sisters that Jev needed to get to know better one day—would be vulnerable in their simple wood homes.

"How many scouts did you bring?" Jev asked again.

"I will speak no more. Tell your elf servant to—"

Lornysh tightened his grip, and the troll hissed. Lornysh spoke in their language of hisses and clucks. The troll spat a reply. Lornysh let his dagger sink deeper, and blood dripped from his prisoner's throat.

The troll threw up his arms and tried to knock Lornysh away, whirling toward the elf with a snarl. Jev rushed forward to sink a dagger in their enemy's back, but Lornysh finished him first, slitting his throat. The troll was dead before he hit the ground.

After hearing about his plans to boil human children, Jev had no sympathy or regret for the troll. "What did you ask about? Their numbers? Did he say anything useful?"

"That elves taste good."

"So, not that useful unless you're planning a menu for a banquet."

Even in the poor lighting, Jev could see the flat look Lornysh gave him.

"We'll find another one that will talk," Lornysh said.

He stalked toward the first one he'd killed and retrieved his arrows.

"We may find answers in that cabin if we can sneak in," Jev said.

"We'll find answers in the throats of our enemies," Lornysh growled and stalked off.

"Guess he didn't like being called tasty," Jev mumbled to himself, following him.

"I can't believe they abandoned us here," Rhi said as twilight deepened in the swamp.

"I can't believe you wanted to go with them to kill trolls." Zenia touched her pack where it rested against the log beside her. She'd had the foresight to bring a lantern in case their trip took longer than expected, but she wouldn't dare light it with trolls roaming the swamp nearby. They might be all over the place, not only in that camp.

"Trolls that are here to invade our kingdom? Of course I did. I mean, I could at least knock them out and pummel them a bit. I could leave the throat-slitting to Lornysh. He doesn't seem to mind that."

Zenia shivered a little. The temperature had dropped, but she knew that wasn't the reason. She could accept Lornysh as a throat-slitter, but the idea of Jev acting as an assassin troubled her. He held his honor so close that it was hard to imagine him finding it acceptable to sneak up on an enemy and stick a dagger in his back. But his honor might also demand he do whatever necessary to protect the people of Kor. And his family.

How far was his land from here? Less than ten miles, she thought. She couldn't truly object to him protecting those he loved. Had there been more people she loved in the city, perhaps she would have been more horrified and affronted by the threat the trolls represented.

Hunkered here in a swamp wasn't the time for feeling sad about the life choices she had made and her lack of family, but as the minutes oozed past, she found herself thinking about how the few people she truly cared about were out here with her. She'd thought she had friends at the temple, or at least good acquaintances, but they'd been so quick to turn their backs on her that maybe they'd never been friends at all. Only Rhi had come out to speak with her after she'd been ostracized. And Jev... She may have only met him a few weeks earlier, but she'd worked so closely with him during that time that she'd come to know him far better than many people she'd known for years. And she'd come to care about him. Maybe even *more* than care about him, if she was honest with herself.

She peered over the log in the direction he and Lornysh had gone, the pungent earthy scent of the moss and fungi offending her city-bred nostrils. It was too dim now to see more than a couple dozen feet away. How long had the men been gone? It seemed like a half hour or even an hour had passed. Long enough for them to have been captured and even killed.

No, surely not. At the least, they wouldn't have gone down without a fight, and she and Rhi were close enough to that camp that they would hear shouts and gunshots. Zenia hadn't heard any noise since the men left, aside from the occasional splash of some creature dropping into one of the stagnant pools. Occasionally, a faint moan came from across a muddy flat in the opposite direction of the encampment. She hadn't figured out what animal was making it.

Rhi gripped her arm. "Do you hear that?"

She was looking in the direction of the moans too. A low, deep one had just floated across the flat.

Zenia nodded. "I'm not sure what's making them. Some animal in pain?"

"Animal? I thought it sounded like a person."

"Who else would be out here?"

"We're not that far from the city. Could be some kid. Could be that Tildar."

They *had* come out here looking for him. Was it possible someone who had gilded drain spouts on his townhouse would be staying in that rude cabin? Or have wandered out into the swamp and been injured?

"We should go investigate," Rhi said.

"Are you hoping to find something to thump?"

"I *am* distressed that Jev and Points didn't think I could help them with the trolls. But whatever is making that noise sounds like it's already been thumped."

"If we wander over there in the dark, we might not find our way back to this spot."

Zenia touched her dragon tear. Technically, she could get it to glow and illuminate the way—or they could light the lantern attached to her pack. But she worried an unfriendly troll would see their light, come over, and thump *them*.

"Wait," she murmured, remembering how she'd used the dragon tear's magic to sense life around her earlier. If she could use it to tell if any trolls or crocodiles were close by, maybe they could safely investigate. And maybe the gem could guide them back to the log too.

The dragon tear vibrated warmly against her chest and emitted a soft blue glow. It seemed to radiate approval of her thoughts. Because it agreed it could do those things or because it was tired of sitting next to a smelly log?

"Is it going to show us the way?" Rhi eyed the gem.

"Let's hope so. Follow me."

Zenia had only taken a few steps toward the muddy flat area when the dragon tear pulsed and drew her to one side. It didn't force her legs to walk that way, but she had the distinct impression it would be wise to obey.

An image sprang into her mind of a person dressed in old-fashioned cotton clothes being caught out there, the mud sucking at his boots. More than sucking at. He struggled but was slowly pulled under the surface.

Quick mud? Zenia shuddered and stepped precisely where the dragon tear wanted her to.

"That isn't the way," Rhi whispered.

"Trust me, it is. Walk exactly where I walk."

The dragon tear guided her like a divining rod pulling a thirsty traveler to water.

"What happens if I don't?" Rhi asked.

"We find out if my dragon tear can rescue you from mud equivalent to quicksand."

"Ah." After a few more steps, Rhi added, "*You* wouldn't try to rescue me?"

"I'd be holding the dragon tear while it did the work. It would be a group effort."

"Comforting."

Once they passed the brown muddy area, the gem guided them back in the direction of the moan. Another one drifted through the swamp, louder now. Maybe it *did* belong to a person.

The air grew less close, and Zenia thought she smelled fresher water. In the darkness, she didn't see a pool, however, until they were almost on top of it. It held clearer water than what they had been passing all day, and she spotted a crude dock thrusting out from the shoreline.

The dragon tear shared an image of the far side of the pool. It opened up and led out into the Jade River. Zenia felt a sense of relief from knowing they could head that direction and find their way home if needed. Such as if they were being chased by angry trolls.

"Is that a boat?" Rhi asked.

Zenia could make out a dark shape on the other side of the dock. It took her a few more steps before she could identify it as a rowboat tied to a post. The dock extended into the pool far enough that there would have been room for at least six of them.

A moan came from the craft, and Zenia jumped.

The dragon tear drew her forward, and she didn't sense alarm or imminent danger from it, but she withdrew her utility knife. She would have preferred the pistol, but her ammo pouch had been soaked when she fell in the other lake. Rhi gripped her bo in both hands.

As Zenia came around the head of the dock, the dragon tear shone its blue light brightly enough to illuminate the contents of the rowboat. A single person lay on his side in the water pooled at the bottom of it. A short, stout person with a red beard.

"Cutter?" Rhi asked uncertainly.

The figure moaned again but also stirred, lifting his head and an arm. An arm with a stump where a hand should have been. Zenia gasped.

"It *is* Cutter," Rhi said. "He lost his hook."

A wave of pain rolled over Zenia, and she gasped again for a different reason. The dragon tear was sharing his emotions—his pain—with her.

"Let's get him out," Zenia said.

Rhi had already started forward. Together, they levered Cutter out of the boat. He was well under five feet tall, but he was stocky and muscular, so it wasn't an easy task. They laid him on the shore— thankfully, it was more pebbles than mud here—and Zenia slung her pack off her shoulders.

"I have a first-aid kit," she said as she dug into an outside pocket.

"I think he's going to need more than a first-aid kit." Rhi held up her hands, Cutter's blood smearing her palms. "It looks like someone left him for dead."

"Hopefully, he'll be able to tell us what happened." Zenia pulled out bandages and a bottle of Grodonol's Pain-No-More.

"Maybe."

They had tried to lay Cutter on his back, but he curled onto his side again, as he'd been in the boat, his legs and arms protectively over his stomach. A gash on his cheek bled profusely, but that wasn't what bothered him.

"We'll have to make friends with a healer and bring him or her on future outings into the wilds." Zenia touched Cutter's shoulder. "Cutter? It's Jev's friend, Zenia. I want to wash and bandage your wound until we can get you back to town. We'll take you to the hospital as soon as we can. Do you understand?"

He was moaning to himself, so he had to be conscious. His eyes were squinted shut though.

"On future outings into the wilds," Rhi said, "maybe we should bring an army instead of a healer. Or an army *and* a healer."

Zenia grimaced, now feeling foolish that they hadn't brought more people. But how could she have anticipated encountering all this a few miles outside of town?

"We'll do the best we can," she said firmly.

CHAPTER 16

J EV DIDN'T LIKE TO THINK of his friend as bloodthirsty, but as he stood guard outside the second tent Lornysh had gone into with an assassin's intent, he had to accept that Lornysh had a heartless streak. Targyon would thank him for slaying enemies so close to the capital, but Jev would have preferred to face the trolls in battle rather than skulking about and striking in the night. Logically, he knew they didn't have another choice, not when there were only two of them, but—

A grunt came from inside the tent, and the flap stirred. The only light came from a campfire burning in front of another tent, and Jev almost missed the movement. He jumped back, facing the entrance as a bare-chested troll surged out with a club in hand.

The troll had sharp eyes and spotted him immediately. The towering scout opened his mouth to yell, but Jev leaped in, slashing toward his head. If he let a troll yell, the entire camp would know he and Lornysh were there and descend upon them. Maybe it was already too late.

The troll jerked his club up to block, but Jev turned the attack into a feint and withdrew before their weapons clashed. He stabbed toward the troll's chest. His foe turned his shoulder, and the blade dug into arm muscle instead of piercing bone and organ. The troll gasped in pain, and Jev winced, fearing the sound would carry.

He launched a series of feints and attacks, hoping to hit a more vital target. The troll parried with his club, wood and steel meeting with a thwack. Too much noise, Jev groaned to himself. But he didn't know how to stop it. On his third rapid thrust, his blade slipped through, catching his foe on the hip. A snarl came from the troll's lips, and he launched himself at Jev.

Jev sprang to the side and ducked as the club swept over his head, close enough to stir his hair. Not allowing himself to feel daunted, Jev leaped back in. He thrust before the troll recovered from his big swing. This time, Jev's blade sank deep into his enemy's flesh, right beside the spine.

The troll's back arched, the club dropping from his fingers. Anticipating he would cry out, Jev lunged close, grabbing him from behind and covering his mouth. The troll bit his hand and elbowed him. Jev grunted, taking a blow to his abdomen, but he raked his short sword across the troll's throat. Hot blood spilled onto his hand, and for a moment, he was back in the Taziira forests, fighting hand-to-hand with elven wardens that had infiltrated his camp, trying to kill the officers in charge. A sergeant and good friend went down to the invaders, and Jev sprang in, enraged as he slit an elf's throat.

Jev stomped the memory down as he released the troll. Others had likely heard the fight, which hadn't been anywhere near as silent or elegant as Lornysh's assassinations. He needed his mind to be in the here and now.

A couple of trolls in nearby tents stepped outside, the firelight silhouetting them. They lifted their noses, sniffing the air like hounds. Jev hoped they smelled only woodsmoke, but he pointed his pistol at them. If they realized an elf and human were sneaking about in their camp, they would raise an alarm. Then silence wouldn't matter any longer.

A touch to Jev's shoulder made him jump.

"In here," Lornysh breathed, the words softer than a breeze.

The trolls at the fire spoke to each other, but they hadn't yet looked in Jev's direction. Lornysh held the tent flap aside, and Jev backed in.

He could smell death, and he was glad it was pitch dark inside. He couldn't see sleeping areas or how many trolls lay unmoving in them.

Lornysh gripped his arm and guided him to the back of the tent. He muttered something, and the flames on his sword came to life, more muted than usual, providing only a small amount of light. It revealed Lornysh crouching before a strongbox.

As Jev's eyes adjusted, he grew aware of dead trolls on blankets, but he focused on the box. A few ink bottles and quills lay in the dirt next to it. Was this the command tent? Lornysh must have chosen it on purpose.

The strongbox was locked, but Lornysh stared at it, and a soft click sounded. He opened the lid, pulled out a folded parchment, and spread it out. He held his fiery blade over it and waved Jev closer so he could see.

It was a map of Korvann and the twenty miles around the city in all directions. The zyndar castles within that area were drawn onto the map, represented by small gray crenelated towers. Jev gritted his teeth when he saw Dharrow Castle with its pond and moat delineated. Someone had drawn a square with a circle around it next to the tower and written words he couldn't read. A similar symbol and words were scrawled by Krox Castle ten miles out of the city on the opposite side. Alderoth Castle, perched on its hill overlooking Korvann, had a red X through it. Down in the city, lines with arrows were pointed along some of the main streets. Invasion routes.

Jev unclenched his jaw and pointed at the writing next to his castle. "What does it say?"

"It's been chosen as a staging area."

Jev curled his fingers tightly around his sword, his knuckles showing white. He seethed as he imagined trolls battering down the front doors or scaling the walls with ropes, invading his home and attacking his cousins and his little nieces and nephews. The staff he'd known all his life and people he'd just met, people who believed themselves safe working for the Dharrows.

"When?" he growled. "When does it start?"

Lornysh shook his head. "It doesn't say. When the scouts report back that everything is ready, likely."

"Everything isn't going to *be* ready." Jev looked at the dead trolls, the ones he'd avoided seeing before, and now, he felt Lornysh's choice perfectly acceptable. "None of these scouts are going to report in."

Lornysh met his eyes, not questioning what Jev meant. "Agreed."

Jev led the way out and stalked straight toward the trolls at the fire.

"Zenia?" Cutter whispered, his voice thick with pain.

"Yes." Zenia was wrapping bandages around his torso to cover the huge stab wounds in his chest and abdomen while Rhi held him propped up. She wished she could give the poor dwarf a hug, but that might hurt more than the bandaging. She'd done her best to clean the wounds, but she hadn't been able to get any of the painkiller potion down his throat yet. "I'm glad to see you're coherent. Want to take a swig from that brown bottle?" She tilted her head toward where it sat on the pebbles next to her.

"Is it alcohol?"

"I think that's one of the ingredients." Zenia tied the bandage she'd been wrapping, uncorked the bottle, and offered it to him.

His hand shook when he lifted it, so she kept one of hers around the bottle and helped him tip the liquid into his mouth.

He spat what had to be curses in dwarven and followed them with, "That tastes like ogre piss. Except thicker. And more rotten."

"It'll numb your pain." She decided not to ask when he'd sampled ogre urine before.

"Alcohol would have done that too."

"No, alcohol would have knocked you out," Zenia said.

"I fail to see how we're disagreeing."

Rhi snorted. "I think I'd rather have alcohol too. I can smell that stuff from here."

"Take another drink," Zenia insisted. Grodonol, the inventor of Pain-No-More, displayed his sense of humor in all his products and this one was no different. Under the light from her dragon tear, she saw the recommended dosage was "three chugs for anything worse than a bee sting."

"You're an awful woman," Cutter declared as she lifted the bottle to his mouth again. "Don't know why Jev wants to have relations with you."

Zenia almost dumped the liquid into his beard. "What?"

"I told him he ought to make you something. Like a spice rack. That's how you let a female know you care."

"A spice rack?" Rhi sounded puzzled. She was no more a chef than Zenia.

"We're not having relations." Zenia reminded herself that Cutter had been missing for days, so Jev might not have had a chance to share the news of their one and only date. "Drink."

"'Course not. He hasn't made you anything."

Cutter sneered, but he let her dump another "chug" in his mouth.

"How'd you get stuck out here, Cutter?" Zenia was glad he was speaking now and not simply moaning in pain. His wounds would need the attention of a healer, but at least she had stopped the bleeding. It had been clear he hadn't been stabbed that long ago. "And is Master Grindmor with you?"

"She *was*." Cutter slumped back in Rhi's arms, issuing another distressed moan. This one had more to do with emotional pain than physical, Zenia sensed. "We've been together the last two—three days? What day is it? We've been trying to bust out of that log prison. Got an axe one time and mowed down a few of those toad-kissing trolls. Thought we'd get out, but which way is out in this damn swamp? We ran but couldn't figure it out before we got caught again. Underground, I can find my way through any maze of tunnels, but out here, all the trees look the same. Don't know why the elves love the damn forest so much."

"How were you separated?" Zenia asked, trying to keep him focused. Once the painkiller kicked in, if it hadn't already, he would get loopy. "Is she still in the cabin?"

"Nah, they took her in the other boat." Cutter waved toward the pool and presumably the river at the other end. "To the city. Something about some ship coming in that they had to get there for. A dwarf ship, I think. They never confided to us, but the trolls had to speak in your language when that sniveling Braksnoth was around. I heard some plans about the invasion. And about them *killing* her." He snarled and straightened, trying to push himself to his feet, but he gasped and grabbed his abdomen, almost pitching over.

It took Zenia and Rhi to keep him from toppling onto his side on the pebbles.

"Easy," Zenia said. "As soon as Jev and Lornysh find us, we'll get back to the city and stop whatever the trolls are doing. Is Tildar—Braksnoth—leading them?"

"They aim to use the master to get on the ship," he said, as if he hadn't heard her question. "Some scheme to get rid of all the dwarves at once. They're going to kill a whole bunch of us! Just to piss off Preskabroto, make sure my people don't align with yours again."

Zenia nodded. "I know. The king does too." Except Targyon wouldn't know anything about this attack—or whatever the trolls meant to launch—on the dwarven ship. Nobody in town knew. "We'll stop it," she assured Cutter, hoping it was the truth.

"*Will* Jev and Lornysh be able to find us?" Rhi whispered. "Once they're done?"

Zenia hesitated. They hadn't left a note or so much as an arrow made from twigs pointing in the right direction.

"Lornysh can find anyone," Cutter muttered. He'd settled down, gripping his stomach and chest again, the pain forcing him to stay still. "By your dragon tear if not by sign."

"Good." Normally, Zenia would have been disturbed, knowing someone could track her, but tonight, she wanted Jev and Lornysh to finish up and find them as quickly as possible. Though a part of her wondered if she and Rhi should jump into the rowboat and take Cutter downriver to find a healer and warn the city right away. How far out was that dwarven ship? How much time did they have?

"How did you two get kidnapped?" Rhi asked. "A bunch of trolls didn't come into the city in the middle of the night and find you in bed together, did they?"

"*Bed? Me?* With the legendary Master Arkura *Grindmor*?"

"I guess he hasn't made her a spice rack yet," Rhi told Zenia.

Cutter shook his head. "You don't proposition a female like her. I just want to become her apprentice. I'd do anything to earn that honor. I swore I'd find her tools, but I was afraid I was just disappointing her. I even tried to pay one of those criminal guilds for information. But nothing came of it except them taking my money. Worthless bastards. Then we got a note that said someone who knew where the tools were hidden would meet us out by that bridge over the river. I figured it for a trap or trick of some kind, but what could I do? I had to get the tools for her. I'd promised I would. What I didn't count on was her insisting on coming out to get them herself. She said she didn't need my help. But I stood up to her and went anyway. I wanted to protect her if there was a trap." Cutter's shoulders slumped. "But I wasn't expecting forty trolls to be hiding under the bridge. Who would have? We downed plenty of them, but there were too many."

Forty? Zenia grimaced at the notion of so many. Just how many were part of this scouting party? And how many were in tents ready to jump into battle with Jev and Lornysh?

"They dragged us back to a log cabin over yonder," Cutter said in a subdued tone. "Tied us up. They've barely been feeding us or giving us water. The tools were there, but we couldn't get to them. Not that they would have helped. They're tools, not weapons. Then tonight, some troll ran in saying it was time, and they dragged us off again. I fought like a gryphon when we got here. There were only twelve of them, you see, so I thought we might have a chance. Might get free and make sure the master wasn't used against our own people."

"What exactly are they planning?" Zenia asked. "You said they mean to use her?"

"Nothing good. They're going to use her to get on board, then attack everyone."

"I thought there were five hundred dwarves coming on that ship," Zenia said. "Would twelve trolls be enough to harm them?"

"They had some boxes with them. Black powder or maybe worse. I sensed magic about them."

Zenia groaned.

"Should we row back to town now?" Rhi asked. "And warn the king?"

Zenia returned the first-aid items to her kit. She'd been thinking the same thing, but was it truly a good idea to split up? Maybe she could somehow tell Jev that they'd found Cutter and that Grindmor had been taken so there was no reason to fight the troll scouts in the swamp, at least not tonight. She had no doubt the king would send men out to deal with them as soon as he learned about the incursion.

"Let me see if I can communicate with Jev." Zenia wrapped her hand around her dragon tear and let her head droop.

"Can it do that?" Rhi asked.

"I'm about to find out."

But as she concentrated, imagining Jev's face in her mind and trying to let the dragon tear know what she wanted, shots rang out.

She spun in the direction they'd come from. The encampment.

"That's them." Rhi let go of Cutter and stood, grabbing her bo from the pebbles. "We have to help."

"Cutter, stay here," Zenia said. "We'll get them and come back for you."

"By the fiery forges of Mount Iksonoth, I'm not staying anywhere." Cutter gasped in pain but managed to stand on his own this time. "Where's my hook? Those mule-humpers ripped it off and threw it somewhere." He stomped along the shoreline. "I heard it hit the rocks."

Zenia wanted to sprint off and leave him—didn't want him to move at all, not with those injuries—but she cursed and silently urged the dragon tear to glow brighter. It flared with blue light, driving back all the shadows on the shoreline. Startled animals squawked and fled into the trees and bushes, the branches rattling.

The dragon tear's blue light glinted off something on the other side of the dock. As Zenia sprinted over, more shots fired in the distance. Was that Jev shooting? Or the trolls? Or both?

She snatched up the hook and the metal and leather assembly that affixed it to the stump on Cutter's arm. "Here."

She raced over and gave it to him. Rhi, who'd been looking in the other direction, ran toward the gunfire as soon as Cutter had it.

"You're a good female," Cutter said, pointing a finger at her. "I'm going to help Jev make you something."

"I'd be honored." A part of her wanted to go slowly and help Cutter, especially when she saw how pained his gait was, but she could do more to help Jev and Lornysh than Rhi could. If she had to, she would implore the dragon tear to burn a horde of trolls, the same way it had crocodiles.

As she sprinted after Rhi, Zenia sensed a hint of pleased glee from the gem.

CHAPTER 17

J EV CROUCHED IN FRONT OF the log cabin, his short sword dripping blood. He fired between the eyes of a troll charging toward him, one of several. He only had a couple of bullets left, but he didn't care. He would use the sword again if he had to. That was how he and Lornysh had started this. They'd killed close to a dozen enemies before one screamed a warning that alerted the rest of them.

Since then, it had been chaos, and there was no longer a point to striving for quiet.

Six or seven trolls lay dead in front of the cabin around Jev and Lornysh. They were using the log structure to block access to their backs. Unfortunately, that left their sides and fronts open for the trolls.

As Jev fired again, careful to make each shot count, Lornysh battled two more a few feet away. His flaming blade burned away the darkness of the night as it slashed, clanging against the axes and swords the trolls wielded. But they had firearms, too, and Jev spotted one aiming at Lornysh, not caring that its buddies were in the way.

Jev fired first, his bullet slamming into the troll's hand. It struck true, and the troll cried out, dropping his weapon. But it wasn't a debilitating enough blow. Snarling, the troll spun toward Jev, yanked out a hatchet, and hurled it.

Jev saw the weapon coming and ducked and rolled to the side. A resonating thud came from above as the axe slammed into the cabin's plank door.

As Jev sprang to his feet, three trolls charged toward him. He fired, but he'd lost track of a bullet somewhere, and the chamber clicked empty. Jev backed up to the log wall, hefting his sword as he jammed the pistol back into its holster. The lanky trolls had long arms, longer than his, and he wished he had a blade with greater reach.

They rushed him at once. Jev jumped to the side, trying to put one troll between him and the other two. He glimpsed the still quivering hatchet shaft out of the corner of his eye and snatched it as he parried a blow from a heavy machete. He darted in close, stabbing swiftly and repeatedly before springing back out again. He tried to stay out of the trolls' reach and also distract them with his blade work. When the one directly in front of him was busy swatting at his sword, Jev threw the hatchet. It thudded into the troll's chest, and he pitched against one of his buddies.

That one would not be distracted for long, but Jev took advantage, hurling a chain of attacks at the lone troll that faced him, at least for the moment. His enemy wielded the machete like a master sword dancer, and Jev's stomach sank when every one of his attacks met steel, the blades ringing in the night as they clashed again and again. But he imagined his family, all his nieces and nephews in danger as trolls stormed Dharrow Castle, and that gave him extra strength, extra energy, and extra speed.

Jev sprang at the troll, slashing high, drawing his attention upward, then kicking him in the knee. He connected solidly enough for cartilage to crunch. For an instant, the troll dropped his defenses, and Jev lunged in. He slammed the point of his sword into his foe's heart, bone crunching along the way.

The other troll had pushed aside his fallen comrade and leaped in from the side before Jev could yank his sword free. He let go of it as an axe swept toward his head. Ducking, he flung himself backward as the troll's weapon sank into the cabin wall.

Jev lunged to his feet, terror pushing aside his rage. He had no weapons left. What now? If they gave him time, he could reload his pistol, but—

The troll freed his axe from the log it had stuck in, hefted it over his head, and charged at Jev.

Jev readied himself to block as well as he could with nothing but feet and fists. Then orange light flared like the noon sun. The troll stumbled, glancing to the side.

At first, Jev thought Lornysh had brightened his sword, but Zenia's voice rang out.

"Back up!"

Not hesitating, Jev scrambled backward. Flames erupted from the mud in front of the cabin. They engulfed the troll, then spread toward four more that had been rushing in to join the fray. Screams pierced the night as fire burned flesh and muscle and bone.

Jev turned away from the brilliance of the light—and the burning trolls as they fell to the ground, screaming and writhing in pain.

Zenia ran to Jev's side as the flames went out, leaving charred corpses behind, just as had happened with the crocodiles. She hugged him fiercely, not seeming to care that he was covered with blood. At least most of it belonged to his enemies. He'd taken a few cuts but nothing that would slow him down. He returned Zenia's hug, but metal clashed nearby as Lornysh continued to fight, and he spotted Rhi using her bo on a troll with an axe.

Jev kissed Zenia's temple and let her go. He plunged his fingers into his ammo pouch so he could reload his pistol.

"Didn't we tell you to stay by that log?" he joked, glancing at her to make sure she hadn't been wounded.

"You thought we would obey you? You being a mere zyndar, and us being a former monk and inquisitor blessed by the Water Order?"

"It crossed my mind." Jev fired at one of the two trolls trying to bring Lornysh down, trusting his friend wouldn't mind if the fight ended early.

Rhi had knocked her troll to the ground and was pummeling him impressively with her bo. When he tried to rise, she kicked him in the face with the strength of a dragon baller sending one of the scaled orbs a hundred yards down the field.

"Remind me not to make that woman angry," Jev said. "Or you either." He glanced at the dragon tear glowing a fierce blue on Zenia's chest.

"You haven't managed yet." Zenia smiled, though she was looking him up and down with concern. She must have noticed some of his cuts.

"Are you sure? I was fairly positive I irked you when you were trying to arrest me and I was evading your attempts."

"No, I like a challenge."

"Where are my trolls, you boulder-cracking fungus lickers?" came a familiar booming voice from the shadows.

"He's talking to you, Zenia," Rhi announced.

"The painkiller is working remarkably well," Zenia said.

"Cutter!" Jev cried after a stunned moment. He peered around until he picked out his friend's stout form limping toward them.

"I even liberated a kindling trimmer to use on them." Cutter shook a two-headed axe as long as he was tall.

"Cutter!" Lornysh yelled. He sprang over the fallen trolls at his feet and ran toward Cutter.

"That's why we left the log," Zenia said.

"An excellent reason." Jev squeezed her around the shoulders, then hurried over to check on Cutter. He looked like he should be in a hospital, not waving giant axes about.

Lornysh gripped Cutter by the shoulders but paused, as if he couldn't decide if he wanted to hug him or shake him. "Where have you been, you young fool?"

"Young?" Cutter protested. "I had my fiftieth birthday during this mess. My captors refused to let me celebrate properly by bringing me a rock pastry."

"Fifty. Hah, you're a child."

"A child in need of a rock pastry."

"Is it hard to stick candles in a rock pastry?" Jev patted Cutter on the back carefully, not wanting to hurt him further, as he imagined pastries made from boulders and drizzled with frosting.

"Candles?" Cutter asked. "What silly tradition is that? You could burn your birthday treat into ashes, much like your girlfriend did those trolls."

Jev gave Zenia an apologetic wave, not wanting to argue with Cutter about what she was to him, not then. But Zenia was barely paying attention. She'd opened the door to the log cabin and was peeking inside.

Jev had no idea what was in there. He and Lornysh had only been using the wall to protect their backs. At one point, he'd thought about diving inside so the trolls could only come at him one at a time, but they hadn't given him an opportunity. Fortunately, Zenia had shown up at a timely moment. When he'd first met her, he never would have imagined her as someone who would end up saving—or at least seriously assisting—him in battle.

"This is problematic," Zenia said, looking back at him and also at Rhi.

As she stepped fully inside, Jev and Rhi followed. Lornysh offered Cutter an arm for support. Cutter clenched his jaw, slung the giant axe over his shoulder, and hobbled toward the door without help.

When Jev stepped into the one-room hunting cabin, he almost stepped on a human body on the floor. The man's chest had been cut open, likely with a massive axe similar to the one Cutter had purloined, and the blood sinking into the dirt floor around him was fresh. Jev didn't think this had happened more than an hour or two ago.

Zenia gazed down at the body while gripping her chin, reminding him of when he'd walked into that dead doctor's office with her. She appeared no more fazed at the sight of this corpse than the last one, though whoever this was had died a far more gruesome death.

"This is—was—Tildar Braksnoth," Zenia said. "His picture was in one of the newspaper articles I read."

Jev had never seen the articles, but the dead man wore an expensive suit and snakeskin boots, and the chain from a gold watch spilled from a bloodied breast pocket. He had definitely been someone with money to spend.

"That's the fellow that was making all the deals with the trolls," Cutter said, leaning against the doorjamb.

Lornysh stood watch outside, his bow visible poking over his shoulder. He and Jev had already discussed that it was unlikely all the trolls had been in camp, that others would be out scouting the countryside and could return at any time.

"This is his land," Cutter added. "That's what he said, anyway. I was blindfolded and gagged and in the corner over there mostly, so I only saw him once, but I heard him talk a bunch of times. He bought this land so the trolls could use it as a staging area for their spies. Before their full invasion force came, the troll scouts were going to try and get into the castle and kill Targyon." Cutter growled and spat at the dead man's boots. "That traitor was going to help them. He drew some maps of the castle for them. In return, they were going to support him with troops as he tried to change the government, get rid of your nobility, and put himself in charge of some new system."

"What kind of *system* would we have if the kingdom was destroyed by trolls?" Zenia asked.

"They had a plan to divvy it up, from what I heard. Swamps and mountains for the trolls, and you humans could keep your farms and cities, so long as the trolls were treated favorably by this Brak-snot fellow once he was in charge."

"So, what happened?" Rhi pointed the tip of her bo at the body.

"I wasn't here for this," Cutter said. "I guess they figured they didn't need him anymore, but I don't know for certain. The trolls carted the master and me off to the boat launch. They're on their way into town to use her to cause trouble and kill a bunch of my kind." Cutter's grip tightened on the axe haft.

"Trouble." Jev gritted his teeth at their plans to kill Targyon. As if he wasn't already furious enough at these invaders. "Lornysh," he barked. "Are you ready to kill more trolls?"

"Always ready," came the prompt reply. "But collect the dwarf's tools first."

Jev had already been stepping out of the cabin.

"What?" He looked around the room.

There wasn't much furniture, and the place smelled of piss. He didn't see any magical tools encrusted in diamonds or made from diamonds. Whatever it was. Grindmor had never described them to Jev.

Zenia walked slowly to a corner and looked down at a small, grimy rug, the only such item in the cabin. She pulled it aside, revealing a couple of boards over a hole in the dirt. "Toolbox here."

"Yes," Cutter said, rushing to her side, though he winced with every step.

Jev vowed to take him to a healer as soon as possible. He just wasn't sure when that would be. If the trolls had left an hour or two ago and had a boat, they ought to already be in the city. What if they were enacting their plan right now?

Zenia and Cutter pulled up the boards and extracted the toolbox. It looked heavy, but Cutter abandoned the axe and clutched it to his chest. He strode toward the door, his jaw set with determination.

Rhi waved at the abandoned axe. "What're you going to do if we're attacked?"

"Hide behind the woman lighting trolls on fire with her mind," Cutter said.

Zenia blinked. "It was the dragon tear."

"Which responds to your mental orders."

Jev strode outside, waving for them to follow. They could discuss Zenia's rock later. For now, he worried they were already too late.

CHAPTER 18

ZENIA FIDDLED WITH HER DRAGON tear and tried not to feel useless as the rowboat surged down the wide Jade River, balmy night air that smelled of the sea and the mangroves breezing past. She sat twiddling her thumbs with Rhi while Lornysh and Jev rowed from the benches at either end. There were only two sets of oars, so it wasn't as if she could help, but she felt like she should be doing something besides looking downriver for the first signs of the city's gas lamps.

Cutter sat on the floor of the boat behind Zenia. She'd offered him her bench, but he'd collapsed down there, seeming more comfortable propped against the side of the craft, the master's toolbox under his arm.

Jev had injuries, too. A fresh gash in his jaw had taken a chunk out of his beard, and as they'd jogged to the dock, Zenia had seen him wince a few times and touch his side and his thigh. His dark clothing hid the blood, but she didn't miss the long cuts in the fabric.

"Are you all right?" Zenia was facing him as he rowed and could see the grim, determined set to his face.

Jev nodded. "It's not hard. We're with the current."

She hadn't meant the rowing, but she didn't correct him. Maybe later he would share more. He ought to be ecstatic at having Cutter back, but Cutter's words about the trolls planning something with the dwarven ship—and his later addendum that they'd planned to kill Targyon—were worrying. She could understand Jev's concern—she was concerned, too—but was used to smiles and quips from him, even when the stakes were high. Without the humor gleaming in his eyes, it was almost like he was someone else.

Maybe that was appropriate since, at the moment, she felt like someone else too. She'd used her dragon tear to kill. Not just animals but intelligent beings with their own culture and language. When she had seen Jev in danger, she had reacted without stopping to consider if there was a less deadly way to subdue them. She supposed that was understandable, but now that she'd had time to think about her actions, she couldn't help second-guessing herself. Also, it made her uncomfortable to realize how easy it had been to kill with the dragon tear.

She thought of Cutter's warnings about the gem. She could see how it could change a person to have that kind of power, how one might start to feel invincible if one could wave a hand and kill. Technically, she could use her pistol to kill a man, too, but with this, she could annihilate someone without leaving any evidence. Something about being able to kill with a thought made it far more horrifying than physically thrusting a dagger into someone's chest. Or firing a bullet into their eye.

Worse, the dragon tear hadn't judged her for the decision to fling fire at the trolls. If anything, it had reacted with glee, and she'd had to fight the urge to turn and burn down the entire camp. Her dream had flashed into her mind—her nightmare—and she'd had some strange sense that she would be getting revenge if she burned everything. But revenge for what? The trolls hadn't invaded the city *yet*.

Zenia rubbed a shaky hand over her face and vowed to wait to ponder it further until they completed their mission and made sure Targyon was safe. If she let doubt creep into her mind now, she might fail to act at an important moment. When she could help a friend in need or even save his or her life.

"Are *you* all right?" Jev asked quietly.

She forced a smile and lowered her hand, aware of Rhi also looking at her. "Fine."

Jev didn't look like he believed her. Maybe later, she would talk to him about it. He might understand. He'd been killing those trolls—he and Lornysh had chosen to go in and kill them. Not merely in self-defense but to defend the city. She couldn't fault them for acting preemptively, but something about meting out justice for a crime that hadn't yet been committed disturbed her. Did it also disturb him? Lornysh, as cool and calculating as he came off, had seemed excited at the chance to slay trolls. For Jev, it had seemed that he was doing what his duty required, as he always did, and he derived no pleasure from it. She appreciated that. It would discomfit her to find out he enjoyed killing.

"You've known her longer than I have, Rhi," Jev said as he continued to row. "Is she lying?"

"Yes, but she'll hold it together and do her job anyway. She always does."

Zenia snorted but couldn't deny the assessment. And she *would* hold it together.

"She might need a hug though," Rhi added, her expression growing sly. She didn't quite wink at Zenia.

"Just don't club her with your bo when you give it," Jev said.

Rhi's expression changed from sly to exasperated. "I meant a *zyndar* hug."

Zenia elbowed her. She didn't need her friend encouraging Jev when she had... discouraged him. It was bad enough Zenia had trouble remembering that herself.

"Oh?" Jev asked. "I had no idea zyndar hugs were superior."

"It's just that Rhi is a horrible hugger." Zenia didn't know if she should extend the silly conversation, but it pleased her that Jev was participating, some of his humor peeking through. "She usually clacks you in the shin with her stick. Even a substandard hug would be superior."

"I know *you're* not judging how I hug," Rhi said. "You don't hug at all. You get stiff when someone tries to wrap their arms around you."

Zenia shifted on the hard bench, now wishing she'd ended the discussion instead of playing along. She didn't *always* get stiff. Just when she was taken by surprise or someone she didn't know that well initiated the hug. Fortunately, the inquisitor robe had kept that to a minimum. She didn't know what it said about her that she'd sometimes *liked* how it acted as a shield.

"I didn't notice that," Jev observed, offering Zenia a warm smile.

It was a simple gesture, but she appreciated it. She wished she could hug him now, but he was rowing. An oar handle in the stomach wouldn't be any better than a bo to the shin.

"There's the river mouth," Rhi said.

Jev's smile faded as he looked over his shoulder. "Lornysh, let's head to shore. We'll have to fight against the river current taking us out into the ocean if we try to row all the way to the docks."

Lornysh did not respond aloud, but they worked together well—and without further communication—to guide the boat to the side of the river as the city came into view, its gas lamps lining the dark streets. They landed at one of the fishing piers that extended into the Jade, left the rowboat, then strode along the riverfront street toward the harbor.

Cutter grunted and took deep, labored breaths as he struggled to keep up with them. Both Lornysh and Jev told him he should stay there and rest, with Jev adding that they could come back to guide him to a healer as soon as they finished this work. Lornysh even offered to break away and escort Cutter to a healer right then. Cutter refused to leave the group, muttering about bringing Master Grindmor her tools. He wouldn't let Lornysh carry them, instead insisting on toting the toolbox along himself.

Zenia stumbled when the harbor came into view and she spotted a huge, towering ship docked at the end of the longest pier. Rising several stories high, it dwarfed the sailboats moored nearby and even the city's two steam-powered warships. She couldn't imagine how anyone could get on or off. There was no way a gangplank could lower all the way to the pier. A rope ladder, maybe.

"It's even bigger than it looked in that spyglass," Jev said.

"That's the *Warhammer*," Cutter said. "One of two of Preskabroto's big steamships. She's less than five years old. My people send her to their mining colonies to loom threateningly over any orcs or ogres that think about disturbing the dwarves there."

"Is it more advanced than our steamships?" Zenia asked.

"Oh, certainly. My people are master engineers." His labored breathing didn't steal the pride from Cutter's tone. "We invented steam engines, you know. While your people were still tying logs together with vines and pushing them around with poles."

"Really," Jev murmured.

"I sense a magical artifact on board," Lornysh said as the group turned, following the waterfront street above the beach. "More than one."

The city was surprisingly quiet with few people in the street, and nobody out on the docks, despite the massive ship that must have come in within the last few hours. Maybe the hour had grown later than Zenia realized. Had the dwarven crew already disembarked and found lodgings in the city? Or would they remain with their ship?

She couldn't see the deck from down below, but she didn't see anyone at the railings. Further, few lamps burned on the ship. The deck appeared to be mostly dark, and only a couple of the dozens—hundreds?—of portholes in the metal hull had lights burning behind them.

"Dwarven artifacts?" Jev asked.

"It wouldn't be surprising if my people brought some magic along," Cutter said.

"The most prominent one is elven." Lornysh looked at Cutter.

"Elven?" Cutter scratched his head with his hook. "That's more surprising. Our people have been allies often, but I can't imagine the Taziir would have been inclined to send magical gifts along for this voyage, given what these dwarves came here to do."

"Work in Korvann?" Zenia wondered if Targyon had spoken to Cutter of his plans before enacting them. Perhaps he'd asked Cutter for advice.

"As friends to humans, yes," Cutter said.

"Any idea what the elven artifact does?" Jev asked.

Lornysh hesitated. "It does seem familiar, but I need to get closer before I'll know."

Zenia found that she could, through her dragon tear, sense what Lornysh was talking about. There seemed to be small magical devices around the ship, perhaps responsible for operating some equipment, but something with a far more prominent signature was placed almost dead center in the ship on one of the middle decks.

She also sensed great heat and energy in the form of steam coming from huge cylindrical boilers in a room at the bottom of the ship. Next to them, coal burned in dozens of furnaces, and in still another room, engines waited to power huge screw-style propellers at the rear of the ship. They were far different from the paddle wheels on the city's riverboats.

The boilers and engines seemed mundane rather than magical, but a hint of curiosity emanated from her dragon tear. She had never seen such massive steam engines. Maybe it hadn't either.

"Are those people dead?" Rhi pointed to the docks.

Zenia almost jumped. Before, she'd thought the docks empty because of the late hour, but she realized that wasn't the reason for the quiet. Dozens of people lay sprawled on the wood planks, none of them moving.

Fear leaped into her chest. Had the trolls already been here? Attacking people left and right? *Killing* people?

"They're not dead," Lornysh said. "They're sleeping."

"Uhm, what?" Rhi asked.

"Magic?" Jev guessed.

"Magic," Lornysh said. "What I sense is something my people call a *hylellela*—a dream weaver. A device with the power to induce sleep and dreams. Some of our holy people use them to enhance the likelihood of receiving meaningful visions. I've encountered the devices often, but they're usually for a single person or perhaps a household. This has been amplified to a greater degree than I've seen before. Some other magical artifact must be linked with the dream weaver."

"Why would a bunch of dwarves—or do we think the trolls were here?— want to make everybody fall asleep?" Rhi asked, then promptly yawned.

Zenia squinted at her, feeling a yawn tugging at her own mouth. They had reached the boardwalk and could have headed out onto the pier where the steamship was anchored, but would they all fall asleep if they got close? She spotted a leg sticking out from behind a stack of crates and realized they might *already* be too close.

"I think you answered your own question." Jev stopped, holding out a hand to halt the group. He was also looking at that leg.

Lornysh tapped his shoulder and pointed up into the capital, beyond the blocks and blocks of buildings and toward Alderoth Crown, the highest hill in the area and the location of Alderoth Castle. Zenia spotted a large clump of lanterns on the road winding from the castle down into the city. They were moving. People heading down into the city on horseback or in steam carriages?

"That's a large procession," Jev remarked and gave Zenia a significant look.

"The king?" she wondered.

Maybe Targyon had received word that the dwarven ship had arrived and was coming down to meet his invited guests. Had the trolls or whoever planted this sleep-inducing artifact anticipated that? Or would it be a pleasant surprise for them when the king delivered himself into their clutches?

"Someone needs to warn him," Zenia said.

"Yes, but not all of us." Jev pointed at the ship. "We need to get on there, find that artifact and cut it out, and stop the trolls from their goal."

"Blowing up the ship," Cutter supplied. "That's what they were talking about."

Jev rocked back on his heels. "Founders, an explosive? Iridium isn't supplying the black powder, is she?"

Zenia spread her arms. "I don't know what she would have to gain, but I wouldn't be shocked if the guilds were involved somehow."

Jev looked at the massive vessel, then waved all around them. "With a large enough explosion, that could take out every ship docked here and all the shops and warehouses down here." His gaze shifted to the nearest snoozing dock workers and sailors. "And however many people are here."

"And on the ship," Cutter said.

"Targyon said five hundred dwarves were coming, didn't he?" Zenia asked.

"Yes." Jev looked at Rhi. "Go warn the king, please. The rest of us will try—*will* figure this out."

"Why me?" Rhi waved her bo. "You may need my help with the trolls."

"Targyon *must* be warned. Tell him to go back to the castle, to stay safe tonight. Until we've handled it."

"But he barely knows who I am. He might not—"

"Tell him I sent you." Jev made his voice harder. "*Go.*"

Zenia imagined he'd used that voice during the war to command his troops. It had the desired effect.

"Yes, Zyndar," Rhi said, then jogged off the docks and into the city.

"Lornysh," Jev said, "how do we get on without falling asleep?"

"I'm not certain. I may have enough innate magic to fight off the effects, though—" a yawn interrupted his words, "—I may not."

Zenia clasped her hand around her dragon tear and groped for a way to formulate her thoughts. Could it protect her from the magic? Shield her somehow? As it had done with physical attacks.

The dragon tear flared with warmth and blue light that shone through Zenia's fingers. An image formed in her mind of her striding toward the ship with the others touching her, staying within the gem's sphere of influence.

"I may be able to protect us," she said.

Lornysh eyed the light seeping between her fingers.

"Touch my shoulders or back, and we'll walk to the ship together."

"What makes you think that will work?" Lornysh asked.

Zenia was reluctant to admit the dragon tear shared ideas with her, especially when Cutter was present, Cutter who'd warned her the gem might be dangerous. "A hunch."

Lornysh's eyes narrowed with skepticism.

Jev stepped close and rested a hand on her shoulder. He nodded to her and drew his pistol. The sign of faith touched her.

Following his lead, Cutter came up and laid a hand on her back. Zenia had never liked people touching her that much—Rhi's joke about finding hugs uncomfortable came to mind—so she had to make herself stand still and not step away. She raised her eyebrows toward Lornysh.

He grumbled something in Elvish but came close enough to put his hand on her other shoulder.

A refreshing surge of energy flowed through Zenia, emanating from her dragon tear. The niggling weariness that had crept over her as soon as she stepped onto the boardwalk vanished.

"Huh," Jev said.

Did he feel it too?

"Your dragon tear is unlike others I've been around," Lornysh stated, sounding displeased rather than full of wakeful energy, but he wouldn't have made the comment if he hadn't felt something. He looked past her to Jev. "It may be too powerful for an untrained wielder. The temptation for her to use it for personal gain will be great."

Zenia opened her mouth to snap that they didn't have time for philosophizing, but Jev spoke first.

"She can handle it." He squeezed her shoulder and pointed toward the dwarven ship.

Lornysh did not object further.

Grateful for the support, Zenia lifted her chin and strode down the pier. She wished she could pat Jev's hand and thank him, but she felt self-conscious with the others so close. She looked over at him, catching his gaze and holding it, and hoped that would convey her feelings. He smiled and squeezed her shoulder again.

As they neared the ship, the gangplank came into view, its location much different than Zenia had imagined. Instead of descending from the upper deck, it thrust out from a doorway in the hull not high above the level of the water. It was extended now with that door open.

They passed more men and women slumbering on the pier and also on the decks of nearby ships. They looked like they had been going about their evening chores when the urge to sleep had swept over them, and they had collapsed where they stood.

"Do we walk right in?" Jev looked past Zenia to Lornysh.

"Now that I've told you about the elven artifact," Lornysh said, "you know as much about this situation as I do."

"That's distressing."

"Indeed."

Lornysh and Cutter shifted closer together behind Zenia, still touching her, so they could walk up the narrow gangplank. Jev frowned, then stepped in front of her, sliding his hand down to clasp hers.

"Will this work?" he asked, leading her up the gangplank. Unwilling to let her go into danger first?

"I think so," Zenia said when the dragon tear didn't object. "If you start to look drowsy, I'll poke you in the butt."

"I prefer squeezes to pokes. Maybe a little pat."

"A pat would keep you awake?"

"If you did it, I assure you it would."

Cutter sighed, and Zenia let the conversation die. But not her awareness of Jev. She noticed the warmth of his hand pressed against hers, the callouses of his palm, the gentleness of his grip. She realized they had never walked and held hands before. She had the urge to thread her fingers between his.

But they were stepping into the metal corridor of a ship full of danger, so she made herself focus on possible threats around them rather than hand-holding. Almost immediately, Jev moved awkwardly around a sleeping dwarf with a beard so thick and bushy Zenia had to jump to avoid stepping on it.

"Up or down?" Jev asked when they reached an intersection with narrow stairs that led up and down. "Or turn down the corridor?"

"Up one level and toward the stern of the boat," Lornysh said.

Jev led the way toward the stairs. They were even narrower than the gangplank had been, and Zenia worried about finding enough room for all of them to remain touching. Another dwarf lay slumped at the base of the steps, snoring loudly and emphasizing the need to stay close to her dragon tear.

A clang echoed down from a deck above them, and Jev paused. That was the first noise they had heard except for snoring.

"Someone's awake," Jev murmured, continuing up.

Zenia felt sweat break out on her palm and hoped Jev wouldn't notice.

"Whoever planted the artifact," Lornysh said. "The trolls, most likely."

"What did they need Master Grindmor for if they had such a device?" Jev whispered.

"To get on board," Cutter growled. "My people never would have lowered the gangplank for trolls. But if they had her... a dwarf wouldn't risk seeing a master cutter hurt. Especially not one as gifted as she is."

Another clang sounded, and their group fell silent. Jev guided them out of the stairwell and down a dark corridor. Mostly dark. A faint green glow came from around a bend up ahead.

Zenia glanced at open doors as they passed tiny cabins. Crew quarters with bunks affixed to the walls. She spotted a couple more sleeping dwarves, but few had been in their cabins when the artifact had been turned on.

Whispers drifted around the bend, the same hisses and clucks Zenia had heard in the swamp. Trolls. How many?

She might be able to use the dragon tear to sense life around her, but she was afraid to give it another task when it was the only thing keeping them awake.

They were almost to the bend when a tug from behind made Zenia pause. Lornysh let go of her. He whirled, jerking his bow from his shoulder and nocking an arrow in one swift gesture.

"Down," Cutter barked.

Zenia crouched as a gunshot fired from behind them. Lornysh loosed his arrow. A bullet clanged off the metal wall beside Zenia's head.

"Look out," she yelled, gripping Jev's hand, wanting to pull him down for safety.

But he was facing the other way, and he released her hand and sprang forward as two trolls with axes burst around the bend. They wore headbands with glowing red gems embedded in them, and they leaped for Jev without any sign of lethargy.

Zenia drew her pistol. Jev had given her dry ammunition back on the rowboat, so her firearm was loaded, but she struggled to find a clear shot as he engaged the two trolls. In the narrow corridor, his body blocked them from her view.

Cutter also released Zenia, roaring as he headed in the other direction and tore a dagger out of a belt sheath. It looked far too large for his hand—he must have acquired it from a troll. He charged back to help Lornysh with the two trolls that had tried to sneak up on them from behind. One of them already leaned against the wall with an arrow sticking out of his chest, but he was still alive, trying to pull out the shaft. When he saw Cutter, he snarled and hefted a sword. Cutter met that snarl with one of his own and lunged in.

Zenia lifted her pistol—since Cutter was shorter than the troll, she had no trouble aiming at his face. But the troll spotted her and crouched low, deliberately staying behind Cutter as the two squared off, blades coming together in screeches of metal.

Farther down the corridor, Lornysh battled the other troll. His sword flared with orange flames, their fiery reflection visible on the smooth metal walls as he stabbed and thrust. Again, Zenia had no opportunity for a clear shot. She almost reached for her dragon tear but worried whatever magical attack she chose might also strike her friends as easily as her foes.

Wondering if she could be of more help to Jev, she turned as he raised his knee and slammed a boot into one of his adversary's stomachs. The troll grunted and stumbled back, but the second one lunged around him and rushed in, swinging an axe. Jev ducked, and the axe whizzed over his head and clanged against the wall.

With Jev squatting low, Zenia had her chance. She fired at the axe-wielding troll as he shifted his weapon, trying to slam it down into Jev. But Jev barreled into his attacker, tackling him and taking him to the deck. Zenia's bullet only grazed the side of the troll's head.

As Jev and the troll wrestled, she had a clear shot of the one behind them, the one he'd kicked. The troll crouched and sprang to leap over the others to get her. She fired at his eye. The bullet landed true this time, and the troll lurched to the side, his head smashing against the wall.

Another pistol fired. This time, it was Jev, his weapon buried in his opponent's stomach. He leaped back, leaving the troll writhing on the deck, then fired again. His second bullet took his foe in the neck. The troll screamed, grabbing the wound and rolling into his buddy.

Jev staggered, putting his hand against the wall for support.

"Are you injured?" Zenia ran forward and gripped his shoulder, imagining an axe gash in his gut.

"What?" He turned bleary eyes toward her. *Sleepy*, bleary eyes.

Zenia willed the energy from her dragon tear to flow into him again. "Grab one of those headbands," she said.

"Souvenir?" He smiled groggily.

She reached down and firmly clasped his hand. "They must be what's keeping the dream artifact from affecting them."

"Ah, good point."

Zenia went with him, making sure to keep a grip on his hand, as he bent to remove a headband. A pained cry came from the corridor behind them. She turned to find Cutter slumped to his knees, his head against the wall. Sleeping? Lornysh was still on his feet, still moving with the grace of a professional dancer as he finished off a troll—one of three that lay crumpled at his feet. Damn, where had that third one in the rear come from?

"Your friend is quite the amazing warrior," Zenia remarked as silence fell.

"I assume you mean Lornysh and not Cutter." Jev reached for a second headband.

"He's injured and snoring, so it wouldn't be fair to judge his martial competence." Zenia waited for Jev to remove the headbands, then led him back toward Cutter. She knelt and rested her free hand on his shoulder, again urging the dragon tear to send wakeful energy into his limbs.

She wished she could also heal his wounds, but when she'd tried that with Lunis Drem a few weeks earlier, the dragon tear hadn't known what to do.

"There aren't any more trolls back there," Lornysh said, walking up with his sword in hand and one of the headbands glowing at his forehead.

Jev had also donned one, and he crouched to one-handedly maneuver the other band onto Cutter's head. Zenia still had Jev's other hand, not positive he'd fully recovered from almost falling asleep during that battle.

"I think they work," Jev told Zenia after a moment, touching his headband.

She nodded as Cutter stirred. "Good."

"You can probably let go of my hand," Jev said. "Though if you'll miss it terribly, you can grab something else that I don't need while fighting."

Zenia snorted and released him. "Like what?"

"I'm sure Rhi could make suggestions if she were here. Cutter, can you get up?" Jev helped him to his feet.

Cutter winced, a groan escaping his lips, but he stoically grabbed the toolbox as he stood. "We need to find Master Grindmor."

"We need to cut off that artifact so she and the rest of the dwarves can find themselves." Jev waved his pistol and headed down the corridor again.

Zenia stayed closer behind him, though she didn't grab anything else of his. She trusted his new headband would keep him awake.

"Cutter," she said, "any idea where someone would go if they wanted to destroy this ship in a huge explosion?"

"All the way down," Cutter said. "The boiler room. They could rig a catastrophic boiler failure and cause a real mess. There's a *lot* of coal stored down there to keep a fire burning long afterward too."

"Artifact first," Jev said, leading them around the bend. "If the dwarf crew wakes up, *they* can deal with it."

"They will be more likely to have the know-how," Cutter said.

As they rounded the bend, the green light grew brighter, flowing out of an open hatchway. Jev led with his pistol as he stepped into the cabin, but there weren't any more trolls. The ones that had rushed out to attack them must have been in charge of the artifact.

Two artifacts, Zenia amended as she poked her head into the cabin. The source of the green glow, a sphere mounted on a small stone pedestal, sat on a wool blanket on the lower of two bunks. A glowing yellow cord linked it to a drab gray box.

Her dragon tear shared with her the sense that both items emitted magic.

"Lornysh?" Jev said. "Are they protected by magic? Or can we walk up and flip a switch? Or slam a sword into them?"

Zenia shifted aside so Lornysh could enter, but she didn't take her gaze from the artifacts. She could tell her dragon tear was focusing on them too. She sensed it examining them with something akin to curiosity.

"It's difficult to tell with the magical power they're emitting," Lornysh said, "but I don't sense that any troll magic—a booby trap, if you will—has been added to them. I'll look for a switch."

Zenia's dragon tear shared an image of the artifacts being incinerated by flame. It also shared an eagerness to handle the matter.

Wait, she thought, her mind on explosions. What if destroying some powerful artifact could cause a backlash? *We'll let Lornysh see if they can simply be turned off.*

She didn't usually speak words to the dragon tear, but from the petulant almost sulking impression she got from it, she knew it understood.

Jev looked over at her, and she remembered the way he had come to her defense earlier, his belief that she could control the dragon tear. And she would.

Wait, she thought again.

The sensation of a long sigh floated through her mind.

"I think this will do it." Lornysh carefully unlinked the cord between the two artifacts, then touched something on the back of the glowing sphere.

The light faded until complete darkness filled the cabin.

"It's off," Lornysh said, then whispered something in his language. His sword glowed with flames again, providing a soft orange illumination.

"How long until all the dwarves wake up?" Jev asked.

"I don't know. It didn't take long to rouse Cutter, but he'd only been out for seconds."

"Not even that long," Cutter said. "I just needed a moment to rest my eyelids."

"Sure, you did," Jev said.

"There's a dwarven relaxation technique that involves placing warm stones over one's eyelids. For a moment, I thought I was doing that."

"Will you show us to the boiler room?" Jev asked him.

"Yes, I—"

"What's that?" Lornysh interrupted.

Cutter frowned at him. "I don't hear anything."

Zenia listened hard, and a faint pulsing sound reached her ears. It seemed to be coming from all around her, from somewhere in the ship.

"I do now," Cutter said.

"Boiler room." Jev nodded to the corridor.

Cutter led them out and back to the stairwell, passing the fallen trolls on the way. They also passed a couple of sleeping dwarves as they descended to the lower levels, none of them stirring yet.

The pulsing noise gradually grew louder, and it made Zenia uneasy. She had never heard anything like it but couldn't believe it signaled anything good.

At the bottom of the stairs, the temperature increased, as if they had walked into a steam hut. Cutter led them into a huge room lit by fires burning in dozens of fireboxes. Thick glass windows in their doors allowed them to see the writhing flames within.

A single dwarf lay in the center of the chamber, a rifle and daggers on the deck next to him. Blood pooled underneath him. This one wasn't sleeping; he was dead.

"He's wearing the engineer's hat," Cutter said. "If anyone would have known how to fix trouble down here, it's him. It *was* him."

"In there," Jev blurted and ran through a wide doorway connecting the furnace room with another one.

Lornysh and Cutter followed him inside, but Zenia halted in the doorway, staring.

This room wasn't lit as well as the other, but she could make out unfamiliar devices connected to cylindrical tanks—the boilers Cutter had mentioned?—and cables draped between and around them. A couple of empty backpacks lay near the door, as well as two dead trolls. They wore headbands, but whatever had happened—a fight with the engineer?—staying awake hadn't been enough to save them.

"Are those... explosives?" Jev turned a slow circle, taking in the cables linking devices affixed to the sides of the boilers. "Because they look a lot more complicated than kegs of black powder."

The strange pulsing noise was louder in here than it had been anywhere else. It seemed to originate with the devices themselves.

"Are they magical?" Zenia asked, the question as much for her dragon tear as for the others.

It emanated a sense of uncertainty, something she'd rarely felt from it. Jev looked at Lornysh.

"I sense magic," Lornysh said, "but I can't tell if it comes from the devices themselves or if it is a protection that was placed to enshroud them."

"I think those are mundane explosives," Cutter said. "*Dwarven* explosives. We have sophisticated ways to blow big holes in mountains to open up new areas for mining, and those look like ones I've seen before. These slag-faced trolls were shopping in everybody's stores before coming out here. Or stealing from stores, more like."

"Blowing holes in mountains?" Jev asked. "What about in ships?"

Zenia stared at him, imagining the devices igniting while they all stood there within the bowels of the steamship.

"I'm a gem cutter, not a miner, but yes, I think there's enough explosive power there to take out the ship and maybe every other ship in the harbor. Maybe a few city blocks. I don't know. The boilers blowing up in addition is going to amplify the power of the explosives. And I agree with Lornysh. I sense some magic, maybe protecting them from meddlers."

Jev cursed. "City *blocks*? Do you know how to disarm them? If we can nullify the magic somehow?" He looked bleakly at Zenia—no, at her dragon tear.

She didn't share with him the uncertainty she felt from it.

Cutter limped toward one of the devices, but he was shaking his head, his expression bleaker than death. "I don't think so, Jev. This isn't anything I ever studied. I can tell you that if we try to simply remove them without knowing what we're doing, we may set them off prematurely."

"How long do we have until they go off *maturely*?" Jev demanded.

"I think…" Cutter lifted the lid on the side of one of the devices, and Zenia gulped. After what he'd said, she couldn't imagine even touching them was a good idea. "Twenty minutes."

Jev thumped his fist against his thigh. "We've got to get this ship away from the pier. And—four founders—we've got to get all the dwarves that are sleeping off it." He spun toward Lornysh and Zenia. "You two, figure out a way to get the dwarves out of here. Wake them up, lift them, throw them over the side, I don't care. I just want everyone off this ship. *Now*."

Jev had never presumed to give Zenia an order before, but she didn't object. She ran out with Lornysh, hoping she could use her dragon tear to wake the dwarves. Maybe one of the crew would know how to disarm the devices.

With a surge of regret, she realized they shouldn't have killed all the trolls. They should have kept them alive to question, or to force *them* to disarm what they had armed. But it might not have mattered. The two trolls who'd likely set this all up had been dead before her team arrived.

As Zenia followed Lornysh into the stairwell, she heard Jev tell Cutter, "Show me to navigation. We've got to get this ship out of the harbor."

CHAPTER·19

J EV FOLLOWED CUTTER THROUGH THE passageways and up several stairwells, wanting to pick him up and carry him. Cutter was moving admirably quickly, given the extent of his injuries, but not quickly enough with that clock counting down.

They never did come out on the upper deck. Cutter led him to the bow of the ship, into a large navigation room with huge glass windows looking out over the waterfront and Korvann. Jev scowled at the reminder of just how close they *were* to the city.

A panel under the windows held a wheel not dissimilar to those for steering kingdom ships, but that was where the similarities ended. A confusing array of levers and switches stretched out to either side of it. Some of them even glowed yellow or blue. With magic? It had to be.

Three dwarves lay sleeping on the metal deck under the control panel.

"Cutter, you know how to steer this thing?" Jev stared at the panel. Was there a *reverse* lever? The ship would have to go backward to leave the dock. He couldn't imagine turning the bulky thing around otherwise.

"Sorry, Jev. I spent most of my life underground. I've been a passenger on one of these ships once, but that's it."

Jev stepped over one of the dwarves and up to the panel. If he could get the ship backed out and turned toward open water, maybe he could find something to tie the wheel in place to keep it on course. Then he could run up on deck and help the others get the dwarves off. Were there lifeboats somewhere? He hoped so.

When he touched the wheel's cool bronze rim, a dome embedded in the center flared to life, and a yellow glow illuminated the switches and levers to either side. Startled, Jev jumped back. The glow disappeared.

"I was afraid of that." Cutter limped up beside him.

"What?"

"I think the ship requires someone to be manning the helm in order to move."

"Why would that be required?"

Cutter shrugged. "So someone won't be tempted to leave it steaming forward without supervision. This was a huge investment for my people. You wouldn't want it smashing into rocks or icebergs."

"But you'd want it blowing up because some saboteurs rigged the boiler room to explode?"

"No, that wouldn't be ideal either."

Jev threw him an exasperated look as he gripped the wheel again. "Why didn't your people take measures to ensure *that* wouldn't happen?"

The wheel flared to life again, highlighting Cutter's weary face, his eyes tight with pain, and Jev regretted yelling at him. "I'm sorry. I'll figure it out. I'll get the ship backed out of here and away from the city. Go find Zenia and Lornysh, will you? Help them get everyone woken up and off the ship."

How they were going to do that in what had to be down to fifteen minutes, Jev had no idea. Judging by the way Cutter shook his head, he didn't either. But he bent and grabbed one of the dwarves on the deck, gasping in pain as he pulled the unconscious female toward the exit.

Jev hunted on the panel for the engine controls, glad he could at least read the Preskabroton labels. He tried not to think about how crazy this was, about how they wouldn't have enough time.

"There's Grindmor," Lornysh said as soon as he and Zenia reached the open upper deck, the salty night air a contrast to the hot, stuffy passageways below. "And a lot of other dwarves."

"Still sleeping." Zenia cursed and ran to the familiar bearded form surrounded by a couple dozen other dwarves, all crumpled where they'd fallen unconscious. She spotted others up and down the deck but not anywhere near the five hundred that were supposed to be aboard. "Any idea how to wake them? Or how we get them all out before..." Zenia tugged at her ponytail. Had she been right to follow Jev's order without questioning it? Was it possible the explosives could be disabled somehow? What if—

"Use the dragon tear," Lornysh said.

"How?"

"Find everyone living on this ship and levitate them down to the docks." He gazed at her intently and expectantly, as if that wasn't the most ridiculous thing Zenia had heard that week.

"Levitate? Like float? Is that possible?"

"A dragon could do it."

"I'm not a dragon."

"*That* is." Lornysh stabbed a finger at her glowing gem, then ran to pick up Master Grindmor. "At the least, it's linked to one and drawing upon its power."

"I don't understand how that could be pos—"

"If you can't get them off that way, I'm going to start throwing dwarves overboard and hope the cold water wakes them up before they drown."

He shook Grindmor, but she didn't stir. A nearby dwarf only snored like a foghorn when Lornysh shoved him toward the railing.

Zenia was skeptical that her dragon tear could lift people—or dwarves—but it had done many things she wouldn't have guessed it could. She concentrated on Grindmor, imagining her rising off the deck, over the railing, and gently down to the pier below.

A chipper image popped into Zenia's head of the world from above. *Far* above. For a dizzying moment, she felt as if she were looking down at the land from a mountaintop. A moving mountaintop. Trees and bushes and trails passed below, and even cattle came into view for a moment. It was like she was a bird. Or... a dragon?

She fought down the dizziness and urged the dragon tear to focus on the dwarves. But Grindmor was already hovering off the deck. As Zenia watched—*gaped*—the dwarf master floated over the railing.

Terrified Grindmor would fall, Zenia focused on keeping her concentration and willing her to safety. She ran to the railing to keep her target in sight. Grindmor, arms and legs dangling limply, floated downward and landed on the pier near the boat.

Zenia spotted someone sitting up near the boardwalk, one of the unconscious sailors they'd passed on the way out to the ship. Four founders, she hoped that meant everyone would wake soon. She spun back toward the deck. Hundreds more dwarves needed to be floated off the ship.

Her dragon tear vibrated with power and warmed in her hand. All the dwarves in sight on the deck were lifted into the air. Zenia willed them over the railing, in awe that it was working, and that Targyon had given her something so powerful. He couldn't possibly have known.

"Worry about that later," she whispered to herself.

She caught Lornysh staring at her as the dwarves floated down to the pier, landing near Grindmor. His eyes were narrowed, his face hard to read, but he was definitely studying her. Or the dragon tear. Or both.

One dwarf stirred as he landed on the pier, lifting his head and looking around in confusion.

"They're waking up," she called to Lornysh, hoping to distract him from scrutinizing her. *He* was the one who'd asked her to do this.

"Good." Lornysh looked toward the hatchway they'd come out of earlier.

Cutter was backing out, dragging an unconscious dwarf by the armpits. Lornysh ran to help him with the load. Zenia, aware of the minutes ticking past, focused on getting the rest of the dwarves off the deck. How she would find all the ones below and get them off in time, she didn't know.

She also didn't know if simply laying the dwarves on the pier down there would keep them safe. If Jev couldn't figure out how to move the ship—

A thrum went through the deck, startling her. The group of dwarves that had been floating toward the railing faltered. She swallowed and concentrated, reminded that the power came from the dragon tear, but she was directing it.

"Jev's got the propellers going," Cutter yelled. "Zenia, can you snap the ropes tying the ship to the pier?"

Zenia lifted a hand to acknowledge the request, but she had to get her batch of dwarves to safety first. They floated downward with a few waking and lifting their heads while en route. A startled cry came from one airborne dwarf, and Zenia's concentration faltered again. The group of them plunged several feet before she regained her focus.

She swore and gripped the railing with one hand, the other tightening around her dragon tear. The heat emanating from it had grown so intense it almost burned her palm.

The dwarves landed safely, a couple of them springing to their feet and looking in all directions.

"Run to safety," she yelled down to them, assuming they would have no idea what was going on. "Into the city!"

She didn't know if they heard her way down there. She shifted her focus to the two thick ropes attaching the steamship to the pier cleats.

"I know you can do fire," she whispered, envisioning flames licking at the ropes.

The dragon tear once again responded with a sensation of enthusiasm. Flames appeared on both ropes, burning them to ash within seconds.

Zenia turned away from the railing to look for more dwarves to float away, but weakness stole over her, and her knees almost buckled. She lurched back and grabbed the railing again for support. Her role was minimal, but drawing upon the dragon tear and channeling its power affected her. Could she possibly get all the dwarves off the ship in time? How many minutes were left?

The deck thrummed again, and a shout came from below. Zenia peered over the railing in time to see two dwarves running down the gangplank. They waved their arms and shouted, pointing back at the ship. Did they know about the explosives? If enough of them woke up, would someone know how to disarm them?

A hand gripped her arm. Lornysh.

"Come. Cutter said most of the remaining dwarves are in a big passenger area down by the gangplank. We just missed them when we came in. He thinks they were being queued up to disembark when the trolls arrived with the artifacts—and Master Grindmor."

He was running as he shared this, and Zenia had to force her wobbly legs to run after him. If most of the dwarves were in one place, maybe she could get them off, even if they didn't wake up in time. She still felt there ought to be a way to defeat the explosives down there, to keep the ship from blowing up, but she had to focus on this.

Another thrum rumbled through the vessel, and it lurched slightly.

"Wait, we have to stop and tell Jev to hold on, not to move the ship yet, or all those dwarves—"

"He can't wait, or he risks your harbor and part of your city being destroyed in the explosion. Come. You'll have to fling the dwarves into the water if the ship moves from the pier."

Though Zenia wanted to disobey, she raced down the stairs after him. There were too many lives at stake to do anything else.

Steering the ship from so high above the water was a mind-boggling experience.

Jev had never even sailed a normal kingdom steamship. Fortunately, nothing but open water lay behind the dwarven vessel, and he'd found the reverse lever. The ship was rumbling slowly away from the pier. As soon as he cleared it, he would turn the engines to full power. With luck, his friends were getting all the dwarves into lifeboats, and there would be a spot left for him. If he could get the ship a mile or two out to sea, that ought to be far enough to ensure the explosion wouldn't affect the harbor.

A shadow stirred in the corner of Jev's eye. He spun away from the control panel as a troll lunged at him, a dagger in hand.

Jev ducked and flung himself out of the way, rolling across the hard deck as the glow from the wheel winked out. He rammed against one of the sleeping dwarves, eliciting a groan.

Hoping they would wake up and help him, Jev jumped up and yanked his pistol out of his holster. The troll had already turned, and it lunged at him again, catching his wrist before he could aim the weapon. Long, powerful fingers tightened, and pain flashed up Jev's arm.

He snarled, refusing to release his pistol. The troll raised his dagger with his other hand. Jev kneed him in the groin and lunged forward, catching his foe's wrist. The knee barely had any effect. The troll only growled and squeezed harder, trying to twist Jev's pistol from his grip.

Jev glimpsed a clock on the wall, and his heart almost stopped when he saw how few minutes were left. Where had the cursed time gone? He couldn't spare even a minute for this.

He pushed with all his might, using his legs as well as his arms, and ducked his chin before ramming his head into his adversary. The troll tried to dodge, but Jev caught him under the chin. The grip on his wrist lessened, and Jev yanked his hand away. Fingernails like claws raked down his arm.

Jev kicked out, trying to push his foe back so he could aim and shoot. But his foot caught on the sleeping dwarf, and he stumbled. The troll sprang for him.

Once again, Jev flung himself to the side, twisting in the air and firing. It was a wild shot, but he caught the troll in the shoulder. A yowl of pain came from those blue lips.

Though Jev hit the deck hard, he turned the fall into a roll again and came up several feet away, his back to a wall. His attacker had to be in pain, but he lunged after Jev. This time, Jev took a split second to aim. His bullet slammed into the troll's cheek.

The troll's momentum kept him coming. Jev scooted aside, but not fast enough. The troll clipped his shoulder as he hit the wall. Jev snarled and shoved him away, ready to shoot again. But his enemy pitched to the deck and didn't move again.

Jev leaped over him, wincing as he glanced at the clock, and returned to the wheel. The yellow glow flared, and the propeller started again. As Cutter had warned him, the ship had halted as soon as he let go of the wheel. Its momentum had been negligible, and it hadn't yet cleared the pier.

Jev pushed levers, hoping the labels were as simple and direct as they seemed. They needed to move faster. If he broke the pier in his attempt to depart swiftly, he would pay Targyon for it later.

Footsteps rang on the deck outside the navigation room. *Now* what?

Careful to keep his hand on the wheel, Jev pointed his pistol at the hatchway.

Zenia and Lornysh raced inside, and he jerked his weapon down.

"We've got all the dwarves off the ship," Zenia panted, sweat streaming down her face. "Except these. Lornysh?"

"On it." Lornysh waved at someone in the passageway outside. "Cutter, three more."

Zenia leaned forward, gripping her knees with her hands, and Jev wanted to grab her and offer her support, but she wasn't close enough.

He couldn't risk taking his hand from the wheel for even a second. Not when there were only— He glanced at the clock.

"Four minutes left," he said. "Get out of here. All of you."

They had finally cleared the pier. Jev pushed the lever to full speed. But the surge of power he expected didn't come. The ship barely picked up speed.

"That can't be as fast as it goes," Jev blurted. "Cutter?"

His friend had made it into the navigation room looking as weary as Zenia if not worse.

"We're in reverse," Cutter said as he grabbed one of the sleeping dwarves—Lornysh was already carrying another out over his shoulder. "I don't think the ship goes backward fast. Can you turn it around?"

Jev glanced at the clock as he imagined the lumbering craft ponderously turning before it could head out to sea. "I'll have to."

There was no way the ship could travel the mile—*miles*—he wanted in time at this speed.

"Zenia," he said.

"You want me to help?" She stepped forward and gripped the edge of the control panel.

She swayed on her feet, and he reached out to steady her. Her dragon tear glowed dully on her chest.

"I want you to get out of here. You, Lornysh, and Cutter." Sweat slithered down Jev's spine as he glanced at the clock again. "Hurry."

"You're going to stay here?"

There wasn't time to explain that someone had to stay to keep the ship moving out to sea. Besides, she wouldn't like hearing that explanation.

"Just long enough to turn it around." Jev nodded firmly to her and met her eyes. It was a lie, but he couldn't bear to give her the truth. "I'll be right behind you."

"Jev, I'm not leaving you here." She frowned at him. Could she tell he was lying? "There has to be a way to keep the explosives from going off."

She swayed again and he gripped her more tightly, keeping her from falling. What had she done to get all the dwarves off the ship in time?

"I've been trying to think of it," Zenia added. "I've just been too busy."

"There's no time," Jev whispered, then raised his voice to yell, "Lornysh! Are you out there?"

Cutter was dragging the last dwarf through the doorway as Lornysh slipped past them, running back in with his hands free. The dwarf opened his eyes and peered around.

"Up, up," Cutter commanded. "We've got to get out of here before the ship blows up."

The dwarf lurched to his feet. "Eh?"

"Follow me."

"Jev?" Lornysh asked as the dwarves disappeared into the corridor. He glanced toward the glass windows overlooking the night sea.

Jev was turning the ship as quickly as he could, but the lumbering craft was as ponderous as he'd feared.

"Help Zenia out of here," Jev said. "Please."

"What?" Zenia shook her head. "Not without you. I'll wait, and we'll all get off together if we can't think of anything. But I'm sure..." She bit her lip.

Jev wanted to kiss that lip. And all of her. It touched him that she didn't want to leave him, but he couldn't let her go down with him.

"And you?" Lornysh asked, stepping up behind Zenia.

"I'll be right behind you," Jev repeated the lie.

Lornysh looked at the dome glowing in the center of the wheel. "Ah."

He gripped Jev's shoulder before grabbing Zenia around the waist and hoisting her off her feet.

"What are you *doing*?" She kicked her feet, trying vainly to wrench her way free.

Jev almost cried out that he loved her, but Lornysh swept her out of the navigation room too quickly, he and his wiry strength unfazed by her struggles. For a moment, Zenia twisted so she could see backward and met Jev's eyes, but she and Lornysh were gone before he could speak.

With tears blurring his own eyes, Jev turned back to the wheel. The ship finally faced out to sea, and he pushed it to maximum. The engines thrummed with satisfying power. For a second, he thought he might yet get the ship far enough away from the harbor that he could run up and fling himself over the railing, that maybe he could swim far enough away before the explosion went off.

But he looked at the clock and feared there wasn't enough time.

"Sorry, Father," he whispered, regretting that the old man would lose his only remaining son and his chosen heir. "Sorry, Zenia," he added, regretting that they'd never have a chance to become... more.

CHAPTER 20

ENIA STOPPED STRUGGLING BECAUSE IT would be foolish to delay, but she wanted to strangle Lornysh as he swept her through the passageways, up the stairs, and out onto the ship's upper deck. He didn't give her an opportunity to escape. Maybe that was for the best, but pure terror gripped her heart as they left Jev farther and farther behind. Would he truly come right behind them?

Even when they reached the now-empty deck, Lornysh didn't put Zenia down.

"I can run on my own," she yelled, even though all her muscles trembled with weariness from all the dwarves she and her dragon tear had hoisted off the ship. As the vessel had pulled away from the pier, she'd had to float them farther before she could let go of her hold, and the gem had grown so hot from the effort that it left a scorch mark on her palm. It was still hot, pinned between her chest and Lornysh's shoulder as he toted her.

She wished she had water to squelch its heat.

Water. Would water douse the explosives in the hold of the ship? Keep them from working the way the swamp water had gotten her bullets too wet to ignite?

"Lornysh," she yelled when he didn't answer—or slow down. "Wait!"

He did not. He sprinted for the railing where Cutter was helping that last dwarf from the navigation room over the side. Zenia didn't realize until Lornysh picked up his speed that he meant to jump with her still clamped to his shoulder. She couldn't keep an alarmed scream from escaping her mouth as he soared over the railing and into the night sky.

She glimpsed the empty deck of the ship behind them—no sign of Jev—and the gas lamps of the city streets in the distance. And then she plunged into icy water, striking hard enough to hurt and to knock the remaining air from her lungs.

Finally, Lornysh let her go, and she clawed her way to the surface.

Shouts came from around them, Cutter and several other dwarves floating nearby.

"Swim to land," Lornysh ordered them all. "Get away from the ship. Now!"

It was steaming off in the other direction, the smoke coming from its massive stacks blotting out the stars overhead.

Zenia and the others weren't as far from the pier as she had expected, and she grimaced, not just because waves splashed her in the face. Because the ship might not be far enough away when it exploded.

Remembering her thought about the water, she wanted to try to rip a hole in the side of the ship, let water pour in and hopefully ruin those explosives. Maybe that would save Jev. Jev who hadn't yet leaped over the side of the ship. Who might still be in that navigation room.

But as she gripped the warm dragon tear and tried to concentrate, a stab of pain in her mind made her gasp. A sense of intense weariness spread over her. She didn't know if it came from the dragon tear or her own body. She tried to fight past it, but blackness edged her vision.

If she passed out, she could drown out here.

A hand gripped her under the armpit. Lornysh.

"I have an idea," Zenia blurted as he pulled her onto her back, kicking with his legs to steer both of them toward the pier. "If we could get—"

A thunderous boom sounded, and fiery white light erupted from the ship. Zenia threw an arm up as the intensity of a sun assaulted her eyes. The explosion. Jev.

Lornysh pulled her harder and faster. She was so numb, she barely felt the icy water streaming past, barely heard anything over the ringing in her ears.

When her back bumped against something, she was confused. Lornysh let go of her, but then hands gripped her from above. She was hauled up a ladder and onto the pier where people—humans and dwarves—stood all around, staring out over the water.

The light from the explosion was dying down, but that only allowed them to see how much of the vessel was gone. What remained was already filling with water as the hull sank deeper and deeper.

As Zenia stared at the wreck, even more numbness crept into her. She dropped to her knees on the pier, barely noticing the hardness of the wood.

Tears leaked from her eyes. Nobody could have survived that. *Jev* couldn't have survived it.

Why hadn't she dragged him away? Why had she let him and his damn zyndar honor decide he should sacrifice himself?

He'd known. He'd said he would be right behind her, but she was positive he'd known he wouldn't make it out. That look he'd given her, that sad smile. It hadn't been a promise that he'd see her again; it had been a goodbye.

She hadn't understood, and she hadn't said it back. She hadn't said any of what she should have said. That she cared about him, that she loved the way he bumped shoulders with her and always tried to make her laugh. That he hadn't cared what a frigid inquisitor she'd been when they met. That he hadn't cared that she was a commoner. That he hadn't cared that she'd walked him into an interrogation session where he'd been tortured by her colleagues. He hadn't cared about *any* of that. He'd still wanted to get to know her, to have a relationship with her.

But what had she done? She'd pushed him away. She'd wanted to be with him, but because he couldn't marry her, she'd refused to have anything to do with him. *Why?* Because of some vow she'd made more than a decade ago? Because of a small chance that she might get pregnant? It wasn't as if he would have turned his back on a child. He would have taken care of her, of the baby. She knew he would.

What had she truly been afraid of? That he would marry someone else someday and watching them together would devastate her? Even if that was true, was it a reason never to love him at all?

She sucked in a deep breath, and her whole body shook. Her lip quivered. There were people all over the docks, staring at the carnage and making hushed comments, but she didn't care. She dropped her head into her hands and cried.

"Someone's out there," a man blurted. "Look!"

"He's injured."

A splash sounded as Zenia lifted her head, her heart pounding.

"Jev?" she whispered.

A strong swimmer stroked in the direction of the ship, silver hair streaming out behind him. She gulped. Was that Lornysh again? He risked a lot if he was seen here now that everyone was awake. The ship might have been full of dwarves who had no grudge against elves, but half of Korvann seemed to have rushed down to the docks due to all the commotion.

But if he was swimming out to save Jev, she would protect Lornysh from anyone who tried to get to him.

Zenia rose to her feet on legs still weak from the night's efforts. She lifted a hand to block out the light of the flames burning on the wreck. There *was* someone in the water. Someone with dark hair. Someone barely moving. Tears sprang back to her eyes.

"Get a healer!" she yelled to anyone who would listen. "That's Jev—Zyndar Dharrow!" She hoped. "He saved us all!"

Lornysh reached Jev—she refused to believe it was anybody else—hooked an arm around his chest and paddled backward toward the docks. Zenia was tempted to jump in and swim out to help, but Lornysh was strong and making good time. With her hands trembling and her heart in her throat, she didn't know how much help she would be.

"Wait," she blurted to herself and wrapped her hand around the dragon tear. A flash of pain came from her palm where the gem's heat had burned her before, but she tightened her grip anyway. "Lift him," she whispered to it. "Bring him here, please."

She concentrated on channeling the thought into the dragon tear for a more focused command, but it understood. A sense of weariness came from it, but it vibrated against her hand, and Jev and Lornysh floated out of the water.

Lornysh lifted his head, looking back in surprise. Jev barely reacted, his limbs hanging limply in the air.

As Zenia stepped back to make room for them on the end of the pier, she looked to make sure someone had obeyed her order to get a healer. It wasn't as if she was zyndar or anyone as far as these people knew.

Thankfully, she recognized people in white robes making their way through the crowd. Air Order mages. Healers, she hoped. Jev had been born under the White Dragon's stars. They should be happy to heal him.

Jev and Lornysh floated closer, and Zenia released the dragon tear. Now, she could see their faces and could tell for certain that it *was* Jev.

His eyes were closed and blood dripped from gashes all over his body. His clothing was so torn, his shoulder and torso were almost bare. Bare and bruised with more severe cuts visible.

"Jev," Zenia whispered, reaching out a hand, distressed by his pain. Was he conscious? Maybe it would be better for him if he wasn't.

The vibrations of her dragon tear faded as Jev settled onto his back on the dock. Lornysh landed on his feet next to him. He took one look at her, then stepped back, pulling his wet hood over his head.

Zenia hoped people were too transfixed on Jev to have seen his ears, but it was only a passing thought. She knelt beside Jev, her focus on him.

She laid one hand on his wet chest and cupped the back of his head with the other, careful to avoid the gouges leaking blood. She could barely see through the tears smearing her vision but saw his eyes were closed.

"Jev," she whispered, bending down, resting her face beside his, wishing she could fling her arms around him in a hug. "Healers are coming. You'll be fine. They'll take care of you."

Something stirred against her cheek. One of his lashes. She turned and found his eyes open. Pain created lines at the corners of them, and he appeared dazed, but he seemed to recognize her.

"You can rest," she said. "The healers are almost here."

"Damn," he whispered, his voice barely audible. "No... private moment... for a kiss?"

"*That's* what's on your mind now?" She almost pointed out that he might be dying, but that wouldn't be a reassuring thing to say. Besides, she had faith the Air Order healers could help him. He'd made it off the ship. He had to make it the rest of the way.

"Was wishing... I'd given you... one," he murmured, eyelids drooping. "Before you left... but guess... I'm not supposed... to do that."

It wasn't an accusation, just a sad forlorn statement, but it sank into her heart like a knife.

"You can," she heard herself whispering. "I love you, Jev."

His eyelids lifted again, and he turned his face toward her. She half expected a joke. Or for him to pass out before he could respond. But he focused on her and said, "I love you too."

"Good." She shifted her hand from his head to his cheek, touching it gently. She wished she could kiss him now but heard voices right behind her.

"Ma'am?" a woman said. "We're healers. Let us in."

Zenia patted Jev's chest and reluctantly rose to her feet. His eyes remained locked onto her, and she smiled at him until the two healers crouched down, blocking their view of each other.

Lornysh, she noted, had disappeared. A wise decision, she was sure. Cutter had moved away from the docks with Master Grindmor to avoid the crowd. Zenia didn't see Rhi, but she didn't see the king's entourage, either, so hopefully, she had found him and warned him to stay away from the waterfront.

The white-robed healers rose to their feet as another mage stepped out of the crowd, her hand around a dragon tear. She focused on Jev, and he was lifted into the air once more.

"What's going on?" Zenia asked the closest healer.

"His injuries are extensive. We will take him to the Temple of the White Dragon in the Air quarter. A carriage is arriving shortly." The healer nodded as Jev floated past.

"I'm going with you."

"There won't be room in the carriage, but you may meet us there if you wish."

Zenia gripped her own dragon tear. She couldn't imagine a healer would have a reason to lie about this or had some nefarious plan to take advantage of Jev's injuries, but she wanted to make sure. The dragon tear understood and showed her the healer's thoughts.

The man's eyebrows twitched—did he sense her gem's touch? She didn't care. Let him know she was inspecting his mind.

Fortunately, she sensed only a genuine interest in caring for Jev from the man and knowledge that it would be easier to do so in the quiet of his temple. He believed Jev had saved the city and should be treated with the utmost respect and care.

Zenia stepped back and let the healer go. She wouldn't delay him, though she *would* follow along. Perhaps Lornysh and Cutter would wish to come too. There was that stream by the Air Order Temple and all those trees. Perfect for an elf to hide among.

She would wait inside, by his bed if they would let her. Then, when he was well, they could discuss how foolish she had been, how it had taken him almost dying for her to realize she wanted to figure out a way to be with him. In whatever way it could be possible. She resolved that it *would* be possible.

EPILOGUE

JEV WOKE IN A BED with a sheet pulled up to his chin, a whitewashed stone ceiling arching overhead. Sunlight slanted in through a single window. Morning sun? Afternoon? He had no idea which way his window faced or how long he'd been out. He hoped he hadn't lost more than a day.

He'd drifted into consciousness a few times while the healers had been working on him and knew he was in the Air Order Temple, but most of the experience was a hazy blur in his mind. For the first time, nobody in a white robe hovered over him, and his body no longer tingled with healing magic. It still ached in places but not the way it had when he first hit the water. The explosion had gone off while he'd been racing across the upper deck toward the railing, and it had felt like a rock golem slamming into his back.

He'd hurt so much, he'd been certain he would drown, that he would never make it to the docks. He needed to thank Lornysh for pulling him to safety. And Zenia. He remembered his numb surprise as a magical power lifted them both out of the water and deposited him at her feet. She'd knelt and hugged him and whispered she loved him. And he'd whispered it back, so thankful the founders had given him a chance to do so. Back on that ship, he'd experienced an amazing number of regrets considering how little time he'd had for thinking.

He still didn't know how they would make a relationship work, but if she wanted to marry him, Jev would talk to her father—and his— and find a way to get the old man to accept her as a daughter-in-law. To walk away from his responsibilities would be unthinkable—and dishonorable—but he could do his best to change his father's mind. He had to try. For Zenia. And for him. To marry someone else and work every day at her side… He couldn't imagine anything making him more miserable.

"Need to tell her that," he mumbled and turned his head.

His skull ached—everything did—but that didn't keep him from looking around the room, hoping to find her sitting in a chair, waiting for him to wake up.

But the room was devoid of furniture, of everything except cabinets and a dresser with a pitcher and wash basin on it. Disappointment filled him.

A soft knock sounded, and the door opened.

Zenia poked her head inside, and Jev's disappointment disappeared. He smiled and lifted his arms, not caring that they were heavier than boulders and covered with a sheet.

Returning his smile, Zenia stepped inside and up to the side of his bed. She bent and hugged him carefully. He had no interest in care, not at that moment. He hugged her hard, pulling her down against him, hoping to keep her close forever.

She smelled good—was that lavender? She must have washed since their adventures in the swamp. He hoped he didn't smell of mud and explosives. Even if he did, she didn't seem to care. She turned her head to kiss his cheek, and a shiver of delight went through him.

"I missed you," he whispered.

"I've been outside your door the whole time, except for a few minutes to wash up. And that only because Rhi insisted. She said my earthy troll-bedewed odor would seep under your door and prevent you from healing."

He snorted. "What about my troll-bedewed odor?"

"You took that bath in the ocean. I also walked in once to find one of the healers sponging off your blood and grime with loving tenderness." She quirked an eyebrow.

"One of the healers sponged me? Was it the man or the woman?"

"The woman. Disappointed?"

"Only that it wasn't you. I'll let you sponge me later if you want." He grinned. She had straightened, letting her arms loosen around him, but her hand remained on his chest. He placed his hand over hers, claiming it. And her. "I'm naked under this sheet, you know."

"Sounds drafty."

He couldn't tell if she liked the idea of him naked under the sheet or not. He supposed he shouldn't assume that because she'd said she loved him she wanted to engage in any physical activities. There was still her vow to herself, after all. She also could have meant… he grimaced. What if she'd been talking about *platonic* love?

"Are you still in pain?" she asked, misreading the reason for his grimace.

"Not too much. I was trying decide if I'd heard—uhm, interpreted—you correctly when we were on the dock. I was a little dazed." He gazed into her eyes, seeking a clue.

Would she pretend it hadn't happened? He was sure it had, dazed or not. She'd been a beautiful sight, bending over him, touching him, and he'd burned it into his memory.

She gazed back at him, then smiled and bent low again. Her lips parted, and she kissed him, not on the cheek this time.

His soul sang as he returned the kiss with all the feeling in his battered body. He lifted his hand and stroked her cheek, again vowing to find a way, so long as she was willing.

A loud knock sounded, more like a banging, and Zenia withdrew. Far, far too soon. But she was still smiling down at him, her eyes twinkling, and he allowed himself to believe there would be more kisses soon.

The door opened.

"Is he going to live?" came Cutter's gruff voice, "or are we going to have to cut him up and sacrifice him to a troll?"

"I have other plans for him," Zenia said as Cutter ambled in.

"Are they sexual plans?" Rhi asked as she walked in behind Cutter.

A third figure slipped in behind them, a green cloak wrapped around his body and his hood up over his silver hair. Lornysh.

"He's an injured man," Zenia said. "That would be inappropriate."

"I bet he could rally himself." Rhi winked at Jev.

He didn't wink back, but the thought, *Yes, yes, I could,* passed through his mind.

"Our desks have likely been filling up with paperwork while we've been off having adventures," Zenia said. "He'll need time to recover, so I thought I'd have him hold folders while I organize everything."

"He's too injured for sex but not for physical labor?" Rhi asked.

Jev lifted a finger. "I'm not too injured for sex."

"Holding folders isn't physical labor," Zenia said, ignoring him. "They're lightweight."

"I've seen your desks. There's at least fifty pounds of paper on them today."

"He can sit down while he holds the folders."

Cutter came up to the opposite side of Jev's bed and prodded him in the shoulder with the top of his hook. "You might want to stay in bed a while longer. These women are making odious plans for you."

"So I hear."

"*My* plans weren't odious," Rhi said. "I was trying to get someone under the sheets with him. Zenia's the one talking about folders."

Lornysh crossed his arms over his chest and leaned against the wall by the door, as if to guard the way in. Or maybe to show that he was far too mature for this conversation.

"I see that *you're* doing fine, Cutter," Jev said. "Did someone heal you?"

"Yes, I was in a room down the hall."

"Is Master Grindmor all right?"

"Yes, Targyon had his personal physician heal her. She's important, you know. He also invited the rest of the dwarves up to the castle until they're able to go out into the city and start their shops. He's promised to replace the tools they brought over that were lost in the explosion—alas, our brilliant steamship is on the bottom of the harbor now."

"Hundreds of dwarves roaming around the castle?" Rhi asked. "They'll destroy the place."

"More likely remodel it," Jev said, thinking of the plumbing and fancy bathroom in Iridium's underground lair. He believed that had been one of the favors she'd wheedled out of Master Grindmor.

"Think they can put some windows in our office?" Zenia asked. "It's very dark even when all the lamps are lit."

"It's the basement office of a secret organization nobody is supposed to know about," Jev said. "It's supposed to be dark and easy to forget about."

"If I could see better, I'd be more efficient at organizing the paperwork. You wouldn't have to hold folders for as long."

"Cutter," Jev said, "how are your people at windows?"

Cutter scratched his jaw with the tip of his hook. "Dwarves don't have much need for windows. We live in underground cities."

"How do you do paperwork down there in the dark?" Zenia asked.

"Dwarves aren't much for paperwork. Most orders and agreements are verbal."

"How can I visit this wondrous place?" Jev asked.

Zenia shot him a dirty look. He smiled beatifically at her.

"You'd need a dwarf to accompany you down, or the guards would send rock golems after you," Cutter said.

"Then it's fortunate that I know a dwarf."

"Ah, but I'm not going anywhere anytime soon. Did I tell you?" Cutter leaned forward, gripping the edge of the bed with his hand. "Master Grindmor decided that I might be worth training. She said to come to her shop first thing next week and she'd test me and see if I have any skills worth honing."

"Might?" Zenia asked.

Cutter's blissful expression suggested he believed he would be taken on. Or maybe he was simply delighted to be given a chance.

"The last I heard," Jev told Zenia, "our grumpy master was insulting Cutter's beard, so this seems to be an improvement in their relationship."

"She's not grumpy. She's focused. And rightfully stern with young dwarves." Yes, Cutter's expression was definitely blissful. "All these years I've waited to meet her and implore her to take me on, and it's finally going to happen. I'm certain. I'll prove to her that my skills are masterful. Oh, but I'm rusty." He leaned back from the bed. "I better go practice." He hurried for the door. "Get well, Jev."

"I'll endeavor to do so."

"Dwarves are quirky, aren't they?" Rhi remarked after Cutter left, the door slamming shut behind him.

"Monks are not quirky?" Lornysh asked, speaking for the first time.

"Of course not. But I'm not a monk anymore. I'm an agent, hoping some captain of the agents will teach me what I'm supposed to do all day at work besides run errands for that zyndar blowhard."

"I assume she means Garlok and not me," Jev said.

Rhi smiled blandly at him.

"Now that things have settled down," Zenia said, "at least for the moment, maybe we can start a training program."

"Have they settled down?" Jev thought of the trolls in the swamp. They might have rescued Grindmor and kept Kor's tenuous relationship with the dwarves from evaporating, but the kingdom might still face the threat of an invasion. "The trolls?"

"Targyon sent a zyndar captain—Krox, I believe his name was—to lead some army troops into the swamp and deal with the troll infestation problem," Zenia said. "If they were indeed just scouts, maybe the main force will decide to abort their invasion plans if those scouts don't return."

"Let's hope," Jev murmured. "Lornysh, do you think the elven ambassador will come back if the troll problem disappears? I know Targyon would like a chance to reestablish relations with your people."

"They may not be ready for that for quite some time, but I'm certain they will want to station another ambassador in your capital city to keep an eye on you. We—" Lornysh stopped and frowned toward the window.

A cloud had drifted over the sun, stealing the brightness in the room, but Jev hadn't heard anything. Lornysh walked to the window and peered outside.

Jev looked at Rhi and Zenia. They shrugged back.

"I must go." Lornysh backed away from the window and yanked his hood over his head. "Watch out for strangers, and stay safe."

He left as swiftly as Cutter had, though the door shut with a whisper instead of a slam.

"Elves are also quirky," Rhi announced.

Jev wondered how he could get Rhi and her quirky observations to follow the others out of the room and leave him alone with Zenia. He appreciated that everyone had come to visit, but that kiss had been quite lovely, and he would enjoy resuming it.

He gazed up at her like a love-smitten teenager. Maybe she would convince Rhi to step outside. She smiled back down at him and patted his arm. That wasn't quite what he'd wanted her to do.

Another knock sounded. Jev sighed immensely.

"How does everybody know I'm awake now?" he wondered.

"My dragon tear told me," Zenia said, her face assuming that uncertain expression she got when she wasn't positive everything her gem could do was a good thing. "I'm not sure how everyone else found out."

He remembered the dreams she'd confessed she was having. Had she dozed enough last night to have another one? Maybe he could convince her to sleep without the dragon tear and see if that changed anything.

The knock sounded again.

"Oh," Rhi said. "This is somebody polite who won't simply barge in if they don't hear a response."

"I didn't know I knew anyone like that," Jev said dryly, then raised his voice to call, "Come in."

His cousin Wyleria entered, her dark brown hair swept back in a bun, and nodded to Rhi and Zenia before smiling at Jev. There was a tinge of uncertainty in that smile. It surprised him. Had she heard he was in worse shape than he was? No, if that were true, she would look delighted to find him awake and alert.

Wyleria stepped inside hesitantly, and Jev had the impression the uncertainty had to do with whether or not he would want to see her. Why wouldn't he?

"Thanks for coming, Wyleria," he said sincerely. "Has word of everything that happened in the city last night made its way out to the castle?"

"Actually, no. I happened to be coming into town to see you this morning, and that's when I learned you were being cared for by healers here." She frowned fiercely at him. "You could have gotten yourself killed."

"Zyndar are always supposed to be prepared to give their lives for their kingdom and the people they're sworn to protect."

"Yes, but you seem to be risking it on a regular basis now."

Hm, she must have heard about his adventures with that creature in the elven embassy. He'd glossed over the dangers of the night, including battling the monster after climbing up the side of the tower without a rope, but perhaps someone had since filled her in.

"Technically, I was doing that during the war too. You just didn't know about it because I was overseas and you didn't see the reports."

"Is that supposed to make me feel better?" Wyleria shared an exasperated sisterhood-of-women look with Rhi and Zenia.

"If it helps," Jev said, "I'll try not to need to risk my life again this week."

"This week? You can't even promise a month?"

"Well, Zenia wants me to hold fifty pounds of folders for her. It's possible I'll be crushed under their weight."

He smiled, but his cousin didn't.

"Oh, Jev," she said. "You're your father's only heir now. You need to take care of yourself."

Jev closed his eyes, feeling smothered. He was glad someone cared, but he'd been without a mother for more than twenty years. He was used to taking care of himself and not having well-meaning but stifling feminine concern thrust upon him. He appreciated that Zenia wasn't the type to stifle or smother. She seemed to accept that their job was dangerous and they would both be in trouble from time to time. He turned his head toward her, his appreciation seeping out in a smile.

Wyleria noticed and frowned. Jev looked away and made his face more stern. He realized that just because he'd confessed his love for Zenia didn't mean anyone else in the family knew—or should know. He wanted to figure out how to deal with his father on his own terms, preferably before news of his plan to do so reached the old man and he had time to hunker down behind mental fortifications.

"Jev," Wyleria said, "I need to speak with you. Several of your cousins and your aunts are planning to visit you later today, but this is important." She glanced at Rhi and Zenia again, no hint of camaraderie and shared anything in her expression now. "In private, please."

Rhi shrugged and walked out. Zenia touched his shoulder, then headed for the door, also without protest. Jev almost wished she *had* protested. He wanted to say that anything Wyleria wanted to say to him could be said in front of her, but… he shouldn't state that. Not yet. One day, he hoped he could.

"What is it?"

As Jev sat up in the bed, arranging his sheets to fully cover his waist, he remembered what Wyleria had said earlier, that she'd been coming to see him even before she heard about the explosion and his injury. Had his father sent her? Or was something going on at home that she needed to tell him about?

Her expression had grown grave. He grimaced, suspecting he wasn't going to like this.

"Some… rumors were brought to your father's attention," Wyleria said carefully, studying not him but the floor.

"Is this about those zyndari sisters who were gossiping about me and Zenia?"

Wyleria lifted her gaze. "You've heard?"

"I've heard there's a surprising amount of gossip related to me lately."

"*Are* you having a relationship with her?" Wyleria asked.

Jev thought of their kiss and almost said, "Yes, so?" But he also thought of Zenia's modesty, or, perhaps more accurately, of that promise she'd made to herself. He wasn't positive she'd changed her mind on that yet and didn't want to disgruntle her by announcing they were a romantic couple.

"We've become good friends," he said. "I don't know yet if it will become more than that."

Wyleria took a deep breath. "I suggest you break it off before it does."

"And why is that?" Even though Wyleria was one of his favorite cousins, and he rarely lost his temper with her, he couldn't keep the coldness out of his tone.

"There hasn't been an official announcement yet since you haven't been told, but your father agreed to a proposal that came in."

Jev's blood chilled in his veins and gripped his heart like an icy vise. "A proposal for what?" he asked, though he knew full well.

"Marriage. To Zyndari Fremia Bludnor."

"One of those teenage sisters trying to manipulate Father into it?" Jev curled his fingers around the edges of his mattress. "Why would he agree to that?"

"She's young, pretty, and her grandfather fought with your father in the Border Wars. He respects the man, says he's smart and brave, and believes his granddaughter will birth strong sons."

"Founders' cracked scales. He said he'd give me through the summer to find someone on my own."

"He didn't confide in me, of course," Wyleria said, "but I got the impression he believes the rumors about you and Zenia. He was also muttering about something you said the other day, asking him about marrying commoners. I gather he's afraid... you'll make a foolish mistake if you're given the time."

"Zenia's *not* a foolish mistake," Jev said hotly before he could consider the wisdom of speaking the words.

Wyleria smiled sadly.

"Not that it should matter a whit, but *she's* smart and brave. Just yesterday, she fought alongside me against trolls in the swamps." Jev flung a hand in the direction of the river, wherever it was from his room. "She figured out who was behind the kidnapping of Master Grindmor—I still don't know how she came up with checking the property purchase logs. If not for her, the dwarf would have been dead and that ship would have blown up in the docks and taken half the city out with it. All *that* ought to matter a lot more than what someone's *grandfather* did fifty years ago."

Wyleria lifted her hands. "Jev, I don't disagree with you, even if an ex-inquisitor wouldn't be my first choice for you."

"That Fremia can't be your first choice either."

"No, she's not. She's a manipulative teenager. You need... I don't know what you need. Time, I think. I'm sorry you won't get it. Your father agreed to a wedding date next month."

Jev groaned and flopped back on his bed, feeling like a thirteen-year-old boy again, completely helpless in the face of his father's mandates. He'd just, as Wyleria pointed out, risked his life for the city, and this was the reward he got?

"Am I too old to run away from home?" he asked bleakly.

"Yes."

"Would it be selfish to wish for another war and that I'd be *sent* away from home?" Not that he truly wanted that, not unless Zenia could be sent away with him. Besides, with trolls skulking around in the countryside, he shouldn't even joke about such things.

"Very much so."

"Damn."

"I'm sorry, Jev. I understand how you feel."

He grunted in skepticism.

"Trust me, I do. My mother recently found out about a relationship I've been having, and she's riding around the countryside right now, visiting zyndari mavens with eligible sons, hoping to arrange a marriage for me."

"Ah." He guessed she did understand. "I didn't think you'd been seeing anyone."

"I am." Wyleria grimaced. "I was."

"A commoner?"

"No, she's the right social class."

"Uh." Jev stared up at the ceiling, his brain taking a while to figure out the ramifications of that pronoun.

"Just the wrong gender," Wyleria added dryly.

"Did you change preferences in the years I was gone, or have I just been dense?"

She chuckled. "You *are* dense, but I was only fifteen when you left and wasn't yet certain of my preferences."

"Huh."

He didn't know what more to say. It was selfish, but he was far more concerned about his own future. Maybe later, when he figured out a way to be with Zenia, he could turn his mind toward helping his cousin. Or at least properly commiserating with her.

For now, he closed his eyes and willed meddling parents all over the world to disappear.

"What do you think they've been talking about in there for so long?" Rhi asked.

Zenia, sitting on a bench beside her, could only shrug. She'd picked up on Wyleria's words that she'd been on her way into the city to discuss something with Jev before she'd heard about his injury. News from home, from his castle. It had to be. A message from his father?

She dreaded what that news might entail but told herself not to worry until she learned what it was. If he told her.

"I couldn't guess," she replied.

"Jev's gift is still on his desk unopened," Rhi said. She'd gone into the office that morning and run into Zyndar Garlok and the king. She'd mentioned Targyon was waiting for a full report.

Zenia would head up to the castle soon to deliver it. Fortunately, she had started preparing a written report while she'd been waiting for the healers to finish with Jev.

"I'm sure he'll open it when he's healed," Zenia said. "He hasn't been up there."

"I once again resisted the urge to shake it."

"Noble," Zenia said.

"I thought so."

"Ma'ams?" A young acolyte in white trousers and a tunic walked up with an envelope. "Is one of you Captain Cham?"

"Yes," Zenia said.

The girl held up the envelope uncertainly. She was eleven or twelve. Zenia wondered if she was an orphan given to the temple to raise, as Zenia had once been, long ago.

"That's the only clue we're giving you," Rhi said.

Zenia snorted and held out her hand. "What is…" She trailed off as she recognized the style of the writing on the envelope, elegant letters written in blue ink.

"Uh oh," Rhi said, apparently recognizing it too. "Another message from your… helper?"

Helper. Was that the right word? She supposed so, since the last two clues she'd received had been warnings, *apt* warnings. But Zenia suspected this *helper* would ask for a favor one day or expect something in return. When she had some free time, whenever that might be, she would try to figure out who was sending these messages and how they were always a step ahead of her.

"Thank you," she told the acolyte. "Where did you find it? Did you see who left it?"

The girl shook his head. "One of our monks brought it in from outside. He said it was leaning against the wall by the door and there wasn't anyone around."

"Of course not." Zenia sighed and opened it as the acolyte returned to her chores.

"How did whoever is sending these know you were here?" Rhi waved toward the columns of the large prayer room.

"Who knows how he or she knows anything?" Zenia drew out the single piece of paper inside and unfolded it. As with the others, it was a short, simple message. "Avoid the elf."

"*The* elf? We only know one. Unless you count that princess that we briefly met at Dharrow Castle."

"It may not refer to Lornysh." Why would it? "But to some elf we have yet to meet."

"Or it could be Lornysh. Maybe he's going to start some trouble."

"He hasn't yet. Why would he?"

"I don't know, but what do we really know about him?"

"He's Jev's friend," Zenia said. "That's enough."

"How much does *Jev* know about him? Do you know?"

"Enough to consider him a friend." Zenia returned the paper to the envelope. She wouldn't conjure up suspicions about someone because of a warning from a mystery person, especially when they had no idea *which* elf the message meant.

"Hm," was all Rhi said.

"It could refer to that scientist we already arrested," Zenia said, though she doubted it, not if this note had just been delivered.

"I guess we'll have to keep our eyes out for pointy-eared suspicious types. And Lornysh."

Zenia frowned at her, recalling that Rhi had conversed with Lornysh a few times while they'd been riding yesterday and other times. Zenia had usually been talking with Jev at those times. "Do you have a reason to mistrust him?"

"He hasn't done anything to me, other than being flinty, but he's secretive, don't you think? We know nothing about him. I asked where he was from and how he liked Korvann once. He stared off into the woods and ignored me."

Zenia held the envelope in both hands and gazed down at it. She would show it to Jev—she didn't think she had mentioned this secret helper yet, and she should do that, regardless of whether this had anything to do with Lornysh. Whatever it had to do with, she had a feeling that more trouble was on the way.

THE END

Printed in Great Britain
by Amazon